The curtain in time that permitted her to pass between centuries had closed...

and Rue had no way of knowing when—or if—it would ever open again. "Through the looking glass," she muttered to herself. "Any minute now, I should meet a talking rabbit."

"Or a United States Marshal," said a gravelly voice.

Rue whirled to see a broad-shouldered cowboy with a badge, his turquoise eyes narrowed in suspicion. This guy was straight out of "Gunsmoke"...but his personal magnetism was high-tech.

His marvelous eyes widened as he took in her jeans and T-shirt. "Where the devil did you get those duds?"

Rue drew a deep breath. "From...another place."

The lawman regarded her dubiously. "You'd better come with me."

Cowboy fantasies were one thing, Rue reminded herself. But this was a trip into the "Twilight Zone," and she had a feeling her ticket was stamped one-way....

Dear Reader,

Each month, Silhouette **Special Edition** publishes six novels with you in mind—stories of love and life, tales that you can identify with—romance with that little "something special" added in.

August is a month for dreams . . . for hot, sunny days and warm, sultry nights. And with that in mind, don't miss these six sizzling Silhouette **Special Edition** novels! Curtiss Ann Matlock has given us *Last of the Good Guys*—Jesse Breen's story. You met him in *Annie in the Morning* (SE#695). And the duo BEYOND THE THRESHOLD from Linda Lael Miller continues with the book *Here and Then*—Rue's story.

Rounding out this month are more stories by some of your favorite authors: Laurey Bright, Ada Steward, Pamela Toth and Pat Warren.

In each Silhouette **Special Edition** novel, we're dedicated to bringing you stories that will delight as well as bring a tear to the eye. For me, good romance novels have always contained an element of hope, of optimism that life can be, and often is, very beautiful. I find a great deal of inspiration in that thought.

What do you consider essential in a good romance? I'd really like to hear your opinions on the books that we publish and on the romance genre in general. Please write to me c/o Silhouette Books, 300 East 42nd Street, 6th floor, New York, NY 10017.

I hope that you enjoy this book and all of the stories to come. I'm looking forward to hearing from you!

Sincerely,

Tara Gavin
Senior Editor
Silhouette Books

LINDA LAEL MILLER
Here and Then

Silhouette Special Edition

Published by Silhouette Books New York

America's Publisher of Contemporary Romance

For Jane and Dick Edwards,
the kind of friends I always hoped I'd have

SILHOUETTE BOOKS
300 East 42nd St., New York, N.Y. 10017

HERE AND THEN

ISBN: 0-373-09762-X

First Silhouette Books printing August 1992

Printed in the U.S.A.

LINDA LAEL MILLER

All right, all right! I admit it! While I thoroughly enjoyed writing every single word of the dozen-plus stories I've done for Silhouette, my grand passion is the historical romance. I *love* painting with the proverbial broad stroke, using nineteenth-century settings, mores, manners.

Some years ago, before I'd started publishing, I ordered Marlys Milheiser's *The Mirror* from my book club. It was the first time-travel story I had ever read, and I was hooked! I consumed it, and was afraid to look into a mirror for days. Later I discovered other time-travel books by such fine authors as JoAnn Simon, Anya Seton and Jude Deveraux. I couldn't get enough of these weird and wonderful tales, and I longed to write one.

And so the BEYOND THE THRESHOLD series began. I was thrilled when my Silhouette editor, Mary Clare Kersten, received the idea with great enthusiasm.

I hope *There and Now* and *Here and Then* bring you as much enjoyment in the reading as they brought me in the writing.

PINE RIVER, WASHINGTON 1892	PINE RIVER, WASHINGTON 1992
Population: 300	Population: 5,500
4 saloons	1 tavern/pool hall
1 U.S. Marshal	5 full-time police officers
One-room schoolhouse	1 elementary school, 1 high school and 1 junior college
1 doctor— Jonathan Fortner, M.D.	15 physicians and 1 hospital
2 churches	6 churches
3 livery stables	4 full-service filling stations
172 horses (within the city limits)	53 horses (outside the city limits)

Chapter One

Aunt Verity's antique necklace lay in an innocent, glimmering coil of gold on the floor of the upstairs hallway. An hour before, when Rue Claridge had been carrying her suitcases upstairs, it had not been there.

Frowning, Rue got down on one knee and reached for the necklace, her troubled gaze rising to the mysterious, sealed door in the outside wall. Beyond it was nothing but empty space. The part of the house it had once led to had been burned away a century before and never rebuilt.

Aunt Verity had hinted at spooky doings in the house over the years, tales concerning both the door and the necklace. Rue had enjoyed the yarns, but being practical in nature, she had promptly put them out of her mind.

Rue's missing cousin, Elisabeth, had mentioned the necklace and the doorway in those strange letters she'd written in an effort to outline what was happening to her.

She'd said a person wearing the necklace could travel through time.

In fact, Elisabeth—gentle, sensible Elisabeth—had claimed she'd clasped the chain around her neck and soon found herself in the 1890s, surrounded by living, breathing people who should have been dead a hundred years.

A chill wove a gossamer casing around Rue's spine as she recalled snatches of Elisabeth's desperate letters.

You're the one person in the world who might, just might, believe me. Those wonderful, spooky stories Aunt Verity told us on rainy nights were true. There *is* another world on the other side of that door in the upstairs hallway, one every bit as solid and real as the one you and I know, and I've reached it. I've been there, Rue, and I've met the man meant to share my life. His name is Jonathan Fortner, and I love him more than my next heartbeat, my next breath.

A pounding headache thumped behind Rue's right temple, and she let out a long sigh as she rose to her feet, her fingers pressing the necklace deep into her palm. With her other hand, she pushed a lock of sandy, shoulder-length hair back from her face and stared at the sealed door.

Years ago there had been rooms on the other side, but then, late in the last century, there had been a tragic fire. The damage had been repaired, but the original structure was changed forever. The door had been sealed, and now the doorknob was as old and stiff as a rusted padlock.

"Bethie," Rue whispered, touching her forehead against the cool, wooden panel of the door, "where are you?"

There was no answer. The old country house yawned around her, empty except for the ponderous nineteenth-century furniture Aunt Verity had left as a part of her estate and a miniature universe of dust particles that seemed to pervade every room, every corner and crevice.

At thirty, Rue was an accomplished photojournalist. She'd dodged bullets and bombs in Belfast, photographed and later written about the massacre in Tiananmen Square, covered the invasion of Panama, nearly been taken captive in Baghdad. And while all of those experiences had shaken her and some had left her physically ill for days afterward, none had frightened her so profoundly as Elisabeth's disappearance.

The police and Elisabeth's father believed Elisabeth had simply fled the area after her divorce, that she was lying on a beach somewhere, sipping exotic tropical drinks and letting the sun bake away her grief. But because she knew her cousin, because of the letters and phone messages that had been waiting when she returned from an assignment in Moscow, Rue took a much darker view of the situation.

Elisabeth was wandering somewhere, if she was alive at all, perhaps not even remembering who she was. Rue wouldn't allow herself to dwell on all the *other* possibilities, because they didn't bear thinking about.

Downstairs in the big kitchen, she brewed a cup of instant coffee in Elisabeth's microwave and sat down at the big, oak table in the breakfast nook to go over the tattered collection of facts one more time. Before her were her cousin's letters, thoughtfully written, with no indications of undue stress in the familiar, flowing hand.

With a sigh, Rue pushed away her coffee and rested her chin in one palm. Elisabeth had come to the house the two cousins had inherited to get a new perspective on her life. She'd planned to make her home outside the little Washington town of Pine River and teach at the local elementary school in the fall. The two old ladies across the road, Cecily and Roberta Buzbee, had seen Elisabeth on several occasions. It had been Miss Cecily who had called an ambulance after finding Elisabeth unconscious in the upstairs hallway. Rue's cousin had been rushed to the hospital, where she'd stayed a relatively short time, and soon after that, she'd vanished.

Twilight was falling over the orchard behind the house, the leaves thinning on the gray-brown branches because it was late October. Rue watched as a single star winked into view in the purple sky. *Oh, Bethie,* she thought, as a collage of pictures formed in her mind... an image of a fourteen-year-old Elisabeth predominated—Bethie, looking down at Rue from the door of the hayloft in the rickety old barn. "Don't worry," the woman-child had called cheerfully on that long-ago day when Rue had first arrived, bewildered and angry, to take sanctuary under Aunt Verity's wing. "This is a good place and you'll be happy here." Rue saw herself and Bethie fishing and wading in the creek near the old covered bridge and reading dog-eared library books in the highest branches of the maple tree that shaded the back door. And listening to Verity's wonderful stories in front of the parlor fire, chins resting on their updrawn knees, arms wrapped around agile young legs clad in blue jeans.

The jangle of the telephone brought Rue out of her reflections, and she muttered to herself as she made her way across the room to pick up the extension on the wall next to the sink. "Hello," she snapped, resentful because she'd felt closer to Elisabeth for those few moments and the caller had scattered her memories like a flock of colorful birds.

"Hello, Claridge," a wry male voice replied. "Didn't they cover telephone technique where you went to school?"

Rue ignored the question and shoved the splayed fingers of one hand through her hair, pulling her scalp tight over her forehead.

"Hi, Wilson," she said, Jeff's boyish face forming on the screen of her mind. She'd been dating the guy for three years, on and off, but her heart never gave that funny little thump she'd read about when she saw his face or heard his voice. She wondered if that meant anything significant.

"Find out anything about your cousin yet?"

Rue leaned against the counter, feeling unaccountably weary. "No," she said. "I talked to the police first thing, and they agree with Uncle Marcus that she's probably hiding out somewhere, licking her wounds."

"You don't think so?"

Unconsciously, Rue shook her head. "No way. Bethie would never just vanish without telling anyone where she was going…she's the most considerate person I know." Her gaze strayed to the letters spread out on the kitchen table, unnervingly calm accounts of journeys to another point in time. Rue shook her head again, denying that such a thing could be possible.

"I could fly out and help you," Jeff offered, and Rue's practical heart softened a little.

"That won't be necessary," she said, twisting one finger in the phone cord and frowning. Finding Elisabeth was going to take all her concentration and strength of will, she told herself. The truth was, she didn't want Jeff getting in the way.

Her friend sighed, somewhat dramatically. "So be it, Claridge. If you decide I have any earthly use, give me a call, will you?"

Rue laughed. "What?" she countered. "No violin music?" In the next instant, she remembered that Elisabeth was missing, and the smile faded from her face. "Thanks for offering, Jeff," she said seriously. "I'll call if there's anything you can do to help."

After that, there didn't seem to be much to say, and that was another element of the relationship Rue found troubling. It would have been a tremendous relief to tell someone she was worried and scared, to say Elisabeth was more like a sister to her than a cousin, maybe even to cry on a sympathetic shoulder. But Rue couldn't let down her guard that far, not with Jeff. She often got the feeling that he was just waiting for her to show weakness or to fall on her face.

The call ended, and Rue, wearing jeans and a sweatshirt, put on a jacket and went out to the shed for an armload of the aged applewood that had been cut and stacked several years before. Because Rue and Elisabeth had so rarely visited the house they'd inherited, the supply had hardly been diminished.

As she came through the back door, the necklace caught her eye, seeming to twinkle and wink from its place on the kitchen table. Rue's brow crimped thoughtfully as she made her way into the parlor and set the fragrant wood down on the hearth.

After moving aside the screen, she laid twigs in the grate over a small log of compressed sawdust and wax. When the blaze had kindled properly, she added pieces of seasoned wood. Soon, a lovely, cheerful fire was crackling away behind the screen.

Rue adjusted the damper and rose, dusting her hands off on the legs of her jeans. She was tired and distraught, and suddenly she couldn't keep her fears at bay any longer. She'd been a reporter for nine eventful years, and she knew only too well the terrible things that could have happened to Elisabeth.

She went back to the kitchen and, without knowing exactly why, reached for the necklace and put it on, even before taking off her jacket. Then, feeling chilled, she returned to the parlor to stand close to the fire.

Rue was fighting back tears of frustration and fear, her forehead touching the mantelpiece, when she heard the distant tinkling of piano keys. She was alone in the house, and she was certain no radio or TV was playing....

Her green eyes widened when she looked into the ornately framed mirror above the fireplace, and her throat tightened: The room reflected there was furnished differently, and was lit with the soft glow of lantern light. Rue caught a glimpse of a plain woman in long skirts running a cloth over the keys of a piano before the vision faded and the room was ordinary again.

Turning slowly, Rue rubbed her eyes with a thumb and forefinger. She couldn't help thinking of Elisabeth's letters describing a world like the one she'd just seen, for a fraction of a second, in the parlor mirror.

"You need a vacation," Rue said, glancing back over her shoulder at her image in the glass. "You're hallucinating."

Nonetheless, she made herself another cup of instant coffee, gathered up the letters and went to sit cross-legged on the hooked rug in front of the fireplace. Once again, she read and analyzed every word, looking for some clue, anything that would tell her where to begin the search for her cousin.

Thing was, Rue thought, Bethie sounded eminently sane in those letters, despite the fact that she talked about stepping over a threshold into another time in history. Her descriptions of the era were remarkably authentic; she probably would have had to have done days or weeks of research to know the things she did. But the words seemed fluent and easy, as though they'd flowed from her pen.

Finally, no closer to finding Elisabeth than she had been before, Rue set the sheets of writing paper aside, banked the fire and climbed the front stairway to the second floor. She would sleep in the main bedroom—many of Elisabeth's things were still there—and maybe by some subconscious, instinctive process, she would get a glimmer of guidance concerning her cousin's whereabouts.

As it was, she didn't have the first idea where to start.

She showered, brushed her teeth, put on a nightshirt and went to bed. Although she had taken the necklace off when she undressed, she put it back on again before climbing beneath the covers.

The sheets were cold, and Rue burrowed down deep, shivering. If it hadn't been for the circumstances, she would have been glad to be back in this old house, where all the memories were good ones. Like Ribbon Creek, the Montana ranch she'd inherited from her mother's parents, Aunt Verity's house was a place to hole up when there was an important story to write or a decision to work out. She'd always loved the sweet, shivery sensation that the old Victorian monstrosity was haunted by amicable ghosts.

As her body began to warm the crisp, icy sheets, Rue hoped those benevolent apparitions were hanging around now, willing to lend a hand. "Please," she whispered, "show me how to find Elisabeth. She's my cousin and the closest thing I ever had to a sister and my very best friend, all rolled into one—and I think she's in terrible trouble."

After that, Rue tossed and turned for a while, then fell into a restless sleep marred by frightening dreams. One of them was so horrible that it sent her hurtling toward the surface of consciousness, and when she broke through into the morning light, she was breathing in gasping sobs and there were tears on her face.

And she could clearly hear a woman's voice singing, "Shall We Gather at the River?"

Her heart thundering against her chest, Rue flung back the covers and bounded out of bed, following the sound into the hallway, where she looked wildly in one direction, then the other. The voice seemed to be rising through the floorboards and yet, at the same time, it came from beyond the sealed door of the outside wall.

Rue put her hands against the wooden panel, remembering Elisabeth's letters. There was a room on the other side, Bethie had written, a solid place with floors and walls and a private stairway leading into the kitchen.

"Who's there?" Rue called, and the singing immediately stopped, replaced by a sort of stunned stillness. She ran along the hallway, peering into each of the three bedrooms, then hurried down the back stairs and searched the kitchen, the utility room, the dining room, the bathroom and both parlors. There was no one else in the house, and none of the locks on the windows or doors had been disturbed.

Frustrated, Rue stormed over to the piano on which she and Elisabeth had played endless renditions of "Heart and Soul," threw up the cover and hammered out the first few bars of "Shall We Gather at the River?" in challenge.

"Come on!" she shouted over the thundering chords. "Show yourself, damn it! Who are you? *What* are you?"

The answer was the slamming of a door far in the distance.

Rue left the piano and bounded back up the stairs, because the sound had come from that direction. Reaching the sealed door, she grabbed the knob and rattled the panel hard on its hinges, and surprise rushed through her like an electrical shock when it gave way.

Muttering an exclamation, Rue peered through the opening at the charred ruins of a fire. A trembling began in the cores of her knees as she looked at blackened timbers that shouldn't have been there.

It was a moment before she could gather her wits enough to step back from the door, leaving it agape, and dash wildly down the front stairs. She went hurtling out through the front door and plunged around to the side, only to see the screened sun porch just where it had always been, with no sign of the burned section.

Barely able to breathe, Rue circled the house once, then raced back inside and up the stairs. The door was still open, and beyond it lay another time or another dimension.

"Elisabeth!" Rue shouted, gripping the sooty doorjamb and staring down through the ruins.

A little girl in a pinafore and old-fashioned, pinchy black shoes appeared in the overgrown grass, shading her eyes with a small, grubby hand as she looked up at Rue. "You a witch like her?" the child called, her tone cordial and un-ruffled.

Rue's heartbeat was so loud that it was thrumming in her ears. She stepped back, then forward, then back again. She stumbled blindly into her room and pulled on jeans, a T-shirt, socks and sneakers, not taking the time to brush her sleep-tangled hair, and she was climbing deftly down through the ruins before she had a moment to consider the consequences.

The child, who had been so brave at a distance, was now backing away, stumbling in her effort to escape, her freck-les standing out on her pale face, her eyes enormous.

Great, Rue thought, half-hysterically, *now I'm scaring small children.*

"Please don't run away," she managed to choke out. "I'm not going to hurt you."

The girl appeared to be weighing Rue's words, and it seemed that some of the fear had left her face. In the next instant, however, a woman came running around the cor-ner of the house, shrieking and flapping her apron at Rue as though to shoo her away like a chicken.

"Don't you dare touch that child!" she screeched, and Rue recognized her as the drab soul she'd glimpsed in the parlor mirror the night before, wiping the piano keys.

Rue had withstood much more daunting efforts at intimidation during her travels as a reporter. She held her ground, her hands resting on her hips, her mind cataloging material so rapidly that she was barely aware of the process. The realization that Elisabeth had been *right* about the necklace and the door in the upstairs hallway and that she was near to finding her, was as exhilarating as a skydive.

"Where did you come from?" the plain woman demanded, thrusting the child slightly behind her.

Rue didn't even consider trying to explain. In the first place, no one would believe her, and in the second, she didn't understand what was going on herself. "Back there," she said, cocking a thumb toward the open doorway above. That was when she noticed that her hands and the knees of her jeans were covered with soot from the climb down through the timbers. "I'm looking for my Cousin Elisabeth."

"She ain't around," was the grudging, somewhat huffy reply. The woman glanced down at the little girl and gave her a tentative shove toward the road. "You run along now, Vera. I saw Farley riding toward your place just a little while ago. If you meet up with him, tell him he ought to come on over here and have a talk with this lady."

Vera assessed Rue with uncommonly shrewd eyes—she couldn't have been older than eight or nine—then scampered away through the deep grass.

Rue took a step closer to the woman, even though she was beginning to feel like running back to her own safe world, the one she understood. "Do you know Elisabeth McCartney?" she pressed.

The drudge twisted her calico apron between strong, work-reddened fingers, and her eyes strayed over Rue's clothes and wildly tousled hair with unconcealed and fearful disapproval. "I never heard of nobody by that name," she said.

Rue didn't believe that for a moment, but she was conscious of a strange and sudden urgency, an instinct that warned her to tread lightly, at least for the time being. "You haven't seen the last of me," she said, and then she climbed back up through the charred beams to the doorway, hoping her own world would be waiting for her on the other side. "I'll be back."

Her exit was drained of all drama when she wriggled over the threshold and found herself on a hard wooden floor decorated with a hideous Persian runner. The hallway in the modern-day house was carpeted.

"Oh, no," she groaned, just lying there for a moment, trying to think what to do. The curtain in time that had permitted her to pass between one century and the other had closed, and she had no way of knowing when—or if—it would ever open again.

It was just possible that she was trapped in this rerun of *Gunsmoke*—permanently.

"Damn," she groaned, getting to her feet and running her hands down the sooty denim of her jeans. When she'd managed to stop shaking, Rue approached one of the series of photographs lining the wall and looked up into the dour face of an old man with a bushy white beard and a look of fanatical righteousness about him. "I sure hope *you're* not hanging around here somewhere," she muttered.

Next, she cautiously opened the door of the room she'd slept in the night before—only it wasn't the same. All the furniture was obviously antique, yet it looked new. Rue backed out and proceeded along the hallway, her sense of fascinated uneasiness growing with every passing moment.

"Through the looking glass," she murmured to herself. "Any minute now, I should meet a talking rabbit with a pocket watch and a waistcoat."

"Or a United States marshal," said a deep male voice.

Rue whirled, light-headed with surprise, and watched in disbelief as a tall, broad-shouldered cowboy with a badge pinned to his vest mounted the last of the front stairs to stand in the hall. His rumpled brown hair was a touch too long, his turquoise eyes were narrowed with suspicion, and he was badly in need of a shave.

This guy was straight out of the late movie, but his personal magnetism was strictly high-tech.

"What's your name?" he asked in that gravelly voice of his.

Rue couldn't help thinking what a hit this guy would be in the average singles' bar. Not only was he good-looking, in a rough, tough sort of way, he had macho down to an art form. "Rue Claridge," she said, just a little too heartily, extending one hand in friendly greeting.

The marshal glanced at her hand, but failed to offer his own. "You make a habit of prowling around in other people's houses?" he asked. His marvelous eyes widened as he took in her jeans, T-shirt and sneakers.

"I'm looking for my cousin Elisabeth." Rue's smile was a rigid curve, and she clung to it like someone dangling over the edge of a steep cliff. "I have reason to believe she might be in . . . these here parts."

The lawman set his rifle carefully against the wall, and Rue gulped. His expression was dubious. "Who are you?" he demanded again, folding his powerful arms. Afternoon sunlight streamed in through the open door to nowhere, and Rue could smell charred wood.

"I told you, my name is Rue Claridge, and I'm looking for my cousin, Elisabeth McCartney." Rue held up one hand to indicate a height comparable to her own. "She's a very pretty blonde, with big, bluish green eyes and a gentle manner."

The marshal's eyebrows drew together. "Lizzie?"

Rue shrugged. She'd never known Elisabeth to call herself Lizzie, but then, she hadn't visited another century, either. "She wrote me that she was in love with a man named Jonathan Fortner."

At this, the peace officer smiled, and his craggy face was transformed. Rue felt a modicum of comfort for the first time since she'd stepped over the threshold. "They're gone to San Francisco, Jon and Lizzie are," he said. "Got married a few months back, right after her trial was over."

Rue took a step closer to the marshal, one eyebrow raised, the peculiarities and implications of her situation temporarily forgotten. "Trial?"

"It's a long story." The splendid eyes swept over her clothes again and narrowed once more. "Where the devil did you get those duds?"

Rue drew in a deep breath and expelled it, making tendrils of her hair float for a few moments. "I come from another—place. What's your name, anyhow?"

"Farley Haynes," the cowboy answered.

Privately, Rue thought it was the dumbest handle she'd ever heard, but she was in no position to rile the man. "Well, Mr. Haynes," she said brightly, "I am sorry that you had to come all the way out here for nothing. The thing is, I know Elisabeth—Lizzie—would want me to stay right here in this house."

Haynes plunked his battered old hat back onto his head and regarded Rue from under the brim. "She never mentioned a cousin," he said. "Maybe you'd better come to town with me and answer a few more questions."

Rue's first impulse was to dig in her heels, but she was an inveterate journalist, and despite the fact that her head was still spinning from the shock of sudden transport from one time to another, she was fiercely curious about this place.

"What year is this, anyway?" she asked, not realizing how odd the question sounded until it was already out of her mouth.

The lawman's right hand cupped her elbow lightly as he ushered Rue down the front stairs. In his left, he carried the rifle with unnerving expertise. "It's 1892," he answered, giving her a sidelong look, probably wondering if he should slap the cuffs on her wrists. "The month is October."

"I suppose you're wondering why I didn't know that." Rue chatted on as the marshal escorted her out through the front door. There was a big sorrel gelding waiting beyond the whitewashed gate. "The fact is, I've—I've had a fever."

"You look healthy enough to me," Haynes responded, and just the timbre of his voice set some chord to vibrating deep inside Rue. He opened the gate and nodded for her to go through it ahead of him.

She took comfort from the presence of the horse; she'd always loved the animals, and some of the happiest times of her life had been spent in the saddle at Ribbon Creek. "Hello, big fella," she said, patting the gelding's sweaty neck.

In the next instant, Rue was grabbed around the waist and hoisted up into the saddle. Before she could react in any way, Marshal Haynes had thrust his rifle into the leather scabbard, stuck one booted foot in the stirrup and swung up behind her.

Rue felt seismic repercussions move up her spine in response.

"Am I under arrest?" she asked. He reached around her to grasp the reins, and again Rue was disturbed by the powerful contraction within her. Cowboy fantasies were one thing, she reminded herself, but this was a trip into the Twilight Zone, and she had an awful feeling her ticket was stamped "one-way." She'd never been on an assignment where it was more important to keep her wits about her.

"That depends," the marshal said, the words rumbling against her nape, "on whether or not you can explain how you came to be wearing Mrs. Fortner's necklace."

Leather creaked as Rue turned to look up into that rugged face, her mind racing in search of an explanation. "My—our aunt gave us each a necklace like this," she lied, her fingers straying to the filigree pendant. The piece was definitely an original, with a history. "Elis—Lizzie's probably wearing hers."

Farley looked skeptical to say the least, but he let the topic drop for the moment. "I don't mind telling you," he said, "that the Presbyterians are going to be riled up some when they get a gander at those clothes of yours. It isn't proper for a lady to wear trousers."

Rue might have been amused by his remarks if it hadn't been for the panic that was rising inside her. Nothing in her fairly wide experience had prepared her for being thrust unceremoniously into 1892, after all. "I don't have anything else to wear," she said in an uncharacteristically small voice, and then she sank her teeth into her lower lip, gripped the pommel of Marshal Haynes's saddle in both hands and held on for dear life, even though she was an experienced rider.

After a bumpy, dusty trip over the unpaved country road that led to town—its counterpart in Rue's time was paved—

they reached Pine River. The place had gone into rewind while she wasn't looking. There were saloons with swinging doors, and a big saw in the lumber mill beside the river screamed and flung sawdust into the air. People walked along board sidewalks and rode in buggies and wagons. Rue couldn't help gaping at them.

Marshal Haynes lifted her down from the horse before she had a chance to tell him she didn't need his help, and he gave her an almost imperceptible push toward the sidewalk. Bronze script on the window of the nearest building proclaimed, Pine River Jailhouse. Farley Haynes, Marshal.

Bravely, Rue resigned herself to the possibility of a stretch behind bars. Much as she wanted to see the twentieth century again, she'd changed her mind about leaving 1892 right away—she meant to stick around until Elisabeth came back. Despite those glowing letters, Rue wanted to know her cousin was all right before she put this parallel universe—or whatever it was—behind her.

"Do you believe in ghosts, Farley?" she asked companionably, once they were inside and the marshal had opened a little gate in the railing that separated his desk and cabinet and wood stove from the single jail cell.

"No, ma'am," he answered with a sigh, hanging his disreputable hat on a hook by the door and laying his rifle down on the cluttered surface of the desk. Once again, his gaze passed over her clothes, troubled and quick. "But I do believe there are some strange things going on in this world that wouldn't be too easy to explain."

Rue tucked her hands into the hip pockets of her jeans and looked at the wanted posters on the wall behind Farley's desk. They should have been yellow and cracked with age, but instead they were new and only slightly crumpled. A collection of archaic rifles filled a gun cabinet, their nickel barrels and wooden stocks gleaming with a high shine that belied their age.

"You won't get an argument from me," Rue finally replied.

Chapter Two

Rue took in the crude jail cell, the potbellied stove with a coffeepot and a kettle crowding the top, the black, iron key ring hanging on a peg behind the desk. Her gaze swung to the marshal's face, and she gestured toward the barred room at the back of the building.

"If I'm under arrest, Marshal," she said matter-of-factly, "I'd like to know exactly what I'm being charged with."

The peace officer sighed, hanging his ancient canvas coat from a tarnished brass rack. "Well, miss, we could start with trespassing." He gestured toward a chair pushed back against the short railing that surrounded the immediate office area. "Sit down and tell me who you are and what you were doing snooping around Dr. Fortner's house that way."

Rue was feeling a little weak, a rare occurrence for her. She pulled the chair closer to the desk and sat, pushing her tousled hair back from her face. "I told you. My name is

Rue Claridge," she replied patiently. "Dr. Fortner's wife is my cousin, and I was looking for her. That's all."

The turquoise gaze, sharp with intelligence, rested on the gold pendant at the base of Rue's throat, causing the pulse beneath to make a strange, sudden leap. "I believe you said Mrs. Fortner has a necklace just like that one."

Rue swallowed. She was very good at sidestepping issues she didn't want to discuss, but when it came to telling an outright lie, she hadn't even attained amateur status. "Y-yes," she managed to say. Her earlier shock at finding herself in another century was thawing now, becoming low-grade panic. Was it possible that she'd stumbled into Elisabeth's nervous breakdown, or was she having a separate one, all her own?

The marshal's jawline tightened under a shadow of beard. His strong, sun-browned fingers were interlaced over his middle as he leaned back in his creaky desk chair. "How do you account for those clothes you're wearing?"

She took a deep, quivering breath. "Where I come from, lots of women dress like this."

Marshal Haynes arched one eyebrow. "And where is that?" There was an indulgent tone in his voice that made Rue want to knuckle his head.

Rue thought fast. "Montana. I have a ranch over there."

Farley scratched the back of his neck with an idleness Rue perceived as entirely false. Although his lackadaisical manner belied the fact, she sensed a certain lethal energy about him, an immense physical and emotional power barely restrained. Before she could stop it, Rue's mind had made the jump to wondering what it would be like to be held and caressed by this man.

Just the idea gave her a feeling of horrified delight.

"Doesn't your husband mind having his wife go around dressed like a common cowhand?" he asked evenly.

Color flooded Rue's face, but she held her temper carefully in check. Marshal Haynes's attitude toward women was unacceptable, but he was a man of his time and all attempts to convert him to modern thinking would surely be wasted.

"I don't have a husband." She thought she saw a flicker of reaction in the incredible eyes.

"Your daddy, then?"

Rue drew a deep breath and let it out slowly. "I'm not close to my family," she said sweetly. For all practical intents and purposes, the statement was true. Rue's parents had been divorced years before, going their separate ways. Her mother was probably holed up in some fancy spa somewhere, getting ready for the ski season, and her father's last postcard had been sent from Monaco. "I'm on my own. Except for Elisabeth, of course."

The marshal studied her for a long moment, looking pensive now, and then leaned forward in his chair. "Yes. Elisabeth Fortner."

"Right," Rue agreed, her head spinning. Nothing in her eventful past had prepared her for this particular situation. Somehow, she'd missed Time Travel 101 in college, and the Nostalgia Channel mostly covered the 1940s.

She sighed to herself. If she'd been sent back to the big-band era, maybe she would have known how to act.

"I'm going to let you go for now," Haynes announced thoughtfully. "But if you get into any trouble, ma'am, you'll have me to contend with."

A number of wisecracks came to the forefront of Rue's mind, but she valiantly held them back. "I'll just...go now," she said awkwardly, before racing out of the jailhouse onto the street.

The screech of the mill saw hurt her ears, and she hurried in the opposite direction. It would take a good forty-five minutes to walk back to the house in the country, and by the looks of the sky, the sun would be setting soon.

As she was passing the Hang-Dog Saloon, a shrill cry from above made Rue stop and look up.

Two prostitutes were leaning up against a weathered railing, their seedy-looking satin dresses glowing in the late-afternoon sun. "Where'd you get them pants?" the one in blue inquired, just before spitting tobacco into the street.

The redhead beside her, who was wearing a truly ugly pea green gown, giggled as though her friend had said something incredibly clever.

"You know, Red," Rue replied, shading her eyes with one hand as she looked up, and choosing to ignore both the question and the tobacco juice, "you really ought to have your colors done. That shade of green is definitely unbecoming."

The prostitutes looked at each other, then turned and flounced away from the railing, disappearing into the noisy saloon.

The conversation had not been a total loss, Rue decided, looking down at her jeans, sneakers and T-shirt. There was no telling how long she'd have to stay in this backward century, and her modern clothes would be a real hindrance.

She turned and spotted a store across the street, displaying gingham dresses, bridles and wooden buckets behind its fly-speckled front window. "'And bring your Visa card,'" she muttered to herself, "'because they *don't* take American Express.'"

Rue carefully made her way over, avoiding road apples, mud puddles and two passing wagons.

On the wooden sidewalk in front of the mercantile, she stood squinting, trying to see through the dirty glass. The red-and-white gingham dress on display in the window looked more suited to Dorothy of *The Wizard of Oz* fame, with its silly collar and big, flouncy bow at the back. The garment's only saving grace was that it looked as though it would probably fit.

Talking to herself was a habit Rue had acquired because she'd spent so much time alone researching and polishing her stories. "Maybe I can get a pair of ruby slippers, too," she murmured, walking resolutely toward the store's entrance. "Then I could just click my heels together and voilà, Toto, we're back in Kansas."

A pleasant-looking woman with gray hair and soft blue eyes beamed at Rue as she entered. The smile faded to an expression of chagrined consternation, however, as the old lady took in Rue's jeans and T-shirt.

"May I help you?" the lady asked, sounding as though she doubted very much that anybody could.

Rue was dizzied by the sheer reality of the place, the woman, the circumstances in which she found herself. A fly bounced helplessly against a window, buzzing in bewilderment the whole time, and Rue felt empathy for it. "That checked dress in the window," she began, her voice coming out hoarse. "How much is it?"

The fragile blue gaze swept over Rue once again, worriedly. "Why, it's fifty cents, child."

For a moment, Rue was delighted. Fifty cents. No problem.

Then she realized she hadn't brought any money with her. Even if she had, all the bills and currency would have looked suspiciously different from what was being circulated in the 1890s, and she would undoubtedly have found herself back in Farley Haynes's custody, post haste.

Rue smiled her most winning smile, the one that had gotten her into so many press conferences and out of so many tight spots. "Just put it on my account, please," she said.

Rue possessed considerable bravado, but the strain of the day was beginning to tell.

The store mistress raised delicate eyebrows and cleared her throat. "Do I know you?"

Another glance at the dress—it only added insult to injury that the thing was so relentlessly ugly—gave Rue the impetus to answer, "No. My name is Rue...*Miss* Rue Claridge, and I'm Elisabeth Fortner's cousin. Perhaps you could put the dress on her husband's account?"

The woman sniffed. Clearly, in mentioning the good doctor, Rue had touched a nerve. "Jonathan Fortner ought to have his head examined, marrying a strange woman the way he did. There were odd doings in that house!"

Normally Rue would have been defensive, since she tended to get touchy where Elisabeth was concerned, but she couldn't help thinking how peculiar her cousin must have seemed to these people. Bethie was a quiet sort, but her ideas and attitudes were strictly modern, and she must surely have rubbed more than one person the wrong way.

Rue focused on the block of cheese sitting on the counter, watching as two flies explored the hard, yellow rind. "What kind of odd doings?" she asked, too much the reporter to let such an opportunity pass.

The storekeeper seemed to forget that Rue was a suspicious type, new in town and wearing clothes more suited, as Farley had said, to a cowhand. Leaning forward, she whispered confidentially, "That woman would simply appear and disappear at will. Not a few of us think she's a witch and that justice would have been better served if she'd been hanged after that trial of hers!"

For a moment, the fundamentals of winning friends and influencing people slipped Rue's mind. "Don't be silly—there're no such things as witches." She lowered her voice and, having dispatched with superstition, hurried on to her main concern. "Elisabeth was put on trial and might have been hanged? For what?"

The other woman was in a state of offense, probably because one of her pet theories had just been ridiculed. "For a time, it looked as though she'd murdered not only Dr. Fortner, but his young daughter, Trista, as well, by setting that blaze." She paused, clearly befuddled. "Then they came back. Just magically reappeared out of the ruins of that burned house."

Rue was nodding to herself. She didn't know the rules of this time-travel game, but it didn't take a MENSA membership to figure out how Bethie's husband and the little girl had probably escaped the fire. No doubt they'd fled over the threshold into the next century, then had trouble returning. Or perhaps time didn't pass at the same rate here as it did there....

It seemed to Rue that Aunt Verity had claimed the necklace's magic was unpredictable, waning and waxing under mysterious rules of its own. Elisabeth had mentioned nothing like that in her letters, however.

Rue brought herself back to the matter at hand—buying the dress. "Dr. Fortner must be a man of responsibility, coming back from the great beyond like that. It would naturally follow that his credit would be good."

The storekeeper went pale, then pursed her lips and sighed, "I'm sorry. Dr. Fortner is, indeed, a trusted and valued customer, but I cannot add merchandise to his account without his permission. Besides, there's no telling when he and that bride of his will return from California."

The woman was nondescript and diminutive, and yet Rue knew she'd be wasting her time to argue. She'd met third-world leaders with more flexible outlooks on life. "Okay," she said with a sigh. She'd just have to check the house and see if Elisabeth had left any clothes or money behind. Provided she couldn't get back into her own time, that is.

Rue offered a polite goodbye, only too aware that she might be stuck on this side of 1900 indefinitely.

Although she power walked most of the way home—this drew stares from the drivers of passing buggies and wagons—it was quite dark when Rue arrived. She let herself in through the kitchen door, relieved to find that the housekeeper had left for the day.

After stumbling around in the darkness for a while, Rue found matches and lit the kerosene lamp in the middle of the table.

The weak light flickered over a fire-damaged kitchen, made livable by someone's hard work. There was an old-fashioned icebox, a pump handle at the sink and a big cookstove with shiny chrome trim.

Bethie actually wanted to stay in this place, Rue reflected, marveling. Her cousin would develop biceps just getting enough water to make the morning coffee, and she'd probably have to chop and carry wood, too. Then there would be the washing and the ironing and the cooking. And childbirth at its most natural, with nothing for the pain except maybe a bullet to bite on.

All this for the mysterious Dr. Jonathan Fortner.

"No man is worth it, Bethie," Rue protested to the empty room, but Farley Haynes did swagger to mind, and his image was so vivid, she could almost catch the scent of his skin and hair.

Desperately hungry all of a sudden, she ransacked the icebox, helping herself to milk so creamy it had golden streaks on top, and half a cold, boiled potato. When she'd eaten, she took the lamp and headed upstairs, leaving the other rooms to explore later.

She'd had quite enough adventure for one day.

In the second floor hallway, Rue looked at the blackened door and knew without even touching the knob that she would find nothing but more ruins on the other side. Maybe she'd be able to get back to her own century, but it wasn't going to happen that night.

Reaching the master bedroom, Rue approached the tall armoire first. It soon became apparent that Bethie hadn't left much behind, certainly nothing Rue could wear, and if there was a cache of money, it wasn't hidden in that room.

Finally, exhausted, Rue washed as best she could, stripped off her clothes and crawled into the big bed.

Farley didn't make a habit of turning up in ladies' bedrooms of a morning, though he'd awakened in more than a few. There was just something about this particular woman that drew him with a force nearly as strong as his will, and it wasn't just that she wore trousers and claimed to be Lizzie Fortner's kin.

Her honey-colored hair, shorter than most women wore but still reaching to her shoulders, tumbled across the white pillow, catching the early sunlight, and her skin, visible to her armpits, where the sheet stopped, was a creamy golden peach. Her dark eyelashes lay on her cheeks like the wings of some small bird, and her breathing, even and untroubled, twisted Farley's senses up tight as the spring of a cheap watch.

He swallowed hard. Rue Claridge might be telling the truth, he thought, at least about being related to Mrs. Fortner. God knew, she was strange enough, with her trousers and her funny way of talking.

"Miss Claridge?" he said after clearing his throat. He wanted to wriggle her toe, but decided everything south of where the sheet stopped was out of his jurisdiction. "Rue!"

She sat bolt upright in bed and, to Farley's guarded relief and vast disappointment, held the top sheet firmly against her bosom.

Farley Haynes was standing at the foot of the bed, his hands resting on his hips, his handsome head cocked to one side.

Rue sat up hastily, insulted and alarmed and strangely aroused all at once, and wrenched the sheets from her collarbone to her chin.

"I sure hope you're making yourself at home and all," Farley said, and the expression in his eyes was wry in spite of his folksy drawl. He wasn't fooling Rue; this guy was about as slow moving and countrified as a New York politician.

Although the marshal hadn't touched her, Rue had the oddest sensation of impact, as though she'd been hauled against his chest, with just the sheet between them. "What are you doing here?" she demanded furiously when she found her voice at last. She felt the ornate headboard press against her bare back and bottom.

He arched one eyebrow and folded his arms. "I could ask the same question of you, little lady."

Enough was enough. Nobody was going to call Rue Claridge "honey," "sweetie" or "little lady" and get away with it, no matter *what* century they came from.

"Don't call me 'little' anything!" Rue snapped. "I'm a grown woman and a self-supporting professional, and I won't be patronized!"

This time, both the intruder's eyebrows rose, then knit together into a frown. "You sure are a temperamental filly," Farley allowed. "And mouthy as hell, too."

"Get out of here!" Rue shouted.

Idly, Farley drew up a rocking chair and sat. Then he rubbed his stubbly chin, his eyes narrowed thoughtfully. "You said you were a professional before. Question is, a professional what?"

Rue was still clutching the covers to her throat, and she was breathing hard, as though she'd just finished a marathon. If she hadn't been afraid to let go of the bedclothes with even one hand, she would have snatched up the small crockery pitcher on the nightstand and hurled it at his head.

"You would never understand," she answered haughtily. "Now it's my turn to ask a question, Marshal. What the *hell* are you doing in my bedroom?"

"This isn't your bedroom," the lawman pointed out quietly. "It's Jon Fortner's. And I'm here because Miss Ellen came to town and reported a prowler on the premises."

Rue gave an outraged sigh. The housekeeper had apparently entered the room, seen an unwelcome guest sleeping there and marched herself into Pine River to demand legal action. "Hellfire and spit," Rue snapped. "Why didn't she drag Judge Wapner out here, too?"

Farley's frown deepened to bewilderment. "There's no judge by that name around these parts," he said. "And I wish you'd stop talking like that. If the Presbyterians hear you, they'll be right put out about it."

Catching herself just before she would have exploded into frustrated hysterics, Rue sucked in a deep breath and held it until a measure of calm came over her. "All right," she said finally, in a reasonable tone. "I will try not to stir up the Presbyterians. I promise. The point is, now you've investigated and you've seen that I'm not a trespasser, but a member of the family. I have a right to be here, Marshal, but, frankly, you don't. Now if you would please leave."

Farley sat forward in his chair, turning the brim of his battered, sweat-stained hat in nimble brown fingers. "Until I get word back from San Francisco that it's all right for you to stay here, ma'am, I'm afraid you'll have to put up at one of the boardinghouses in town."

Rue would have agreed to practically anything just to get him to leave the room. The painful truth was, Marshal Farley Haynes made places deep inside her thrum and pulse in response to some hidden dynamic of his personality. That was terrifying because she'd never felt anything like it before.

"Whatever you say," she replied with a lift of her chin. Innocuous as they were, the words came out sounding defiant. "Just leave this room, please. Immediately."

She thought she saw a twinkle in Farley's gem-bright eyes. He stood up with an exaggerated effort and, to Rue's horror, walked to the head of the bed and stood looking down at her.

"No husband and no daddy," he reflected sagely. "Little wonder your manners are so sorry." With that, he cupped one hand under her chin, then bent over and kissed her, just as straightforwardly as if he were shaking her hand.

To Rue's further mortification, instead of pushing him away, as her acutely trained left brain told her to do, she rose higher on her knees and thrust herself into the kiss. It was soft and warm at first, then Farley touched the seam of her mouth with his tongue and she opened to him, like a night orchid worshiping the moon. He took utter and complete command before suddenly stepping back.

"I expect you to be settled somewhere else by nightfall," he said gruffly. To his credit, he didn't avert his eyes, but he didn't look any happier about what he'd just done than Rue was.

"Get out," she breathed.

Farley settled his hat on his head, touched the brim in a mockingly cordial way and strolled from the room.

Rue sent her pillow flying after him, because he was so insufferable. Because he'd had the unmitigated gall not only to come into her bedroom, but to kiss her. Because her insides were still colliding like carnival rides gone berserk.

Later, ignoring Ellen, who was watchful and patently disapproving, Rue fetched a ladder from the barn and set it against the burned side of the house. At least, she thought, looking down at her jeans and T-shirt, she was dressed for climbing.

She still wanted to find Elisabeth and make sure her cousin was all right, but there were things she'd need to sustain herself in this primitive era. She intended to return to the late twentieth century, buy some suitable clothes from a costume place or a theater troupe, and pick up some old currency at a coin shop. Then she'd return, purchase a ticket on a train or boat headed south and see for herself that Bethie was happy and well.

It was an excellent plan, all in all, except that when Rue reached the top of the ladder and opened the charred door, nothing happened. She knew by the runner on the hallway floor and the pictures on the wall that she was still in 1892, even though she was wearing the necklace and wishing as hard as she could.

Obviously, one couldn't go back and forth between the two centuries on a whim.

Rue climbed down the ladder in disgust, finally, and stood in the deep grass, dusting her soot-blackened hands off on the legs of her jeans. "Damn it, Bethie," she muttered, "you'd better have a good reason for putting me through this!"

In the meantime, whether Elisabeth had a viable excuse for being in the wrong century or not, Rue had to make the best of her circumstances. She needed to find a way to fit in—and fast—before the locals decided *she* was a witch.

Ellen had draped a rug over the clothesline and was busily beating it with something that resembled a snowshoe. Occasionally she glanced warily in Rue's direction, as though expecting to be turned into a crow at any moment.

Rue wedged her hands into the hip pockets of her jeans and mentally ruled out all possibility of searching Elisabeth's house for money while the housekeeper was around. There was only one way to get the funds she needed, and if she didn't get busy, she might find herself spending the night in somebody's barn.

Or the Pine River jailhouse.

The idea of being behind bars went against her grain. Rue had once done a brief stint in a minimum-security women's prison for refusing to reveal a source to a grand jury, but this would obviously be different.

Rue headed for the road, walking backward so she could look at the house and "remember" how it *would* look in another hundred years. A part of her still expected to wake up on the couch in Aunt Verity's front parlor and discover this whole experience had been nothing more than a dream.

Reaching Pine River, Rue headed straight for the Hang-Dog Saloon, though she did have the discretion to make her way around to the alley and go in the back door.

In a smoky little room in the rear of the building, Rue found exactly what she'd hoped for, exactly what a thousand TV Westerns had conditioned her to expect. Four drunk men were seated around a rickety table, playing poker.

At the sight of a woman entering this inner sanctum, especially one wearing pants, the cardplayers stared. A man sporting a dusty stovepipe hat went so far as to let the unlit stogie fall from between his teeth, and the fat one with garters on his sleeves folded his cards and threw them in.

"What the hell . . . ?"

After swallowing hard, Rue peeled off her digital watch and tossed it into the center of the table. "I'd like to play, if you fellas don't mind," she said, sounding much bolder than she felt.

The man in the stovepipe hat had apparently recovered from the shock of seeing the wrong woman in the wrong place; he picked up the wristwatch and studied it with a solemn frown. "Never seen nothin' like this here," he told his colleagues.

Being one of those people who believe that great forces come to the aid of the bold, Rue drew up a chair and sat down between a long-haired gunfighter type in a canvas duster and the hefty guy with the garters.

"Deal me in," she said brightly.

"Where'd you get this thing?" asked the one in the high hat.

"K mart," Rue answered, reaching for the battered deck lying in the middle of the table. She thought of bumper stickers she'd seen in her own time and couldn't help grinning. "My other watch is a Rolex," she added.

Stovepipe looked at her in consternation and opened his mouth to protest, but when Rue shuffled the cards deftly from one hand to the other without dropping a single one, he pressed his lips together.

The gunfighter whistled. "Son of a— Tarnation, ma'am. Where'd you learn to do that?"

Rue was warming to the game, as well as the conversation. "On board Air Force One, about three years ago. A Secret Serviceman taught me."

Stovepipe and Garters looked at each other in pure bewilderment.

"I say the lady plays," said the gunslinger.

Nobody argued, perhaps because Quickdraw was wearing a mean-looking forty-five low on his hip.

Rue dealt with a skill born of years of practice—her grandfather had taught her to play five-card draw back in Montana when she was six years old, and she'd been winning matchsticks, watches, ballpoint pens and pocket change ever since.

Rue had taken several pots, made up mostly of coins, though she had raked in a couple of oversize nineteenth-century dollar bills, in this game when the prostitute in the pea green dress came rustling in.

The woman's painted mouth fell open when she saw Rue sitting at the table, actually playing poker with the men, and her kohl-lined eyes widened. She set a fresh bottle of whiskey down on the table with an irate thump.

"Be quiet, Sissy," Quickdraw said, talking around the matchstick he was holding between his teeth. "This here is serious poker."

Sissy's eyes looked, as Aunt Verity would have said, like two burn holes in a blanket, and Rue felt a stab of pity for her. God knew, nineteenth-century life was hard enough for respectable women. It would be even rougher for ladies of the evening.

Quickdraw picked up Rue's watch, which was lying next to her stack of winnings, and held it up for Sissy's inspection. "You bring me good luck, little sugar girl, and I'll give you this for a trinket."

"I think I may throw up," Rue murmured under her breath.

"What'd you say?" Stovepipe demanded, sounding a little testy. Losing at poker clearly didn't sit well with him.

Rue offered the same smile she would have used to cajole the president of the United States into answering a tough question at a press conference, and replied, "I said I'm sure glad I showed up."

Sissy tossed the watch back to the table, glared at Rue for a moment, then turned and sashayed out of the room.

Rue was secretly relieved and turned all her concentration on the matter at hand. She had enough winnings to buy that horrible gingham dress and rent herself a room at the boardinghouse; now all she needed to do was ease out of the game without making her companions angry.

She yawned expansively.

Garters gave her a quelling look, clearly not ready to give up on the evening, and the game went on. And on.

It was starting to get embarrassing the way Rue kept winning, when all of a sudden the inner door to the saloon crashed open. There, filling the doorway like some fugitive from a Louis L'Amour novel, was Farley Haynes.

Finding Rue with five cards in her hand and a stack of coins in front of her, he swore. Sissy peered around his broad shoulder and smiled, just to let Rue know she'd been the one to bring about her impending downfall.

"Game's over," Farley said in that gruff voice, and none of the players took exception to the announcement. In fact, except for Rue, they all scattered, muttering various excuses and hasty pleasantries as they rushed out.

Rue stood and began stuffing her winnings into the pockets of her jeans. "Don't get your mustache in a wringer, Marshal," she said. "I've got what I came for and now I'm leaving."

Farley shook his head in quiet, angry wonderment and gestured toward the door with one hand. "Come along with me, Miss Claridge. You're under arrest."

Chapter Three

Farley Haynes set his jaw, took Miss Rue Claridge by the elbow and hauled her toward the door. He prided himself on being a patient man, slow to wrath, as the Good Book said, but this woman tried his forbearance beyond all reasonable measure. Furthermore, he just flat didn't like the sick-calf feeling he got whenever he looked at her.

"Now, just a minute, Marshal," Miss Claridge snapped, trying to pull free of his grasp. "You haven't read me my rights!"

Farley tightened his grip, but he was careful not to bruise that soft flesh of hers. He didn't hold with manhandling a lady—not even one who barely measured up to the term when it came to comportment. To his way of thinking, Rue Claridge added up just fine as far as appearances went.

"What rights?" he demanded as they reached the shadowy alley behind the saloon. He had the damnedest, most unmarshal-like urge to drag Rue against his chest and kiss her, right then and there, and that scared the molasses out of him. The thought of kissing somebody in pants had never so much as crossed Farley's mind before, and he hoped to God it never would again.

"Forget it," she said, and her disdainful tone nettled Farley sorely. "It's pretty clear that around this town, I don't *have* any rights. I hope you're enjoying this, because it won't be long until you find yourself dealing with the likes of Susan B. Anthony!"

"Who?" Farley hadn't been this vexed since the year he was twelve, when Becky Hinehammer had called him a coward for refusing to walk the ridgepole on the schoolhouse roof. His pride had driven him to prove her wrong, and he'd gotten a broken collarbone for his trouble, along with a memorable blistering from his pa, once he'd healed up properly, for doing such a damn-fool thing in the first place.

He propelled Miss Claridge out of the alley and onto the main street of town. Pine River was relatively quiet that night.

They reached the jailhouse, and Farley pushed the front door open, then escorted his captive straight back to the jail's only cell.

Once his saucy prisoner was secured, Farley hung his hat on a peg next to the door and put away his rifle. It didn't occur to him to unstrap his gun belt; that was something he did only when it was time to stretch out for the night. Even then, he liked to have his .45 within easy reach.

He found a spare enamel mug, wiped it out with an old dish towel snatched from a nail behind the potbellied stove, and poured coffee. Then he carried the steaming brew to the cell and handed it through the bars to Miss Claridge. "What kind of name is Rue?" he asked, honestly puzzled.

This woman was full of mysteries, and he found himself wanting to solve them one by one.

His guest blew on the coffee, took a cautious sip and made a face. At least she was womanly enough to mind her manners. Farley had half expected her to slurp up the brew like an old mule skinner and maybe spit a mouthful into the corner. Instead, she came right back with, "What kind of name is Farley?"

If she wasn't going to give a direct answer, neither was he. "You're a snippy little piece, aren't you?"

Rue smiled, revealing a good, solid set of very white teeth. Folk wisdom said a woman lost a tooth for every child she bore, but Farley figured this gal would probably still have a mouthful even if she gave birth to a dozen babies.

"And *you're* lucky I know you're calling me 'a piece' in the old-fashioned sense of the word," she said pleasantly. "Because if you meant it the way men mean it where— when—I come from, I'd throw this wretched stuff you call coffee all over you."

Farley didn't back away; he wouldn't let himself be intimidated by a smudged little spitfire in britches. "I reckon I've figured out why your folks gave you that silly name," he said. "They knew someday some poor man would rue the day you were ever born."

A flush climbed Rue's cheeks, and Farley reflected that her skin was as fine as her teeth. She was downright pretty, if a little less voluptuous than he'd have preferred—or would be, if anybody ever took the time to clean her up.

Considering that task made one side of Farley's mouth twitch in a fleeting grin.

He saw her blush again, then lift the mug to her mouth with both hands and take a healthy swig.

"God, I can't believe I'm actually drinking this sludge!" she spat out just a moment later. "What did you do, boil down a vat of axle grease?"

Farley turned away to hide another grin, sighing as he pretended to straighten the papers on his desk. "The Presbyterians are surely going to have their hands full getting *you* back on the straight and narrow," he allowed.

Rue stared at Farley's broad, muscular back and swallowed. She was exhausted and confused and, since she hadn't had anything to eat in almost a century, hungry. She kept expecting to wake up, even though she knew this situation was all too real.

She sat on the edge of the cell's one cot, which boasted a thin, bare mattress and a gray woolen blanket that looked as though it could have belonged to the poorest private in General Lee's rebel army.

"Did you ever get around to having your supper?" Farley's voice was gruff, but there was something oddly comforting about the deep, resonating timbre of it.

Rue didn't look at him; there were tears in her eyes, and she was too proud to let them show. "No," she answered.

Farley's tone remained gentle, and Rue knew he had moved closer. "It's late, but I'll see if I can't raise Bessie over at the Hang-Dog and get her to fix you something."

Rue was still too stricken to speak; she just nodded.

Only when the marshal had left the jailhouse on his errand of mercy did Rue allow herself a loud sniffle. She stood and gripped the bars in both hands.

Maybe because she was tired, she actually hoped, for a few fleeting moments, that the key would be hanging from a peg within stretching distance on her cell, like in a TV Western.

In this case, fact was not stranger than fiction—there was no key in sight.

She began to pace, muttering to herself. If she ever got out of this, she'd write a book about it, tell the world. Appear on *Donahue* and *Oprah*.

Rue stopped, the nail of her index finger caught between her teeth. Who would ever believe her, besides Elisabeth?

She sat on the edge of the cot again and drew deep breaths until she felt a little less like screaming in frustration and panic.

Half an hour had passed, by the old clock facing Farley's messy desk, when the marshal returned carrying a basket covered with a blue-and-white checkered napkin.

Rue's stomach rumbled audibly and, to cover her embarrassment at that, she said defiantly, "You were foolish to leave me unattended, Marshal. I might very well have escaped."

He chuckled, extracted the coveted key from the pocket of his rough spun trousers and unlocked the cell door. "Is that so, Miss Spitfire? Then why didn't you?"

She narrowed her eyes. "Don't be so damn cocky," she warned. "For all you know, I might be part of a gang. Why, twenty or thirty outlaws might ride in here and dynamite this place."

Farley set the basket down and moseyed out of the cell, as unconcerned as if his prisoner were an addlepated old lady. Rue was vaguely insulted that the lawman didn't consider her more dangerous.

"Shut up and eat your supper," he said, not unkindly.

Rue plopped down on the edge of the cot again. Farley had set the basket on the only other piece of furniture in the cell, a rickety old stool, and she pulled that close.

There was cold roast venison in the basket, along with a couple of hard flour-and-water biscuits and an apple.

Rue ate greedily, but the whole time she watched Farley out of the corner of one eye. He was doing paperwork at the desk, by the light of a flickering kerosene lamp.

"Aren't you ever going home?" she inquired when she'd consumed every scrap of the food.

Farley didn't look up. "I've got a little place out back," he said. "You'd better get some sleep, Miss Claridge. Likely as not, you'll have the ladies of the town to deal with come morning. They'll want to take you on as a personal mission."

Rue let her forehead rest against an icy bar and sighed. "Great."

When Farley finally raised his eyes and saw that Rue was still standing there staring at him, he put down his pencil. "Am I keeping you awake?"

"It's just..." Rue paused, swallowed, started again. "Well, I'd like to wash up, that's all. And maybe brush my teeth." *In my own bathroom, thank you. In my own wonderful, crazy, modern world.*

Farley stretched, then brought a large kettle from a cabinet near the stove. "I guess you'll just have to rinse and spit, since the town of Pine River doesn't provide toothbrushes, but I can heat up some wash water for you."

He disappeared through a rear door, returning minutes later with the kettle, which he set on the stove top.

Rue bit her lower lip. It was bad enough that the marshal expected her to bathe in that oversize bird cage he called a cell. How clean could a girl get with two quarts of water?

"This is a clear violation of the Geneva Convention," she said.

Farley looked at her over one sturdy shoulder, shook his head in obvious consternation and went back to his desk. "If you hadn't told me you and Lizzie Fortner were kinfolk, I'd have guessed it anyway. Both of you talk like you're from somewhere a long ways from here."

Rue sagged against the cell door and closed her eyes for a moment. "So far away you couldn't begin to comprehend it, cowboy," she muttered.

Farley's deep voice contained a note of distracted humor. "Since I didn't quite make out what you just said, I'm going to assume it was something kindly," he told her without looking up from those fascinating papers of his.

"Don't you have something waiting for you at home—a dog or a goldfish or something?" Rue asked. She didn't know which she was more desperate for—a little privacy or the simple comfort of ordinary conversation.

The marshal sighed and laid down his nibbed pen. His wooden chair creaked under his weight as he leaned back. "I live alone," he said, sounding beleaguered and a little smug in the bargain.

"Oh." Rue felt a flash of bittersweet relief at this announcement, though she would have given up her trust fund rather than admit the fact. Earlier, she'd experienced a dizzying sense of impact, even though Farley wasn't touching her, and now she was painfully aware of the lean hardness of his frame and the easy masculine grace with which he moved.

It was damn ironic that being around Jeff Wilson had never had this effect on her. Maybe if it had, she would have a couple of kids and a real home by now, in addition to the career she loved.

"You must be pretty ambitious," she blurted out. The sound of heat surging through the water in the kettle filled the quiet room. "Do you often work late?"

Farley put down his pen again and scratched the nape of his neck before emitting an exasperated sigh. "I don't plan on spending my life as a lawman," he replied with a measured politeness that clearly told Rue he wished she'd shut up and let him get on with whatever he was doing. "I've been saving for a ranch ever since I got out of the army. I mean to raise cattle and horses."

At last, Rue thought. Common ground.

"I have a ranch," she announced. "Over in Montana."

"So you said," Farley replied. It was plain enough that, to him, Rue's claim was just another wild story. He got up and crossed the room to test the water he'd been heating. "Guess this is ready," he said.

Rue narrowed her eyes as he came toward the cell, carrying the kettle by its black iron handle, fingers protected from the steam by the same rumpled dish towel he'd used to wipe out the mug earlier.

"I'm not planning to strip down and lather up in front of you, Marshal," she warned, standing back as he unlocked the cell door and came in.

He laughed, and the sound was unexpectedly rich. "That would be quite a show," he said.

Rue wasn't sure she appreciated his amusement. She just glared at him.

Farley set the kettle down in the cell, then went out and locked the door again. He handed Rue a rough towel and a cloth through the bars, then ambled over to collect his hat and canvas duster.

"Good night, Miss Claridge." With that, he blew out the kerosene lantern on his desk, plunging the room into darkness except for the thin beams of moonlight coming in through the few windows.

It was remarkable how lonely and scared Rue felt once he'd closed and locked the front door of the jailhouse. Up until then, she'd have sworn she wanted him to go.

She waited until she was reasonably sure she wouldn't be interrupted before hastily stripping. Shivering there in that cramped little cell, Rue washed in the now-tepid water Farley had brought, then put her clothes back on. After wrapping herself in the Civil War blanket, she lay down on the cot and closed her eyes.

Although Rue fully expected the worst bout of insomnia ever, she fell asleep with all the hesitation of a rock dropping to the bottom of a deep pond. She awakened to a faceful of bright sunlight and the delicious smell and cheerful sizzle of bacon frying.

At first, Rue thought she was home at Ribbon Creek, with her granddaddy cooking breakfast in the ranch house kitchen. Then it all come back to her.

It was 1892 and she was in jail, and even if she managed to get back to her own time, no one was ever, *ever* going to believe her accounts of what had happened to her.

She would definitely write a novel. A movie would inevitably follow. Priscilla Presley could play Rue, and they could probably get Tom Selleck for Farley's role, or maybe Lee Horsely....

Rue rose from the bed and immediately shifted from one foot to the other and back again.

"'Morning," Farley said with a companionable smile. He was standing beside the stove, turning the thick strips of pork in a cast-iron skillet.

"I have to go to the bathroom," Rue told him impatiently. "And don't you dare offer me a chamber pot!"

The marshal's white teeth flashed beneath his manly mustache. Expertly, he took the skillet off the heat, setting it on a trivet atop a nearby bookshelf, then ambled over to face Rue through the bars.

"Don't try anything," he warned, gesturing for Rue to precede him into freedom.

She stepped over the grubby threshold, concentrating on appreciating the sweet luxury of liberty, however brief it might be.

The marshal ushered her outside and around the back of the small building. Behind it was a small, unpainted cabin, and beyond that was an outhouse.

Rue wrinkled her nose at the smell, but she was in no position to be discriminating.

She went inside and, peering through the little moon some facetious soul had carved in the door, saw Farley standing guard a few feet away, arms folded.

When they were back in the jailhouse, he gave her soap and a basin of water to wash in before setting the bacon on to finish cooking. Rue felt a little better after that, though she longed for a shower, a shampoo and clean clothes.

"I suppose you'll be releasing me this morning," she said after Farley had brought her a metal plate containing three perfectly fried slices of bacon, a dry biscuit and an egg so huge, it could have been laid by Big Bird's mother. "After all, if playing poker were a crime, you'd have to arrest Stovepipe and Garters and Quickdraw."

Farley, who was perched on the edge of his desk, consuming his breakfast, laughed. Then he chewed a bite of bacon with such thoroughness that Rue grew impatient.

Finally, he responded. "I reckon you're referring to Harry and Micah and Jim-Roy, and you're partly right. It isn't against the law for *them* to play poker, but Pine River has an ordinance about women entering into unseemly behavior." Farley paused, watching unperturbed as Rue's face turned neon pink with fury. "You not only entered in, Miss Claridge—you set up housekeeping and planted corn."

"That's the most ridiculous thing I've ever heard!" Rue thought about flinging her plate through the bars like a Frisbee and beaning Farley Haynes, but she hadn't finished her breakfast and she was wildly hungry. "It's down-right discriminatory!"

Farley went to the stove and speared himself another slab of bacon from the skillet. "Nevertheless," he went on, "I can't ask the good citizens of this town to support you for-ever."

"If you'd just wire Elisabeth in San Francisco—"

"Nobody's heard from Jon and Lizzie," Farley inter-rupted. "They were in such a hurry to get started on their honeymoon, they didn't bother to tell anybody where they were going to stay once they got to California. They weren't planning to return until Jon's hand has healed and he's ready to start doctoring again."

Rue finished her breakfast with regret. Although loaded with fat and cholesterol, the food had tasted great. "People have mentioned a little girl. Did they take her with them?"

Farley nodded. "Yes, ma'am. Looks like we'll just have to wait until Jon decides to write a letter to somebody around here. When he left, he wasn't thinking of much of anything besides Lizzie."

After handing her empty plate through the bars, Rue folded her arms and sighed. "They're really in love, huh?"

The marshal's blue eyes sparkled. "You might say that. Being within twelve feet of those two is like being locked up in a room full of lightning."

Rue took comfort in the idea that this whole nightmare might not have been for nothing. If Bethie was really happy and truly in love with the country doctor she'd married, well, that at least gave the situation some meaning.

"I understand there was a fire and that nobody really knows how Dr. Fortner and his little girl escaped."

Farley stacked his plate and Rue's neatly on the trivet and poured the bacon grease from the frying pan into a crockery jar. "That's right. Of course, what's important is, they're alive. There are a lot of goings-on in this world that don't lend themselves to reasoning out."

"Amen," agreed Rue, thinking of her own experiences.

After fetching a bucket of water from outside, Farley put another kettle on to heat.

"You are going to give back my poker winnings, aren't you?" Rue asked nervously. She needed that money to buy some acceptable clothes and pay for a room. Provided she could find someone willing to rent her one, that is.

Farley took a mean-looking razor from his desk drawer, along with a shaving mug and a brush. "It'd serve you right if I didn't," he said calmly, studying his reflection in a cracked mirror affixed to the wall near the stove. "But I'll turn the money over to you as soon as I decide to let you go."

Rue's temper simmered at his blithely officious attitude, but she held her tongue. It was a technique she usually remembered after a conflagration, not before.

She watched, oddly fascinated, when Farley poured water from the kettle into a basin and splashed his face. Then, after moistening his shaving brush, he turned the bristles in the mug and lathered his beard.

Presently, he began using the straight razor with what seemed to Rue to be extraordinary skill.

The whole process was decidedly masculine, and it had a very curious—and disturbing—effect on Rue. Every graceful motion of his hands, every turn of his head, was like a caress; it was as though Farley were removing her clothes and taking the time to explore each new part of her as he bared it. And that odd feeling that she'd just collided with a solid object was back, too; she gripped the bars tightly to hold herself up.

When Farley gave her a sidelong look and grinned, she felt as though the bones in her pelvis had turned to warm wax.

Rue had spent a lot of time on a ranch, and she'd traveled and met people, read hundreds of books, watched all sorts of movies, so she had a pretty fundamental understanding of what was happening in her body. What she *didn't* comprehend was exactly what it would be like to make love, because that was something she hadn't gotten around to doing quite yet. It wasn't that she was scared or even especially noble—she just hadn't found the right man.

Farley finished shaving, humming a little tune all the while, rinsed his face and dried it with the towel draped around his neck.

The jailhouse door opened, and Rue noticed that Farley's hand flashed with instinctive speed and grace to the handle of the six-gun riding low on his hip.

His fingers relaxed when a big woman dressed in black bombazine entered. Her eyes narrowed in her beefy face when she caught sight of the prisoner. Two other ladies in equally somber dress wedged themselves in behind her.

"Something tells me the Presbyterians have arrived," Rue murmured.

"Worse," Farley whispered. "These ladies head up the Pine River Society for the Protection of Widows and Orphans, and they're really mean."

The trio stared at Rue, their mouths dropping open as they took in her jeans, sneakers and T-shirt.

"Poor misguided soul," one visitor said, raising bent fingers to her mouth in consternation and pity.

"Trousers!" breathed another.

The heavy woman whirled on Farley, and Rue noticed that a muscle twitched under his right eye.

"This is an outrage!" the lady thundered, as though he were somehow to blame for Rue's existence. "Where on earth did she get those dreadful clothes?"

"I can speak for myself," Rue said firmly, and the other two women gasped, evidently at her audacity. "This is called a T-shirt," Rue went on, indicating the garment in question, "and these are jeans. I know none of you are used to seeing a woman dressed the way I am, but the fact is, these clothes are really quite practical, when you think about it."

"Well, I never!" avowed the leader of the pack.

Rue's mouth twitched. "Never what?" she inquired sweetly.

Farley rolled his eyes, but offered no comment. It was plain that, although he wasn't really intimidated by these women, he wasn't anxious to cross them, either.

"Are you a saloon woman?" demanded the leader of the moral invasion. The moment the words were out of her mouth, she drew her lips into a tight line and retreated a step, no doubt concerned that sin might prove contagious.

Rue smiled. "No, Miss— What was your name, please?"

"My name is *Mrs.* Gifford," that good lady snapped.

Holding one hand out through the bars, Rue smiled again, winningly. "I'm very glad to meet you, Mrs. Gifford. My name is Rue Claridge, and I'm definitely not a 'saloon woman.'" She dropped her voice to a confidential whisper. "Just between you and me, I think I'm probably overqualified for that kind of work."

Mrs. Gifford turned away and gathered her bombazine-clad troops into a huddle. While the conference went on, Rue stood biting her lower lip and wondering whether or not Farley would turn her over to these people. She thought she'd rather take her chances with a lynch mob, if given the choice.

Farley scratched the back of his neck and sighed. Judging from his body language, Rue was pretty sure he wanted to let her go and get on with the daily business of being a living, breathing antique.

Finally, Mrs. Gifford approached the cell again. "There will be no more prancing up and down the street in trousers and no more poker playing," she decreed firmly.

Under any other circumstances, Rue would have defended her right to dress and gamble as she liked, but she wasn't about to risk getting herself into still more trouble. For all she knew, *Mr.* Gifford was a judge with the power to lock her away in some grim prison.

"No more poker playing," Rue conceded in a purposely meek voice. "As for the—trousers, I promise I won't wear them any farther than the general store. I mean to go straight over there and buy a dress as soon as the marshal here lets me out of the pokey."

The delegation put their heads together for another consultation. After several minutes, Mrs. Gifford announced, "Rowena will walk down to the mercantile and purchase the dress," she said, indicating one of the other women.

"Great," Rue responded, shifting her gaze to the marshal. "Will you give Rowena fifty cents from my winnings so I can get out of here?" If the Society tried to make her go with them, she'd make a break for it.

Rowena, who was painfully thin, her mousy brown hair pulled back tightly enough to tilt her eyes, swallowed visibly and backed up when Farley held out the money.

"Poker winnings," she said in horror. "My hands will never touch filthy lucre!"

Now it was Rue who rolled her eyes.

"*I'll* get the dress," Farley bit out furiously, grabbing his hat from its peg and putting on his long canvas duster. A moment later, the door slammed behind him.

The church women stared at Rue, as though expecting her to turn into a raven and fly out through the barred window.

Thank God I didn't land in seventeenth-century Salem, Rue thought wryly. *I'd surely be in the stocks by now, or dangling at the end of a rope.*

Basically a gregarious type, Rue couldn't resist another attempt at conversation, even though she knew the effort was probably futile. "So," she said, smiling the way she did when she wanted to put an interviewee at ease, "what do you do with yourselves every day, besides cooking and cleaning and tracking down sinners?"

Chapter Four

When Farley returned from his mission to the general store, looking tight jawed and grim, he opened the cell door and handed a wrapped bundle to Rue.

Rue's fiery, defiant gaze swept over Mrs. Gifford and her cronies, as well as the marshal, as she accepted the package. "If you people think I'm going to change clothes with the four of you standing there gawking at me, you're mistaken," she said crisply.

Farley seemed only too happy to leave, although the Society hesitated a few moments before trooping out after him.

If she hadn't been so frazzled, Rue would have laughed out loud at the sheer ugliness of that red-and-white gingham dress. As it happened, she just buttoned herself into the thing, tied the sash at the back and tried with all her might to hold on to her sense of humor.

When the others returned, Farley slid his turquoise gaze over Rue in an assessing fashion, and she thought she saw the corner of his mouth twitch. The ladies, however, were plainly not amused.

"Just let me out of here before I go crazy!" Rue muttered.

Farley unlocked the cell again and stepped back, holding the door wide. In that moment, an odd thought struck Rue: she would miss being in close contact with the marshal.

Their hands brushed as he extended the rest of her poker winnings, and Rue felt as though she'd just thrust a hairpin into a light socket.

"I'll try to stay out of trouble," she said. All of a sudden, her throat felt tight, and she had to force the words past her vocal cords.

Farley grinned, showing those movie-cowboy teeth of his. "You do that," he replied.

Rue swallowed and went around him, shaken. She'd been in an earthquake once, in South America, and the inner sensation had been much like what she was feeling now. It was weird, but then, so was everything else that had happened to her after she crossed that threshold and left the familiar world on the other side.

The Society allowed her to leave the jailhouse without interference, but the looks the women gave her were as cool and disapproving as before. It was plain they expected Rue to go forth in sin.

Once she was outside, under a pastel blue sky laced with white clouds, Rue felt a little stronger and more confident. The air was fresh and bracing, though tinged with the scent of manure from the road. Rue's naturally buoyant spirits rose.

She set out for the house in the country, determined to take another crack at returning to her own time. Not by any stretch of the imagination had she given up on finding Elisabeth and hearing her cousin tell her face-to-face that she was truly happy, but Rue needed time to regroup.

She figured a couple of slices of pepperoni pizza with black olives and extra cheese, followed by a long, hot bath, wouldn't hurt her thinking processes, either.

Soon Rue had left the screeching of the mill saw and the tinny music and raucous laughter of the saloons behind. Every step made her more painfully conscious of the growing distance between her and Farley, and that puzzled her. The lawman definitely wasn't her type, and besides . . . talk about a generation gap!

When Rue finally reached Aunt Verity's house, she stood at the white picket fence for a few moments, gazing up at the structure.

Even with its fire-scarred side, the place looked innocent, just sitting there in the bright October sunshine. No one would have guessed, by casual observation, that this unassuming Victorian house was enchanted or bewitched or whatever it was.

Rue drew a deep breath, let it out in a rush and opened the gate. With her other hand, she touched the necklace at her throat and fervently wished to be home.

The gate creaked as she closed it behind her. Rue proceeded boldly up the front walk and knocked at the door.

When the crabby housekeeper didn't answer, Rue simply turned the knob and stepped inside. *Remarkable,* she thought, shaking her head. Bethie and her new husband were off in California and the maid had probably left for the day, and yet the place was unlocked.

"Hello?" Rue inquired with a pleasantry that was at least partially feigned. She didn't like Ellen and would prefer not to encounter her.

There was no answer, no sound except for the loud ticking of a clock somewhere nearby.

Rue raised her voice a little. "Hello! Anybody here?"
Again, no answer.

Rue hoisted the skirts of her horrible gingham dress so she wouldn't break her neck and bounded up the front stairway. In the upper hall, she stood facing the burned door for a moment, then pushed it open and climbed awkwardly out onto a charred beam, praying it would hold her weight.

The antique necklace seemed to burn where it rested against her skin. Clutching the blackened doorjamb in both hands and closing her eyes, Rue whispered, "Let me go home. *Please*, let me go home."

A moment later, she summoned all her courage and thrust herself over the threshold and into the house.

When she felt modern carpeting beneath her fingers, jubilation rushed through Rue's spirit, though there was a thin brushstroke of sorrow, too. She might never see her cousin Elisabeth again.

Or Farley.

Rue scrambled to her feet and gave a shout of delight because she was back in the land of indoor plumbing, fast food and credit cards. Looking down at the red-and-white dress, with its long skirts and puffy sleeves, she realized the gown was tangible proof that she actually had been to 1892. No one else would be convinced, but Rue didn't care about that; it was enough that *she* knew she wasn't losing her mind.

After phoning the one restaurant in Pine River that not only sold but delivered pizza, Rue stripped off the dress, took a luxurious bath and put on khaki slacks and a white sweater. She was blow-drying her hair when the doorbell rang.

Snatching some money off the top of her bureau, Rue hurried downstairs to answer.

The pizza delivery person, a young man with an outstandingly good complexion, was standing on the porch, looking uneasy. Rue smiled, wondering what stories he'd heard about the house.

"Thanks," she said, holding out a bill.

The boy surrendered the pizza, but looked at the money in confusion. "What country is this from?" he asked.

Rue could smell the delicious aromas rising through the box, and she was impatient to be alone with her food. "This one," she replied a little abruptly.

Then Rue's eyes fell on the bill and she realized she'd tried to pay for the pizza with some of her 1892 poker winnings. The mistake had been a natural one; just the other day, she'd left some money on her dresser. Apparently, she'd automatically done the same with these bills.

"I'm a collector," she said, snatching back the bill. "Just a second and I'll get you something a little more...current."

With that, Rue reluctantly left the pizza on the hall table and hurried upstairs. When she returned, she paid the delivery boy with modern currency and a smile.

The young man thanked her and hurried back down the walk and through the front gate to his economy car. He kept glancing back over one shoulder, as though he expected to find that the house had moved a foot closer to the road while he wasn't looking.

Rue smiled and closed the door.

In the kitchen, she consumed two slices of pizza and put the rest into the refrigerator for later—or earlier. In this house, time had a way of getting turned around.

On one level, Rue felt grindingly tired, as though she could crawl into bed and sleep for two weeks without so much as a quiver of her eyelids. On another, however, she was restless and frustrated.

As a newswoman, Rue especially hated not knowing the whole story. She wanted to find her cousin, and she wanted to uncover the secret of this house. If there was one thing Rue was sure of, it was that the human race lived in a cause-and-effect universe and there was some concrete, measurable reason for the phenomenon she and Elisabeth had experienced.

She found her purse and the keys to her Land Rover and smiled to herself as she carefully locked the front door. Maybe the dead bolt would keep out burglars and vandals, but here all the action tended to be on the *inside*.

Rue drove into town, past the library and the courthouse and the supermarket, marveling. It had only been that morning—and yet, it had *not* been—that the marshal's office and the general store and the Hang-Dog Saloon had stood in their places. The road, rutted and dusty and dappled with manure in Farley's time was now paved and relatively clean.

Only when she reached the churchyard did Rue realize she'd intended to come there all along. She parked by a neatly painted wooden fence and walked past the old-fashioned clapboard church to the cemetery beyond.

The place was a historical monument—there were people buried here who had been born back East in the late seventeen hundreds.

Rue paused briefly by Aunt Verity's headstone, crouching to pull a few weeds, then went on to the oldest section. Almost immediately, she found the Fortner plot, a collection of graves surrounded by a low, iron fence.

She opened the little gate, which creaked on rusty hinges, and stepped inside.

Jonathan Fortner's grave was in the center and beside his stone was another one, marked Elisabeth Fortner. Rue felt tears sting her eyes; maybe Bethie was still alive in that other dimension, but she was long dead in this one. So were her husband and all her children.

After she'd recovered from the shock of standing beside Bethie's grave, Rue studied the other stones. Sons, daughters, sons-in-law and daughters-in-law, even grandchildren, most of whom had lived to adulthood, were buried there. Obviously, Jonathan and Elisabeth's union had been a very fruitful one, and that consoled Rue a little. More than anything else, her cousin had wanted a lot of children.

When Rue turned, she was startled to see a handsome young man crouched by the metal gate, oiling the creaky hinges. He smiled, and something about the expression was jarringly familiar.

"Friend of the family?" he asked pleasantly. Rue had him pegged for the kind of kid who had played the lead in all the high school drama productions and taken the prettiest girl in his class to the prom.

Rue allowed herself a slight smile. "You might say that. And you?"

"Jonathan and Elisabeth Fortner were my great-great-grandparents," he said, rising to his feet. He looked nothing like Bethie, this tall young man with his dark hair and eyes, and yet his words struck a note of truth deep inside Rue.

For a moment, she was completely speechless. It seemed that every time she managed to come to terms with one element of this time-travel business, another aspect presented itself.

Rue summoned up a smile and offered her hand. "I guess you could say Bethie—Elisabeth—was my great-great-cousin. My name is Rue Claridge."

"Michael Blake," he replied, clasping her fingers firmly.

Rue searched her memory, but she couldn't recall Aunt Verity ever mentioning this branch of the family. "Do you live in Pine River, Michael?"

He shook his head and, once again, Rue felt a charge of recognition. "Seattle—I go to the university. I just like to come out here once in a while and—well—I don't know exactly how to explain it. It's like there's this unseen connection and I'm one of the links. I guess this is my way of telling them—and myself—that I haven't broken the chain."

Rue only nodded; she was thinking of the overwhelming significance a simple decision or random happenstance could have. If Bethie hadn't stumbled into that other dimension or whatever it was, then Michael would probably never have existed. In fact, just a few months before, when Elisabeth had not yet stepped over the threshold to meet and fall in love with her country doctor, there had surely been no Michael Blake. That would explain why Aunt Verity had never talked about him or his family.

On the other hand, Michael had grown to youthful manhood; he had a life, a history. He was as solid and real as anyone she'd ever met.

Rue's head was spinning.

"Are you all right?" Michael asked, firmly taking her elbow and helping her to a nearby bench. "You look pale."

Rue sat down gratefully and rubbed her right temple with a shaking hand. "I'm fine," she said hastily. "Honestly."

"I could get you some water...."

"No," Rue protested. "I'm okay. Really."

Michael brought a small black notebook from his jacket pocket, along with a stub of a pencil. "My grandmother would really like to meet you, since you're a shirttail relation and everything. She lives with my mom and dad in Seattle. Why don't you give her a call sometime?"

Rue grinned at the ease with which he invited a total stranger into the inner circle of the family, but then that was the sort of thing kids did. "Thanks, Michael."

He wedged one hand into the pocket of his jacket, holding the can of spray lubricant in the other. "Well, I guess I'd better be getting back to the city. Nice meeting you."

"Nice meeting you," Rue said hoarsely, looking away. *Did you think about what it means to change history, Bethie?* she thought. *I know I never did.*

Michael had long-since driven away in a small blue sports car when Rue finally rose from the bench and went to stand beside her cousin's grave once again.

"Maybe I should just leave it all alone," she murmured as a shower of gold, crimson and chocolate-colored leaves floated down onto the little plot from the surrounding maple trees. "Maybe it would be better to walk away and pretend I believe the official explanation for your disappearance, Bethie. But I just can't do it. Even though I know I could stir up ripples that might be felt all the way into this century, I have to hear you say, in person, that you want to stay there. I have to look into your eyes and know that you understand your decision."

And I have to see Farley Haynes again.

The stray, ragtag thought trailed in after the others, and Rue immediately evicted it from her mind. For all practical intents and purposes, Farley was just a figment of her imagination, she reminded herself, little more than a character she'd seen in a movie or read about in a book.

The idea left a keen, biting sense of loneliness in its wake, but Rue was determined to accept the fact and get on with her life.

Of course, before she could do that, she had to see Bethie just once more.

Instead of going home, Rue drove into Seattle.

She visited a coin shop first, where she purchased an expensive selection of bills and coins issued between 1880 and 1892. After that, Rue visited a dusty little secondhand store tucked away in an alley behind a delicatessen, and bought herself a graceful ivory gown with tatting on the cuffs and collar, and a waist-length capelet to match. A little searching unearthed a pair of brown, high-button shoes and a parasol.

Rue coughed as the shop's proprietress shook out the ancient garment and prepared to wrap it. "Is this a theatrical costume, or was it a part of a real wardrobe?"

The other woman smiled wistfully. "I suspect this gown came from a camphor trunk in someone's attic, since it's in relatively good condition. If you'll look closely at the handwork, you'll see it's made to last."

"Is it washable?"

"I wouldn't try that. The fabric is terribly old; water or dry-cleaning solution might dissolve the fibers."

Rue nodded, feeling fond of that romantic old relic of a dress already, and hoping she could make it hold together long enough to get back to 1892, have a couple of practical calico dresses made and find Elisabeth. Between her poker winnings and the old currency she'd purchased at the coin shop, Rue figured she'd have enough money to catch a boat or a train to San Francisco, where Elisabeth and Jonathan were supposed to have gone.

As Rue was driving back to Pine River, a light rain began to fall. She found a classical station on the car radio—Rue's musical tastes covered the full range, but on that particular night, Mozart had the greatest appeal.

It truly startled her to realize, just as she reached the outskirts of Pine River, that there were tears on her face.

Rue rarely cried, not because she was in any way above it, but because she'd long ago learned that weeping solved nothing. In fact, it usually just complicated matters.

Nevertheless, her cheeks seemed as wet as the windshield, and her feelings were an odd, explosive tangle. Methodically, she began to separate them.

Meeting Michael Blake had given her a shattering sense of the gossamer threads that link the past with the present and the future. If for some reason Elisabeth changed her mind about staying in 1892 and following through with the new destiny she'd created for herself by making that choice, Michael and a lot of other people would simply be obliterated.

To make matters worse, the problem wouldn't stop with Michael's generation. Whole branches of the family tree that might have lived and loved, laughed and cried, would never come into being at all.

Rue's hands began to tremble so badly that she had to pull over to the side of the road and sit with her forehead resting against the steering wheel.

Finally, after several minutes, she was able to drive on, but she was still crying, and there were more feelings to be faced and dealt with.

Next came the most prickly fact of all, the one Rue could no longer deny: she was lonely. From an emotional standpoint, she sometimes felt as though everyone on the planet had stepped into a parallel dimension. She could see them and hear their voices, but they seemed somehow inaccessible, forever out of reach.

Only her grandfather, Aunt Verity and Elisabeth had been able to reach through the invisible barrier to touch her, and now they were all gone.

Rue sniffled. There was one positive aspect to this experience she and Elisabeth shared, however: it opened the door to all sorts of possibilities. Maybe the philosophers and poets were right and she *would* see her loved ones again someday. Maybe Aunt Verity and Gramps were carrying on happy lives in some other time and place, just as Elisabeth seemed to be.

It was all too mystical for a pragmatic mind like Rue's.

Darkness had fallen by the time she reached home but, as always, the atmosphere of the house was friendly.

After carefully hanging up the dress she'd purchased and setting the high-button shoes side by side on the floor of the armoire, Rue went downstairs and made supper: a grilled cheese sandwich and a cup of microwave soup.

She was too tired and overwrought to think clearly or make further plans. After a warm bath, Rue crawled into bed, read two chapters of a political biography and promptly drifted off to sleep.

In the early hours of the morning, Rue dreamed she was back in Baghdad, at the start of the Gulf War, hiding out in the basement of a hotel with several other news people and trying not to flinch every time a bomb exploded. She forcibly woke herself from the nightmare, but the loud noises continued.

Rue's fingers immediately rushed to the necklace at her throat. Once again, the pendant felt warm, almost hot, to the touch. And the predawn air reverberated with gunshots.

Muttering, Rue tossed back the covers and stumbled through the hallway to the sealed door. Sure enough, it opened when she turned the knob, and now she could hear drunken male laughter and the nervous whinnying of horses on the road, though the thick darkness prevented her from seeing anything.

There was more shooting, and Rue cringed. Obviously, a few of the boys where whooping it up, as they used to say on TV, and that made her furious. Someone could be shot!

She gripped the sooty sides of the doorframe and yelled, "Hey, you guys! Knock it off before you hurt somebody!"

Surprisingly, an immediate silence fell. Rue listened for a moment, smiled and closed the door. True, she had unfinished business in 1892, but she wasn't going to attend to it in her nightgown.

There was no point in trying to go back to sleep, thanks to the James Gang. Rue set up her portable computer at the kitchen table and brewed a cup of herbal tea in the microwave. Then she sat down, her toes hooked behind the rung of her chair, and began tapping out an account of the things that had happened to her. Like Bethie with her letters, Rue felt a fundamental need to record her experiences with an orderly succession of words.

Rue had been writing steadily for over half an hour, and the first thin light was flowing in through the window above the sink, when suddenly the keyboard vanished from beneath her fingertips.

Rue looked up, stunned to see that the room had changed completely. Dr. Fortner's cast-iron cookstove stood near the back door. There was no tile, only rough wood flooring, and the wooden icebox had returned, along with the bulky pump handle and the clunky metal sink.

Just as quickly, the modern kitchen appeared. The computer keyboard materialized in front of Rue, and the sleek appliances stood in their customary places.

Rue swallowed hard, remembering the time she'd been standing in the front parlor, looking into the mirror above the mantel. The room had altered that day, too, and she'd even caught a glimpse of a woman dusting a piano.

These experiences gave new credence to Aunt Verity's hazy theory that the necklace had a mind of its own.

She sat back in her chair, pressing her palms to her cheeks, half expecting to find she had a raging fever. Instead, her face felt cool.

After a few moments spent gathering her composure, Rue got out Elisabeth's letters and read them again, carefully, word by word. Not once did Bethie mention seeing a room change; she'd gone back and forth between the present and the past all right, but only by way of the threshold upstairs.

Clearly, the common denominator was the necklace.

Rue rubbed the antique pendant thoughtfully between her thumb and forefinger. She, unlike her cousin, had twice caught glimpses of that other world while just going about her business. Did that mean the invisible passageway between the two eras was changing, expanding? If that were the case, it might also shrink just as unpredictably, or disappear entirely.

Forever.

Rue sighed and shoved splayed fingers through her hair, then began pounding at the keys of her computer again, rushing to record everything. She had always believed that reality was a solid, measurable thing, but there was something going on in and around the house that superceded all the normal rules.

There were no more incidents that day, and Rue spent the time resting and making preparations to return to old-time Pine River. She carefully aired and pressed the fragile dress she'd bought, watched a few soap operas and made herself a tuna sandwich for lunch.

Then on a foray into the dusty attic, she found one of Aunt Verity's many caches of unique jewelry and helped herself to a brooch and set of tarnished, sterling combs.

Later, in her bedroom, she put on the dress and sat at the vanity table, putting her hair up and learning to use the combs strategically. When she'd mastered the technique, Rue sat looking at her reflection for a long time, liking the wistful, romantic image she made.

The faintly musty scent of the fabric was a subtle reminder, however, that she and the garment belonged to two distinctly different times.

Carefully, Rue unpinned her hair, took off the dress and got back into her jeans and sweatshirt. She felt a strong draw to 1892, but she wasn't quite ready to go back. She needed to gather all her internal forces and make this trip count.

Just to make certain there wouldn't be any unscheduled visits to the Outer Limits, Rue unclasped the necklace and carefully placed it inside an alabaster box on the vanity. She wondered briefly if the pendant was capable of slipping back and forth between then and now all on its own.

That concept caused Rue a case of keen, if momentary, panic. She reached for the necklace, drew back her hand, reached again. Finally, she turned purposefully and walked away, determined not to be held hostage by a chunk of antique gold on a chain.

The pull of the necklace was strong, though, and Rue had to leave the house to keep away from it.

She decided to call on the Buzbee sisters, the two spinsters who lived on the other side of the road, and find out if they could shed any light on the situation.

Roberta Buzbee, a plain and angular woman, greeted Rue at the door. She seemed pleased to have company and, after explaining that her sister was "indisposed," invited Rue in for tea.

They sat in the front parlor before a blazing applewood fire. It was a cozy room, except for the shrunken head prominently displayed on top of the piano. Rue didn't ask how the sisters had come to acquire the memento because she was pretty sure Miss Roberta would tell her. In detail.

"Have there been any developments in the search for your cousin Elisabeth?" Miss Roberta asked. The sisters had been among the first people Rue had spoken with when she'd arrived in Pine River and begun to look for Bethie, and she knew they'd never bought the official theories.

Rue shrugged and avoided the older woman's gaze for a moment, wishing she dared admit the truth. The situation was simply too delicate. "I'm going to find her," she said, and all the considerable certainty she possessed was contained in those words. "No matter what it takes, no matter what I have to do, I'm going to see Bethie and make sure she's okay."

Miss Roberta nodded primly and took a graceful sip of her tea.

Rue cleared her throat softly and began again. "Miss Roberta, have other people disappeared from that house? Temporarily or permanently?"

The other woman looked distinctly uncomfortable. "Not just that. People have *appeared*, too," she confided. "Folks in old-timey clothes, mostly."

This was new to Rue; she scooted to the edge of her chair. "Like who?" she asked, wide-eyed.

"Well, there was a woman—never liked her. Verity took her under her wing, though, and she finally left town. Once in a while, Sister and I catch sight of a buggy that comes along and turns in at your driveway. And there's another woman who can be seen hanging out clothes on a fine spring morning."

Ellen, Rue thought. Lizzie's housekeeper. "Ghosts?" Rue asked, to keep the spinster talking.

Miss Roberta clucked her tongue. "Oh, my, no. There aren't any such things—just places where the curtain between our time and theirs has worn a little thin, that's all. Time's all of a piece, Sister and I believe, like a big tapestry. Would you like some lemon cookies? I just baked them this morning."

Rue loved homemade sweets, no matter how agitated her state of mind might be, and she eagerly agreed.

While her hostess was in the kitchen, though, Rue was restless. She picked up a small book that was lying on the coffee table—the title, *My Life in Old Pine River,* suggested the subject was local history. She began thumbing through page after page of old pictures in the center of the book.

Rue's heart twisted when she came across a photograph of Elisabeth standing with the townsfolk in front of a new-looking covered bridge, a slight and mysterious smile curving her lips.

Chapter Five

Seeing an impossibly old photograph of Elisabeth left Rue shaken. Even though she knew from personal experience that time travel was possible, the mysteries of it all still boggled her mind.

"Is something wrong, dear?" Miss Roberta asked as she appeared in the doorway with the promised cookies. "You look as though you wouldn't trust your knees to hold you up."

Rue sighed and rubbed her temple. "This picture..."

Miss Roberta put the platter of cookies down on the coffee table and bent to look at the book in Rue's lap.

Even as she acted, Rue knew discretion would have been a better course than valor, but she was tired of being the only one who knew. She needed the understanding and support of another human being.

She tapped the page lightly with an index finger, and when she spoke, her voice was thready and hoarse. "This woman, standing here by the bridge...this is Elisabeth."

The spinster perched gracefully on the arm of the sofa, took the volume from Rue and raised it for a closer view. "My land, that does *look* like Elisabeth. I've been through this book a thousand times.... This little girl sitting on the big rock by the stream grew up to be our mother...but I swear I've never noticed this woman. Well, well, well. What do you make of that?"

"What, indeed?" Rue murmured, longing to take an aspirin.

Miss Roberta was pensive. "Maybe she was an ancestor of yours. That would account for the resemblance. What I can't understand is how something so obvious could have escaped my attention."

Rue accepted the book when it was offered and scrutinized the picture again. The woman standing in that crowd was definitely Elisabeth herself, not just someone who resembled her, and the handsome, dark-haired man at her side was probably Jonathan Fortner.

Rue smiled, though she could just as easily have cried, so fragile were her emotions. Elisabeth and Jonathan looked right together.

"Next thing you know," Miss Roberta said irritably, "we'll be appearing on *Unsolved Mysteries,* the whole lot of us. We'll have our pictures on the front of those dreadful newspapers they sell at the supermarket, and all because of that troublesome old house of Verity's."

Lowering her head for a moment to hide her smile, Rue nodded. She suspected the neighbor woman secretly hoped an explosion of notoriety would thrust the boundaries of Pine River outward, thus bringing some excitement to an otherwise humdrum town.

Rue ate a cookie and finished her tea, but only to be polite. Now that she'd seen the photograph of Elisabeth, she was more anxious than ever to make contact with her cousin. Bethie looked happy in that old picture, but that didn't mean she wasn't in over her head in some way. After all, during her marriage to Ian McCartney, Elisabeth had put a brave face on things, but she'd also been miserable for the duration.

Dr. Fortner looked like a hard-headed, autocratic type, though there was no denying he was a formidable hunk, and the male sex had virtually ruled the world in the nineteenth century. Maybe the good doctor was dominating Elisabeth in some way, forcing her to stay when she really wanted to come back to her own time.

Just the idea made Rue's blood simmer. Nobody, but *nobody* was allowed to mistreat Elisabeth.

When she could leave without seeming hasty, Rue thanked Miss Roberta for the cookies and tea, and set out for the other side of the road. By that time, it was already getting dark, and a crisp autumn wind was stirring the flame-colored trees.

Reaching the house, Rue built a fire and then carefully assembled all the items she'd purchased for her journey back to 1892—the dress, the brown high-button shoes, the musty, fragile old money, the silver combs.

Since she hadn't bought stockings, Rue made a concession and wore panty hose. She put on a bra, too, because there were certain comforts she just wasn't willing to sacrifice, even for the sake of authenticity. Besides, nobody in 1892 was going to get a look at her underwear, anyway.

Once she'd donned the dress—she had to suck in her stomach and fasten the buttons in front, then turn the gown around again and put her hands through the armholes—Rue did up her hair. Then, reluctantly, wishing she could wear her sneakers as she had before, she slipped her feet into the pinchy-toed shoes.

She folded the money she'd bought in the coin shop, along with the funds she'd won in the poker game, and tucked the bundle securely into her bodice. The hated red-and-white gingham dress was carefully folded into a neon pink designer sports bag, along with a toothbrush and toothpaste, a paperback book, a bottle of aspirin and some snack-size candy bars.

Once she was seated at the kitchen table, the bag perched on her lap, Rue put on the necklace and waited. A sense of urgent excitement buzzed in her stomach, and she was certain something was about to happen.

Rue sat waiting for so long that she finally unzipped the bag and brought out the novel. She was halfway through chapter two when suddenly the necklace started to vibrate subtly and the light changed, dimming until she could barely see.

The first thing Rue was aware of after that was an incredibly bad smell. The second was the moon shape cut out of the crude wooden door in front of her.

Realizing she'd landed in somebody's outhouse, Rue bolted to her feet, sending the book and the sports bag tumbling to the floor. *"Yuk,"* she grumbled, snatching up her belongings again and then turning the loosely nailed piece of wood that served as a primitive lock and bolting out into the sunlight.

An elderly cowboy touched his hat and smiled at her, and the gaps between his teeth made Rue think of a string of Christmas-tree lights with some of the bulbs burned out. "No hurry, ma'am," he said. "I can wait."

Rue's face throbbed with the heat of embarrassment. It was disconcerting enough to be flung back and forth between two different centuries. Landing helter-skelter in somebody's privy was adding insult to injury.

She hurried past a line of laundry flapping in the breeze, not recognizing the house in front of her or the ones on either side, possessed by an entirely new fear. Maybe she wasn't in 1892, or even in Pine River, for that matter.

Rue's hand tightened on the handle of her bag. Reaching a side gate in the white picket fence, she opened it and stepped out onto a wooden sidewalk. She glanced wildly up and down the street, looking for anything familiar.

She swayed slightly, so great was her relief when she saw Farley come out of a saloon and amble toward her, holding his rifle casually in one hand. With his free hand, he pushed his hat back a notch, and the sigh he gave was one of exasperation.

"You're back," he said.

Rue wrinkled her nose. "How long was I gone?"

Farley's marvelous turquoise eyes narrowed as he studied her. "How long were you...what the sam hill are you talking about?"

"An hour?" Rue shrugged and smiled charmingly, pleased that she was confusing Marshal Haynes. He deserved it for being so arrogant. "Two hours? A week?"

"I haven't seen you in about four days." He frowned, and his expression was pensive now. "I figured you'd gone back to your folks or something."

Rue wanted to ask if he'd missed her, but she couldn't quite bring herself to take the risk. "I've been...around," she said, holding out the skirts of the gown she'd bought especially for this trip. "Like my dress?"

Farley wasn't looking at her outfit, however. He was staring at the blindlingly pink bag she was carrying. "That's the damnedest colored satchel I've ever seen," he muttered, reaching out to touch the material. "Where did you get that?"

"Nordstrom," Rue answered with a slight grin. "It's a store in Seattle." Obviously, she couldn't go into much more detail. As it was, if Farley went looking for the place in the Seattle *he* knew, he'd never find it.

"Where are you staying?" he asked suspiciously.

Much as Rue enjoyed Farley's company, she had no desire to do another stretch in his jail. She looked around, biting her lip, and fortunately caught sight of a sign swinging from the lowest branch of an elm tree in a yard down the street. "There," she said. "At Mrs. Fielding's Rooming House."

Farley sighed again. "That's interesting," he commented at some length, "because Geneva Fielding only takes in gentleman boarders, as a rule."

Rue bit her lower lip. "Okay, so I lied," she blurted out in a furious whisper. "If I'd told you the truth, you wouldn't have believed me. I don't *have* a place to stay, since you won't let me set foot inside Elisabeth's house, but you don't need to worry. I'm not going to loiter or anything. I plan to buy a ticket on the next stagecoach out of town."

The marshal raised one eyebrow. "That so? There won't be one leaving for nearly a week."

"Damn!" Rue ground out. If it weren't for the inconvenience this news was bound to cause her, she would have laughed at the expression of shock on Farley's face. She set the bag on the sidewalk and placed her hands on her hips. "Now I suppose you're going to say it's illegal for a lady to swear and I'm under arrest!"

One corner of Farley's mouth twitched almost imperceptibly. "It's true enough that a lady can't cuss on the street and still be within the law. Thing is, I'm not sure whether that ordinance could cover *you* or not."

Rue opened her mouth, closed it again. As a child, she'd been a tomboy, and as an adult, she'd thought more in terms of being a woman than a lady. It hurt that Farley wasn't sure how to classify her.

He allowed her a smile so brief it might have been nothing more than a mirage, then took her elbow in his free hand. "Miss Ella Sinclair takes in roomers now and again. Do you still have that poker money you won the other night?"

It was a moment before Rue could speak, since a series of small shocks was still jolting through her system from the place where Farley was touching her. "Ah...er...yes, I have a little money." She swallowed hard, awed at the cataclysmic shifts taking place in the deepest, most private passages of her spirit. Farley began to walk purposefully onward, and Rue hurried to keep up. "I've got to be careful, though, because I don't know how much I'll need for train fare to San Francisco."

"It'll cost you about seventy-five cents to go from here to Seattle by stage. As for the train ticket, that'll be considerably more."

Mentally, Rue was counting the currency tucked into her bodice, but she kept having to start over because of the distracting sensations Farley's grip on her elbow was causing. She figured she probably had enough money for the trip, provided she skimped on meals and didn't run into any emergencies.

"Is there a place around here where a woman can get a job?" she asked. Farley stopped in front of a narrow blue house with a white weather vane on the roof.

His look was one of wry annoyance as he cocked his thumb back toward the main part of town. "Sure. They're always looking for dancing girls at the Hang-Dog Saloon."

"Very funny," Rue whispered, stepping away from him. "I'll have you know that I'm a trained journalist, with a college education...."

Farley grinned. He plainly knew full well that what he was going to say would infuriate Rue, and so did she... long moments before he actually spoke. "I guess that's where your kinfolks went wrong. Sending you to college, I mean. That's probably how you got all those muddleheaded ideas you're always spouting."

After telling herself silently that it would be immature to stomp on the man's instep, Rue managed to reply in a relatively moderate tone of voice. "It would serve you right if I told you *exactly* where I got all my 'crazy ideas,' Mr. Haynes. However, since you'd almost certainly be too boneheaded to absorb the information, I won't bother." She opened the gate latch. "Goodbye."

Farley was right beside Rue as she strode up the flagstone walk. "You'll need me to vouch for you," he said, his eyes laughing at her even though his sensual mouth was somber. "Even that might not be enough, given the reputation you've made for yourself in this town by wearing pants, playing poker and getting yourself thrown into jail."

Before Rue could answer, the front door of the house swung open and a woman appeared. She was tall, with blue eyes and thin, blond hair, and she wore a paisley shawl pulled tightly around her shoulders. Her smile was tremulous and hopeful—and it was entirely for Farley.

A laughable stab of jealousy knifed through Rue, but she didn't feel at all amused.

Farley touched his hat brim in a courtly way. "Miss Ella, this is... er... a friend of mine. Miss Rue Claridge." Rue didn't miss the fact that he'd remembered her last name, though she had no idea what conclusions to draw from the discovery. "She needs a place to stay, just until the stage pulls out on Tuesday."

Miss Ella folded her arms and assessed Rue with disapproving eyes, and her nostrils flared slightly in rebellion. "I'm sorry, Farley." Her voice was irritatingly shrill. "I don't have a single room left."

"Then I guess she'll just have to stay at my place," Farley said, resigned. With that, he took hold of Rue's elbow again and propelled her back toward the gate.

Miss Ella took only a few moments to weigh the implications of that. The hard leather heels of her shoes clicked purposefully against the floorboards of the porch as she hurried after Farley and Rue. "Wait!" she warbled. "There is Mama's old sewing room.... It's just a matter of moving out a few trunks and the like."

Rue smiled to herself, though in some ways she'd found the idea of being Farley's houseguest appealing.

Farley winked at her, causing Rue's heart to go into arrest for at least five beats, before turning to look back at Miss Ella. "That's very kind of you," he said cordially.

For the first time, it occurred to Rue that Farley Haynes was a well-spoken man, for a small-town, nineteenth-century marshal. Silly questions boiled up in her heart and rose into her mind like vapor, and Rue was grateful that he'd be going on about his business soon. Hopefully before she made a complete fool of herself.

Sure enough, he escorted the ladies only as far as the porch, then tugged at his hat brim, muttered a polite farewell and left.

Rue felt as though she'd been abandoned on a distant planet.

The look in Miss Ella's eyes was not a friendly one as the woman opened the front door and swept into the thin, blue house.

Rue followed, lugging her pink bag. By that time, sleeping in somebody's barn sounded a shade more inviting than rooming with Miss Ella Sinclair.

"That'll be one dollar in advance," the spinster said, holding out one hand, palm up.

Pulling her money from her bodice embarrassed Rue, but she did it defiantly all the same, to let the landlady know she wasn't intimidated. "Here," she said, peeling off a bill.

"Thank you," Miss Ella replied crisply. "I'll just go and ready up that room I mentioned." With that, she swept off, leaving Rue standing awkwardly in the front parlor, still holding her bag.

The landlady returned in a surprisingly short time for someone who'd allegedly had to move trunks out of a sewing room. Of course, Rue knew there had never been a shortage of beds in this house in the first place; Miss Sinclair was smitten with Farley, and she didn't want him taking in a female boarder.

Rue's quarters turned out to be a closet-size room wedged underneath the stairway. There was very little light and even less air. Someone had made a disastrous attempt at decoration, papering the place with hideous red cabbage roses against a pea green background. It looked as though a child had stood on the threshold and pitched overripe tomatoes at the walls.

"Dinner is at seven," Miss Ella announced. "Please be prompt, because Papa is always ravenous when he returns from a day at the bank."

Rue nodded and set her bag on the foot of the narrow cot she'd be sleeping on every night until the stagecoach came through and she could be off to Seattle. It hardly looked more comfortable than the bed in Pine River's solitary jail cell.

"Thank you." Rue rushed on without thinking, and the instant the question was out of her mouth, she regretted it. "Where's the bathroom?"

"There's a chamber pot underneath the bed," the land-lady answered with a puzzled frown. "And as for bathing, well, each boarder is assigned one particular night when he can bathe in the kitchen. Yours will be..." She paused, tapping her mouth with one finger as she considered. "Thursday."

Rue sat down on the edge of the cot with a forlorn sigh. She didn't mind being in the wrong century, she didn't even mind boarding in a house where she wasn't wanted, but not being able to take a shower every day was practically un-bearable.

Miss Ella waggled her fingers in farewell and went out, closing the squeaky door behind her.

Rue got out her paperback book, stretched out on the lumpy cot and sighed. She'd stayed in worse places, though most of them had been in third-world countries.

Somewhere between chapters four and five, Rue dozed off. When she awakened, she had a headache and cramps in all her muscles, and she was clutching her sports bag like some pitiful orphan abandoned at Ellis Island.

Since crying wasn't a workable method of operation, she got up, poured tepid water from a chipped pitcher into a mismatched bowl and splashed her face. After that, she opened the window a crack and took a few deep breaths.

Soon Rue was feeling better. She ferreted out the supply of candy bars tucked away in her bag and ate a single piece, then decided to brave Miss Sinclair's parlor. She would borrow a cloak, if she could, and go out for a walk before dinner.

The landlady was nowhere to be found, as it happened, but a young woman who introduced herself as Miss Alice

McCall volunteered a long woolen cape. Gratefully, Rue wrapped herself against the evening chill and went out.

There were no streetlights in this incarnation of Pine River, and certainly no neon signs. The blue-gray color of television screens didn't flicker beyond the windows, but oil lanterns sent out a wavering glow.

A crushing wave of loneliness washed over Rue, a bruising awareness that the lights behind those thick panes of glass didn't shine for her.

She was a stranger here.

In the center of town, the golden glimmer of lamps spiced with bawdy piano tunes spilled out of the saloon windows into the streets. Rue was drawn not by the drinking and the ugliness, but by the light and music.

The sudden flare of a match startled her, and she jumped. Farley was leaning against the outer wall of the feed and grain, his trusty rifle beside him, smoking a thin brown cigar.

"Looking for a poker game?" he inquired dryly.

Rue tossed her head to let him know just how much contempt she had for his question, then gestured toward the cigar. "Those things will kill you," she said. She didn't really expect to turn Farley from his wicked ways; she just wanted to make conversation for a few minutes.

He chuckled and shook his head. "You have an opinion on just about everything, it seems to me."

Rue sighed. It wasn't the first time someone had called her opinionated, and it probably wouldn't be the last. "There are worse things," she said, drawing her borrowed cloak more tightly around her. She hoped she would catch up with Elisabeth before too long, because she didn't have the clothes for cold weather.

"I can't deny that," Farley confessed good-naturedly. He started walking along the board sidewalk, and Rue just naturally strolled along beside him.

"Miss Sinclair is—what did you people call it?—oh, yes. She's sweet on you, Marshal. She's set her cap for you."

Now it was Farley who sighed. "Umm," he said.

"Typical male answer," Rue replied briskly. "Who are you, Farley? Where did you go to school?"

His boots made a rhythmic and somehow comforting sound on the wooden walk as he moved along, keeping a thoughtful silence. Finally, he countered, "Why do you want to know?"

"I'm just curious," Rue said. They'd reached the end of the main street, and Farley crossed the road and started back the other way, the ever-present rifle in his hand. "You're educated, and that isn't all that common in the old...in the West."

Farley laughed, and the sound was low and rich. The smell of his cigar was faint and somehow a comfort in the strangeness of that time and place. "My pa was a hard-scrabble farmer in Kansas," he said, "and my ma never got beyond the fourth grade in school, but she loved books, and she taught me to read from the Bible and the *Farmer's Almanac*. Once in Texas, I herded cattle for a man who must have had two hundred books in his house, and he let me borrow as many as I could carry." Farley paused, smiling as he remembered. "I stayed on with that outfit for three years, even though the money wasn't for spit, and I read every damn one of those books."

Rue felt a swell of admiration, along with the usual jangling this man always caused in her nervous system. And she wished she could take him by the hand and show him the library her grandfather had built up on the ranch in Montana. "Awesome," she said.

"Awesome," Farley echoed. They were passing one of the saloons, and he glanced in over the swinging doors, apparently just making sure all was well with the warm-beer set. "I've never heard that word used that way."

Rue smiled. "Kids say 'awesome' in . . . Seattle." It was true enough. They just weren't saying it *yet*. "I'm impressed, Farley. That you've read so many books, I mean."

"If you ever want to borrow any," he said with an endearing combination of modesty and shyness Rue had never dreamed he was capable of, "just let me know. I've got some good ones."

They had reached the residential part of town, and Rue knew seven o'clock must be getting close. "Thanks," she said, lightly touching Farley's arm. "I might do that."

The instant her fingers made contact with the hard muscles of his forearm, Rue knew she'd made a mistake. The ground seemed to tremble beneath her feet, and she felt more than slightly dizzy.

When Farley leaned his rifle against a building and gripped the sides of her waist to steady her, the whole situation immediately got worse. He gave a strangled groan and bent his head to kiss her.

His tongue touched either side of her mouth, then the seam between her lips. She opened to him as she had never done for another man, and he took full advantage of her surrender.

Much to Rue's chagrin, it was Farley who finally broke away. He gripped her shoulders and held her at a distance, breathing hard and muttering an occasional curse word.

"I'll see you back to the Sinclair place," he said after a long time.

Rue was shaken and achy, wanting the marshal of Pine River as she had never in her life wanted a man before. "Farley, what's wrong?" she asked miserably.

He took her elbow and started hustling her along the walk. "Nothing. You're leaving for Seattle on Tuesday and I'm staying here to start a ranch. Let's remember that."

For the first time, Rue fully understood how Elisabeth could care enough about a man to give up every comfort and convenience of the twentieth century. Her own attraction to Farley Haynes had just reached a frightening pitch.

She swallowed. "I guess you'll marry someone like Miss Sinclair, once you're ready to settle down. A man out here needs a wife."

Farley didn't look at her. "I guess so," he said, and his voice sounded gruff. They'd reached the Sinclair's front gate, and he reached down to unfasten the latch. "In the future, Miss Claridge," he said tightly, "it might be a good idea if you didn't go out walking after dark. It's not safe or proper, and the good people of the town don't set much store by it."

Rue was riding an internal roller coaster, had been ever since Farley had kissed her, and she'd exhausted her supply of sensible remarks. "Good night," she said, turning and rushing toward the house.

The Sinclairs and their boarders were just sitting down to supper, and Rue joined them only because she was famished. This was one night when she would definitely have preferred room service.

"What do you do, Miss Claridge?" the head of the household asked pleasantly. He was a tall, heavy man with slate gray hair and a rather bulbous red nose. "For a living, I mean?"

His daughter smiled slyly and lowered her eyes, obviously certain that the new boarder was about to make a fool of herself.

"I'm an heiress," Rue said. The statement was true; it was just that her money was in another dimension, stamped with dates that would be nothing but science fiction to these people. "My family has a ranch in Montana."

"What brings you to Pine River, Miss Claridge?" asked the young woman who had loaned Rue her cloak earlier.

"I came to see my cousin, Elisabeth Fortner."

Mr. Sinclair put down his fork, frowning, but his daughter did not look at all surprised. Of course, Rue would have been the subject of much female conjecture in the dull little town.

"Jonathan's wife?" Mr. Sinclair inquired, frowning heavily. "The woman we tried for murder?"

"Yes," Rue answered. "The woman you tried...and acquitted."

Pointing out Elisabeth's innocence of any crime didn't seem to lighten the mood at the table. It was as though being accused had been enough to taint not only Bethie, but all who came before and all who could come after.

Once again, Rue wondered how happy her cousin could expect to be in this town. Probably the memory of Elisabeth McCartney Fortner's murder trial would live on long after Bethie herself was gone, and time would undoubtedly alter the verdict.

"More chicken and dumplings, Miss Claridge?" cooed Miss Sinclair with particular malice.

Rue's stomach had suddenly closed itself off, refusing to accept so much as one more forkful of food. "No, thank you," she said. Then she excused herself from the table, carried her dishes into the kitchen and took refuge in her room under the stairway.

After making a reluctant trip to the privy behind the house—Rue refused to use the chamber pot under any circumstances—she washed and brushed her teeth, then climbed into bed. There was one lamp burning on the bedside stand, but the oil was so low that reading was out of the question.

Rue turned down the wick until the room was in darkness, then lay back on her pillow, thinking about Farley and the way she'd felt when he kissed her. She raised one hand to her chest, amazed at the way her heart was pounding against her breastbone, and that was when she made the frightful discovery.

The necklace was gone.

Chapter Six

Rue bounded out of bed, lit the lamp and tore through her sheets and blankets in a panic. There was no sign of the necklace.

Only too aware that she would be trapped in this backward century if she didn't find the antique pendant, she sank to her knees and went over every inch of the floor.

Rue was rifling through her sports bag when the last of the lamp oil gave out and the tiny room went dark. For a long moment, she just knelt there on the splintery wood, breathing hard and fighting a compulsion to scream hysterically.

Finally, reason prevailed. She couldn't retrace her steps through town until morning. Flashlights hadn't been invented yet and, besides, if Farley caught her out prowling the sidewalks at that hour, he'd probably toss her back in jail just on general principle.

Lying very still, Rue forced herself to concentrate on her breathing until she was calmer. Soon her heartbeat had slowed to its regular rate and the urge to rush wildly around Pine River upending things in search of the missing necklace had abated slightly. For all her self-control, Rue didn't manage to sleep that night.

Finally the sun peeked over the blue-green, timber-carpeted hills, and Rue bolted out of her room like a rubber-tipped dart shot from a popgun. She'd long since washed, dressed and brushed her teeth.

She went over every step she'd taken the day before, hoping to find the necklace wedged between one of the boards in the sidewalk or lying beside the Sinclairs' gate or on the path to the privy. After a full morning of searching, however, Rue still had no necklace, and she was pretty forlorn.

In a last-ditch effort, she made her way to Farley's office. The front door was propped open with a rusty coffee can filled with ordinary speckled rocks.

"Hello?" Rue called, peering around the frame.

Farley was just hanging his hat on its customary peg, and a large, rumpled-looking man was snoring away on the cot in the cell.

When Farley smiled in recognition, Rue felt as if two of the floorboards had suddenly switched places beneath her feet. "Good day, Miss Claridge," the marshal said.

He acted as though he hadn't kissed her the night before, and Rue decided to go along with the pretense.

She stepped into the room reluctantly, torn between approaching the marshal and bolting down the sidewalk in utter terror. Rue hadn't felt this awkward around a guy since junior high. "I wonder if you would mind checking your lost-and-found department for my necklace," she said, sounding as prim as Miss Ella Sinclair or one of the Society.

Farley's dark eyebrows knit together for a moment, then he went to the stove and reached for the handle of the coffeepot. "We've never seen the need for a lost-and-found department here in Pine River," he said with a good-natured patience that nonetheless rankled. "Folks pretty much know what belongs to them and what doesn't."

Rue sagged a little. "Then no one has reported finding a gold necklace?"

Farley studied her sympathetically and shook his head. "Coffee?"

Rue had never been a frail woman, but these were stressful circumstances, and she knew a dose of Farley's high-octane brew would probably turn her stomach inside out. "No, thanks," she said distractedly. "Did you know it's been proven that caffeine aggravates P.M.S.?"

"What aggravates what?"

"Never mind." Rue turned to go, muttering. "I've got to find that necklace...."

There was nowhere else to look, however, so Rue returned to the Sinclair house. The place was empty and, since she'd probably missed lunch, Rue headed for her room. As she was opening the door, a distraught, feminine moan drifted down the stairway.

Holding the skirts of her secondhand dress, Rue swept around the newel post and up the stairs. The sound was coming from beneath the first door on the right. She knocked lightly. "Hello? Are you all right in there?"

"Yes." The answer was a fitful groan.

Rue opened the door a crack and saw Alice McCall lying on a narrow bed in her chemise. A crude hot-water bottle lay on the lower part of her stomach.

"Cramps?" Rue inquired.

"It's the curse," Alice replied, whispering the words as though confessing to some great sin.

Remembering the aspirin in her bag, Rue said, "I think I can help you. I'll be right back." She raced downstairs to her room to fetch the miracle drug she'd brought from her own century and then, after pausing in the kitchen to battle the pump for a glass of water, returned to Alice's room.

The poor girl was pale as death, and her wispy, reddish blond hair was limp with perspiration.

She looked at the pair of white tablets in Rue's palm and squinted. "Pills?"

"They're magic," Rue promised with a teasing lilt to her voice. Aspirin would probably work wonders for someone who had never taken it before. "Just swallow them and you'll see."

Alice hesitated only a moment. Then she took the tablets and washed them down, one by one, with delicate sips of water.

"Would you like me to fix you a cup of tea?" Rue asked.

"You're very kind, but, no," Alice responded, her face still pinched with pain. It would be a while before the aspirin worked.

Rue sat down at the foot of the bed, since there was no chair, and took in the small, tidy room at a glance. Although Alice's bedroom had a window and the wallpaper was actually tasteful, the place was as sparsely furnished as a monk's cell. Two dresses hung on pegs on the wall, one for everyday and one for Sundays and special occasions. Over the bureau, with its four shallow drawers, was a mirror made of watery greenish glass. A rickety washstand held the requisite pitcher and bowl.

Above the bed was a calendar, clearly marked 1892, with a maudlin picture of two scantily clad children huddling close in a blizzard. The month of October was on display, and the twenty-third was circled in a wreath of pencil lines.

"Is your birthday coming up?" Rue asked, knowing Alice had seen her glance at the calendar.

Alice smiled wanly. "No. That's the day of the Fall Dance at the schoolhouse."

Rue wondered if Alice, like Miss Ella Sinclair, was sweet on Marshal Haynes. The idea took a little of the sparkle off her charitable mood. "Are you hoping to dance with anybody special?"

Color was beginning to return to Alice's cheeks, though Rue couldn't be sure whether that was due to the aspirin or the prospect of spending time with that special someone. "Jeffrey Hollis," she confided. "He works at the mill."

"Are the two of you dating?"

Alice looked puzzled. "Dating?"

"Courting," Rue corrected herself.

Alice laughed softly. "*I* am definitely courting Jeffrey," she replied, "but I think somebody will have to tell him that he's supposed to be courting me in return." She lay back on the pillow, her lashes fluttering against her cheeks, and then, without further adieu, she floated off to sleep.

Rue covered her newfound friend with a plaid woolen blanket and sneaked out of the room. Back in her own quarters, she ate another candy bar, read two more chapters of her book, and closed her eyes to meditate on the problem of the lost necklace.

Mentally, she retraced every step she'd taken the day before, from the moment she'd found herself in a stranger's privy until she lay down in bed and realized the pendant was gone. And again the chilling thought came to her that that weird, spooky piece of jewelry might have taken to traveling through time all on its own.

Rue squeezed her eyes shut and dragged in a series of slow, deep breaths in an effort to keep her cool, all the while feeling like a one-woman riot.

If she got stuck in this place, she vowed silently, she would pay Elisabeth back by moving into her house like a poor relation. She would stay for fifty years and consciously work at getting more eccentric with every passing day.

Rue brought herself up short. She refused to worry about the future or about the missing necklace. It was time to stop thinking about problems and start looking for solutions.

The first order of business was to find Elisabeth. Once she'd done that, once she knew for a fact that her cousin really wanted to stay in the Victorian era, she could worry about getting home. Or about making a life for herself right there in old Pine River.

With Farley.

She imagined cooking for him, pressing his shirts, washing his back.

The images stirred hormones Rue hadn't even known she had, and a schoolgirl flush rolled from her toes to the roots of her hair in a single crimson wave.

Good grief! she thought, bolting upright on the cot. *Cooking? Ironing? Washing his back? What's happening to me? I'm regressing at warp speed!*

Rue sighed and rose from the bed. Lying around in her room in the middle of the day was a waste of daylight. She would check on Alice, then go out and retrace her steps again. Maybe she would find the necklace, or maybe some earthshaking idea would come to her.

Miss McCall was still sleeping, and some of the color had returned to her cheeks, so Rue knew the aspirin was doing its work. She closed the door of Alice's room carefully and turned toward the front stairway.

Mr. Sinclair was standing there, barring her way, a worrisome smile on his face. He was a portly man, with gray hair, shrewd brown eyes, florid cheeks and a somewhat bulbous nose.

"Miss Claridge," he said, as though Rue might have forgotten her name and he was generous enough to enlighten her.

Rue retreated a step, feeling uneasy. She'd seen that look in a man's eyes many times during her travels, and she knew the banker had decided to make a pass. "Good afternoon," she said warily, with a little nod.

"Exploring the house?" He crooned the words, and somehow that was more unnerving than if he'd shouted them.

Rue raised her chin a notch, still keeping her distance. "Of course not," she said with cool politeness.

"Your room is on the first floor, I believe." Sinclair's eyes never linked with hers all the while he was speaking. Instead, his gaze drifted over her hair, her throat, her shoulders and then her breasts.

"I was looking in on Miss McCall," Rue said, folding her arms to hide at least one part of her anatomy from his perusal. "She's suffering from—feminine complaints."

In the next instant, the master of the house reached out with one beefy hand and took hold of Rue's jaw. While his grip was not painful, it was definitely an affront, and she immediately tried to twist free.

"Now, now," Sinclair murmured, as though soothing a fractious child, "don't run away. I wouldn't want to have to tell Farley I caught you going through my personal belongings and get you thrown back into jail."

Rue felt the blood drain from her face. This kind of bore was easy enough to deal with in her own time, but just then the year was 1892 and Sinclair was probably among the most influential men in town. "What do you want?" she asked, hoping she was wrong.

She wasn't.

He ran a sausage-size thumb over her mouth. "Just an hour of your time, Miss Claridge. That's all."

Rue thrust herself away from him. "I wouldn't give you a *moment*," she ground out, "let alone an hour!"

Smiling genially, Sinclair hooked his thumbs in his vest pockets. "That's a pity. More jail time will surely ruin what little is left of your reputation."

Rue inched backward toward the stairway leading down to the kitchen. "I'll deny everything. And Farley will believe me, too!" She wasn't too sure about that last part, but she wanted to keep Sinclair distracted until she was out of lunging distance.

His bushy eyebrows rose in mocking amusement. "Silly child. What the marshal believes doesn't amount to a hill of beans. Not against the say-so of a man who controls everybody's finances."

Knowing she had reached the stairs, Rue whirled and raced down them. She snatched her bag from the little room she had occupied so briefly and fled out the front door.

Now, for all practical intents and purposes, she was homeless. She couldn't go back to her own century because she'd lost the necklace, and since Farley would probably take Sinclair's word over hers, arrest was no doubt imminent.

Much as Rue enjoyed Farley's company, she wasn't about to be locked up again. One stretch in the hoosegow on trumped up charges was more than enough; she had no intention of serving another.

Even so, Rue was forced to admit to herself that she was drawn to Farley's quiet strength. She made her way through the deep grass behind the mercantile and the Hang-Dog Saloon, stopping now and then to crouch down when she heard voices. After nearly half an hour of evasion tactics, she reached the little barn behind the marshal's house and slipped inside.

Farley's horse, a big roan gelding, nickered companionably from its stall.

"At least somebody around here likes me," Rue said, looking around the small structure and deciding the loft would make the best hiding place.

After letting out a long sigh, she tossed her bag up and then climbed the rickety ladder—not an easy task in a long skirt.

The hay in the loft was sweet smelling, and afternoon sunlight flooded in through a gap in the roof. Rue sat crosslegged and automatically unzipped the side flap on her bag, since that was where she had hidden her money.

The currency, like Aunt Verity's necklace, had vanished.

Rue gave a little cry of frustration and fell backward into the hay. A few minutes later, she checked the main compartment of the bag, but nothing was missing. Evidently the thief—possibly even Sinclair himself—had stumbled upon the money first and been content with that.

Despite her fury, Rue had to smile, wondering what the robber would have made of her miniature candy bars and other modern inventions.

Following that, she took the advice her grandfather had given her long ago and quietly accepted the fact that she was in big trouble. As much as she would like things to be different, the reality was that her money was gone, one of Pine River's most prominent citizens planned to accuse her of stealing, and she'd lost the only means she'd had of returning to her own time. Only when she'd faced these problems squarely would solutions begin to present themselves.

At least, she *hoped* solutions would begin to present themselves. Nothing came to her right away.

The sun was setting and crickets were harmonizing in the quack grass outside the barn when she heard sounds below and rolled over to peer through a crack between the floorboards of the loft.

Farley was there. He filled a feedbag and slipped it over the gelding's head, then began currying the animal. The graceful play of the muscles in the marshal's back and shoulders did odd things to Rue's heartbeat, but she couldn't help watching him work.

The lawman caught her completely off guard when he suddenly whirled, drew his pistol and pointed it at the underside of the loft.

"All right, just come down from there," he ordered. "And keep your hands where I can see them."

Some days, Rue reflected dismally, it just didn't pay to get out of bed.

"Don't shoot, Marshal," she said. "It's only me, Rue Claridge, Pine River's Most Wanted."

When Rue peered over the top of the ladder, Farley was just sliding his pistol back into its holster. He'd hung his hat on a peg on the wall, and his attractively rumpled brown hair glimmered even in the fading light. "What the hell are you doing up there?" he demanded, setting his hands on his hips.

Rue sighed and swung her legs over the side of the loft, gripping the pink sports bag in one hand. "Holding, of course. When Mr. Sinclair put the moves on me, I told him to get lost, and he said he'd have you arrest me...."

Farley scratched his head, obviously impatient and puzzled.

Rue tossed her bag to the floor and then climbed resignedly down the ladder to face her fate. "Here." She held out her hands, wrists together. "Handcuff me."

The marshal looked sternly down his nose at Rue. "You've gone and gotten yourself thrown out of the only boardinghouse that would have you?"

Sudden color pulsed in Rue's cheeks. "Didn't you hear a word I've said? Sinclair wanted me to—to be intimate with him. I refused, of course, and he said he'd have me arrested for robbing his house."

Farley's turquoise eyes narrowed. "Let's see that satchel," he said brusquely.

Rue resented the invasion of privacy, but she also knew she had no real choice, so she handed over the bag.

The marshal turned it end over end, trying to find the opening, and Rue finally reached out and pulled back the zipper herself.

Farley stared at the small mechanism as though it were a bug under a microscope. "What the—"

"It's called a zipper," Rue said with a sigh. "They won't be invented for another twenty-five or thirty years, so don't bother looking for them in your favorite store."

Now Farley studied Rue with the same thoroughness as he'd examined the zipper on her neon pink bag. "You don't talk like anybody I've ever known before, except for Mrs. Fortner, of course. Where did you come from?" he asked quietly.

Rue folded her arms. She might as well tell the truth, she decided, since nobody was going to believe her anyway. "The future. I came from the far end of the twentieth century." She snatched the bag from his hands, suddenly anxious to convince him, to have one person on the face of the earth know what was happening to her. "Here," she said, pulling the paperback spy novel out and thrusting it in Farley's face. "Look. Did you ever see a book like this before, with a soft cover? And read the copyright date."

Farley turned the book in his hands, clearly amazed by the bright red cover and the gold-foil lettering spelling out the title and the author's name.

"Nobody can come from the future," he insisted stubbornly, but Rue could see that the paperback puzzled him.

"I did," she said. After setting the bag down, she politely took the book, opened it to the copyright page and held it out again. "There. Read that."

Farley took in the printed words, then raised baffled eyes to Rue's face. "It's a trick," he said.

"How could it be?" Rue demanded, growing impatient even though she'd known she would never convince him. "Paperback books and zippers don't exist in 1892, Farley!"

"You could have gotten those things at some fancy science exhibition in St. Louis or Chicago or somewhere." Clearly, Farley meant to stand his intellectual ground, even though it was eroding under his feet. "All I know is, it's got to be some kind of hoax."

Rue rolled her eyes. Then she bent and pulled out one of her precious snack-size candy bars. "How about this?" she challenged, holding out the morsel. "Did I get this at an exhibition, too?"

Farley frowned, examining the wrapper.

"You have to tear off the paper," Rue prompted. "Then you eat what's inside."

Farley looked suspicious, but intrigued, also. He tore away the paper, letting it drift to the floor.

Rue picked the litter up and crumpled it on one hand, while Farley carried the candy bar over to the doorway and studied it in the last light. The look of consternation on his face was amusing, even under the circumstances.

"Go ahead, Farley," she urged. "Take a bite."

The marshal glanced at her again, then nibbled cautiously at one end of the chocolate bar. After a moment, he smiled. "I'll be damned," he muttered, then consumed the rest of the candy. "Got any more of those?"

"Yes," Rue answered, thrusting out her chin, "but I'm not going to let you wolf them down. Especially not when you're about to arrest me for something I didn't do."

"I'm not going to arrest you," Farley replied reasonably, looking at Rue with curious amusement. "We've only got one jail cell here in Pine River, as you know, and it's already occupied. I'll just have to give you my bed and bunk out here in the barn until you get on that stage next Tuesday."

Rue didn't protest, nor did she turn the conversation back to the reality of time travel. Farley was still telling himself he was the victim of some elaborate prank, no doubt, but at least she had the satisfaction of knowing she'd planted the seed of possibility in his mind. Maybe after some rumination, he'd begin to take the idea seriously.

It the meantime, they were clearly going to pretend nothing out of the ordinary was going on.

If someone had to sleep in the barn, Rue reasoned, better Farley than she. She lowered her eyes. "There's a problem with my leaving on the stage," she confessed. "Somebody snitched all my money."

Farley sighed. "With luck like yours, it's purely a wonder you ever managed to win at poker the other night," he said, gesturing toward the door. "Come on, Miss Rue. Let's go in and rustle up some supper. We'll figure out what to do with you later."

Rue picked up her bag, straightened her shoulders and preceded him through the doorway of the barn. An inky twilight was working its way down the timbered hills toward them, and there was a bite in the air.

The inside of Farley's log cabin was cozy and surprisingly neat. Books lined one whole wall, from roof to floor, and a stone fireplace faced the door. An attached lean-to housed a small kitchen area, and Rue suspected the tattered Indian blanket hanging from the ceiling hid Farley's bed.

She went to stand beside the fireplace, hoping the warmth would dispel the sweet shivers that suddenly overtook her. She had a peculiar sense, all of a sudden, of being a piece on some great celestial board game, and she'd just been moved within easy reach of both victory and defeat.

"Hungry?" Farley asked, clattering metal against metal in the lean-to kitchen.

"Starved," Rue said, too tired, confused and frustrated for any more deep thought. She'd missed both breakfast and lunch, and the candy bars weren't taking up the slack.

Farley came out of the lean-to. "The stew'll be warmed up in a few minutes," he said. As he went around the cabin lighting kerosene lamps, he seemed uncharacteristically nervous.

Rue, on the other hand, felt totally safe. "So you're a cook as well as a reader," she said, wanting to hear him talk because she liked the sound of his voice, liked knowing he was there.

He grinned and shook his head. "No, ma'am," he replied. "My food is provided as a part of my wages, like this cabin. The ladies of the town take turns cooking for me."

The thought made Rue violently jealous, and that was when she realized the horrible truth. Somehow, she'd fallen in love with Farley Haynes.

Talk about Mr. Wrong.

"Oh," she said finally.

Farley shook his head and crouched to add wood to the fire. "Maybe you shouldn't stand so close," he said, and his voice was suddenly hoarse. "Ladies have been known to catch their skirts afire doing that."

Rue moved away to look at Farley's collection of books, and her voice shook when she spoke. "Have you really read all these?"

"Most of them more than once," Farley replied. She heard him retreat into the lean-to, then he called to her to join him. "Stew's warm," he said.

After drawing a deep breath, raising her chin and pushing back her shoulders, Rue marched into the tiny kitchen.

Farley had set a place for her at the small, round table, and there was a lantern flickering on a shelf nearby. The atmosphere was cozy.

He ladled stew into two bowls, set a loaf of hard bread on a platter and sat down across from her.

Once she'd taken several bites of the stew, which was delicious, Rue was a little less shaky, both inwardly and outwardly. She smiled at Farley. "This is quite a place you've got here."

"Thank you," Farley replied, "but I'll be glad when I can take up ranching and let somebody else wear my badge."

A bittersweet sadness touched Rue's heart. "Have you got a place picked out?" she asked, breaking off a piece of bread.

Farley nodded. "There's a half section for sale north of town. I've almost got enough for the down payment, and the First Federal Bank is going to give me a mortgage."

"Mr. Sinclair's bank," Rue murmured, feeling less festive.

Farley was chewing, and he waited until he'd swallowed to answer. "That's right."

An autumn wind tested the glass in the windows, and Rue was doubly glad Farley had taken her in. "If there was any justice in this world, you'd go right over there and arrest that old lecher right this minute for sexual harassment."

A modest flush tinted Farley's weathered cheekbones. "He hasn't broken the law, Rue. And that means he can't be arrested."

"Why?" Rue demanded, only vaguely registering the fact that Farley had called her by her first name. "Because he's a man? Because he's a banker? I was innocent of any crime, and that didn't keep you from slapping *me* behind bars."

"I've never slapped a woman in my life," Farley snapped, looking outraged.

Rue sat back in her chair, her eyes brimming with tears she was too proud to shed. "It's hopeless," she said. "Absolutely hopeless. You and I speak different languages, Farley Haynes."

"I would have sworn we were both talking English," he responded, reaching calmly for his glass of water.

"I give up!" Rue cried, flinging out her hands.

Farley reached for her bowl and carried it to the stove. "What you need," he said, "is some more stew."

Rue watched him with a hunger she would have been too embarrassed even to write about in the privacy of her journal, and she swallowed hard. "Stew," she said. "Right."

Chapter Seven

The stew was remarkably good, hot and savory and fresh, and Rue consumed the second helping without quibbling. She was fiercely hungry, and the food eased her low-grade headache and the shaky feeling that invariably overtook her when she failed to eat regular meals.

After supper, Farley heated water on the stove, and Rue insisted on washing the dishes. It was fun, sort of like playing house in an antique store.

The lean-to was a small place, though, and when Farley poured himself a cup of coffee and then lingered at the table, flipping thoughtfully through a stack of papers, Rue was more painfully conscious of his presence than ever. She tried not to think about him, but it was an impossibility. He seemed to fill the little room to its corners with his size, his uncompromising masculinity and the sheer strength of his personality.

In Rue's opinion, the effect on her nerves, her muscles and her most-secret parts was all out of proportion to the circumstances, strange as they were. She felt like a human volcano; lava was burning and bubbling in the farthest reaches of her body and her spirit. Simple things like drying the chipped crockery bowls they'd eaten from and setting them on the shelves took on the significance of epic poetry.

She was wrestling with the enormous enamel coffeepot, trying to pour herself a cupful, when she felt Farley looming behind her. He displaced her grip on the pot's handle and filled her cup.

He was only standing at her back, it was nothing more dramatic than that, yet Rue felt a devastating charge radiate from his body to hers. In the next moment, the invisible field, woven of lantern light, cosmic mystery, half-forgotten dreams and stardust enfolded her, and she sagged backward against Farley's steely stomach and chest.

Farley made no sound. He simply took the cup from Rue's hand, set it on the stove and closed his strong arms lightly around her waist. For all that she had never been in such trouble, even on her most memorable assignments as a journalist, Rue felt as though she'd stumbled upon some magical sanctuary where nothing and no one could ever hurt her.

In the meantime, the seismic tumult was building inside Rue, gaining force moment by moment. She knew the inevitable eruption would be more than physical; it would be an upheaval of the soul, as well. And she wanted it despite the danger.

Presently—whether a minute or an hour passed, Rue could not have said—Farley raised his hands slowly, gently, to weigh her breasts. When his thumbs moved over her nipples, making them harden and strain against the fabric of her dress, Rue groaned and tilted her head back against his shoulder.

He touched his lips to her temple, warming the delicate flesh there, and then he bent his head slightly to nibble the side of her neck. Rue would have throttled any other man for taking such liberties, but her need for Farley had sneaked up on her, and it was already so pervasive that she couldn't tell where the craving stopped and her own being began.

When he lifted her into his arms, Rue's logical left brain finally struggled to the surface and gurgled out a protest, but it was too late. The fanciful right side of her brain was hearing rapturous symphonies, and the notes drowned out all other sounds.

Farley carried her out of the kitchen—Rue was vaguely aware of the fire as they passed the hearth—then he took her behind the Indian blanket that served as a curtain. There was a look of grim resignation on his face as he laid her on the neatly made bed and stood gazing down at her for a long moment. It was as if he thought she'd cast a spell over him and he was trying to work out some way to break it.

She couldn't tell him that she was under an enchantment, too, that she had never done anything like this before. All she could do was lie there, all but the most primitive essence of her identity seared away by the heat of her desire, needing him. Waiting.

He took off her funny, old-fashioned shoes and tossed them aside, then began unbuttoning her dress. Only when she lay completely naked on his bed, totally vulnerable, did he speak.

"God help me," he said in a raw whisper, "I've wanted to see you like this since that day I found you wandering in Doc Fortner's house. I've wanted to touch you...."

Rue took his hand in hers, emboldened by the turquoise fire in his eyes and the frantic fever in her own spirit, and pressed his palm and fingers to her breast. "Touch me," she said softly, and the words were both a plea and an affirmation.

Farley complied for a long, torturously delicious interval, then while Rue waited in sweet agony, he withdrew. She watched, dazed, as he removed his clothes.

His body had the stealth and prowess of a stalking panther as he stretched out beside her on the rough, woolen blanket that served as a bedspread. Then he kissed her, first caressing her lips with his, then commanding her mouth to open for the entrance of his tongue.

The conquest was a triumphant one, far more potent than any ordinary kiss. Rue's body arched beside Farley on the bed, and he reached beneath her to cup her bottom in one hand and press her close against his thighs and the solid demand of his manhood.

She was afraid when she felt him, terrified of his size and power, and yet this knowledge did nothing to stem the furious tide of her passion.

Farley kissed Rue, again and again, all the while caressing and shaping her with his hands, until she was in a virtual delirium of need. Perspiration shimmered on every inch of her flesh, and tendrils of her hair clung wetly to her neck and temples.

At last, Farley positioned himself between her legs, then put his hands under her shoulder blades and raised her breasts for conquering. When he captured one eager nipple with his mouth, Rue cried out in despairing surrender, begging him to take her.

For all her travels, for all her reading and her sophistication, when Farley entered her, Rue was startled. There was pain, and it lingered, but it was also promptly overshadowed by a consuming, joyous rage made up of heavenly light and dragon's fire.

Rue pressed her hands to Farley's back, and the play of his muscles under her palms was as much a part of their lovemaking as the ferocious rhythm of joining and parting that was even then transforming them both.

For all the breathless promise of the past half hour or so, when Rue finally achieved satisfaction, she was all but swept away by the force of it. She strained beneath Farley in wild, glorious and totally involuntary spasms, her teeth clenched against the shouts of triumph rattling in the back of her throat. She was just settling back to the bed, breathless and disoriented, when Farley clasped her bottom hard in his hands, pressed her tightly against him and made a series of deep, abrupt thrusts. To Rue's surprise, she reached another climax when Farley had his; her release was a soft, languid implosion, like a blessing on the tempest that had preceded it.

When he'd finally spent the last of his energy, Farley collapsed beside Rue, his breathing hard and raspy. She pressed her face into the taut, moist flesh on his shoulder, at once hiding from her lover and seeking him out.

"I knew it would be like that," Farley muttered after they'd lain entwined for a long time, listening to the beating of each other's hearts, the crackle of the fire and the night sounds of the lively timber town beyond the cabin walls.

Rue's eyes filled with tears, but she wasn't mourning the time before, when she and Farley had been innocent of each other. No matter what happened, whether she lived the rest of her life with this man or without him, in this century or another, she'd given herself truly and totally to Farley Haynes, and she would never forget the splendor of it.

"I thought it was a lie," she finally confessed. "What people said about making love, I mean. I never knew—until now."

Farley sighed and raised his head to look through her eyes, as though they were clear as windowpanes, and straight into her soul. He kissed her forehead and then rested his scratchy chin where his lips had just touched. "I'm sorry," he said, his voice low and hoarse. "I offered you safe haven here, and then I took advantage."

Rue had just been transported to a whole other plane of womanhood, and the journey had had just as great an impact on her senses and emotions as being tossed from one time period to another. She was incapable, for the moment, of working out whether Farley's apology was appropriate or not. "It's not as though you threw me down on the bed and forced me," she pointed out, loving the feel of his back, supple skin over firm muscles. "I wanted you."

Farley drew back to search her eyes again, and the gesture made her feel more naked than she had earlier when he'd methodically relieved her of her clothes. "You are the most forward-thinking female I have ever encountered," he said somberly, but then a grin broke over his face. "I think I like that about you."

Rue swallowed, and her ability to think in rational terms was beginning to dissipate like fog in bright sunshine. Farley was joined to her, and he was getting hard again, and she didn't want him to leave her. "Stay inside me, Farley. Please."

Bracing himself by pressing his hands on the mattress on either side of her, Farley began to move slowly. "I'll find out the truth about you," he said, his words growing short and breathy as he increased his pace, "if it's the last thing I ever do."

Pressing her shoulders deep into the feather pillows and tilting her head back in magnificent surrender, Rue gasped out, "I'd love to tell you—I'd love to show you the place I came from. . . ." And from that moment on, Rue was beyond speaking.

Farley dipped his head to lave one of her distended nipples with his tongue. His attentions were merciless and thorough, and soon Rue was pitching under him like a wild mare trying to shake off a rider.

Once that session had ended, Rue cuddled against Farley's side—his rib cage had about as much flexibility as the staves of a wooden barrel—and promptly drifted off to sleep. When she awakened, the Indian blanket that separated the bed from the rest of the cabin was framed in silvery moonlight and Farley's side of the mattress was empty.

Rue scrambled off the bed, found one of Farley's shirts hanging from a peg in the wall and shoved her arms through the sleeves. The clock on the plain, board mantel over the fireplace read 3:17 and despite the fact that she had no claim on the marshal's time, a sense of alarm crowded her throat.

Obviously, Farley had gone out for some reason—maybe there had been shouts or a frantic knock at the door or even shots fired, and she'd been too drunk on lovemaking to hear. In fact, she hadn't even noticed when Farley left.

Rue's imagination tripped into overdrive. She'd seen enough Clint Eastwood movies to know what awful things could happen to a lone lawman. The difference was that now she wouldn't be able to toss away her popcorn box, fish her car keys out of her purse and go home to an apartment filled with modern conveniences. This was the real thing, and she just happened to be hopelessly in love with the peace officer in question.

On some level, Rue had known from the moment she met Farley that something significant was going to happen between them. But she hadn't expected the event to be on a par with the destruction of the dinosaurs or the formation of the Grand Canyon.

Rue groped her way into the lean-to kitchen, blinded by her emotions rather than a lack of light, and looked at herself in Farley's shaving mirror. Except that her hair was tangled and she was wearing a man's shirt, she seemed unchanged. Inside, however, Rue was wholly different; she'd been converted, not into someone else, but into a better, richer and more genuine version of herself.

Trembling, Rue poured a cup of coffee from the pot on the stove and sank into one of the two chairs at the table. Since it had been sitting on the heat for hours, the brew was black as coal oil and only slightly more palatable. Rue figured there was probably enough caffeine in the stuff to keep her awake well into the next century—be it the twentieth or the twenty-first—but she took a second sip anyway.

Through the closed windows and thin walls of Farley's house, Rue could hear the sounds of laughter and bad piano music and an ongoing argument between a man and a woman. She was overwhelmingly relieved when the door opened and the marshal himself walked in.

He set his rifle in the corner, hung his hat and long canvas duster on their pegs and then began unfastening his gun belt. All the time, he watched Rue in the dim, icy glow of the moonlight.

Rue didn't want to express her relief at seeing him; she didn't have the right. "I hope I didn't keep you from your work," she said with as much dignity as a person wearing only a man's shirt and a glow of satisfaction can be expected to summon up.

Farley didn't answer. He simply came to the table, took Rue's hand and brought her to her feet. He took her back to the bedside, and she crawled under the covers, her heart turning to vapor and then gathering in her throat like a summer storm taking shape on the horizon.

She watched as Farley took off his clothes for the second time that night, more shaken than before by his magnificence and quiet grace.

He stretched out beside her under the blankets and with a few deft motions of one hand, relieved her of the long shirt she wore. Having done that, Farley curved one arm around Rue and arranged her close against his side, her head resting on his shoulder.

Farley did not make love to Rue; instead, he simply held her, sheltering her in his solidity and strength. For Rue, the experience was, in its own way, just as momentous as full surrender had been earlier. The simple intimacy met fundamental needs that had not only been unsatisfied before, but unrecognized.

Rue slept soundly that night and awakened with the first light of dawn, when Farley gently displaced her to get out of bed.

"What do I do now?" Rue asked softly. Sadly. "I can't stay here. The whole town will know if I do."

"The whole town already knows," Farley answered, pulling on a pair of dark trousers and disappearing around the edge of the blanket curtain. "There aren't many secrets in a place like Pine River."

Rue slipped under the covers with a groan of mortification, but she could still hear the clatter and clink of stove lids, the working of a pump handle, the opening and closing of a door.

Presently, the smell and sounds of sizzling bacon filled the air, along with the aroma of fresh coffee. Rue got up, struggled back into her clothes and peered around the blanket.

She could see Farley in the lean-to, standing at the stove. The sight of him, with his hair wetted down and combed, a meat fork in one hand, filled her with a tenderness so keen that it was painful.

Rue approached hesitantly. For the first time in her life, she didn't know what to say.

Farley turned a strip of bacon in the black skillet and ran his turquoise eyes companionably over her length. For an instant, Rue was beneath him again, in the throes of complete physical and spiritual communion, and the sensation left her disconcerted.

The marshal made short work of her poetic mood. "If you're sore," he said, "I've got some balm out in the barn."

Rue sighed. This was the same man who had evoked such violently beautiful responses from her the night before and had later held her snugly against his side, making no demands. Now he was offering her the same medicine he would use on a cow or a horse.

"Thanks," she answered belatedly, "but I'll be fine."

Farley shrugged, took two plates down from a shelf and began dishing up breakfast.

"Interesting," she murmured thoughtfully, pulling back a chair.

He set a plate filled with fried food in front her. "What's interesting?"

"You," Rue reflected. "You're a nineteenth-century male, and here you are cooking for a woman. Even waiting table."

Farley arched an eyebrow. "It's that or risk letting you do the cooking," he replied.

Rue laughed, but her amusement faded as daylight strengthened the thin glow of the lanterns and reality settled in around her. It was morning now; the enchanted night was over and she was stranded in the wrong century, with the wrong man.

"Farley, what am I going to do?" she asked again. "My money is gone, I don't have anywhere to stay and it's beginning to look like my cousin and her husband are going to make their home in San Francisco and never contact anybody in Pine River again."

"Jon and Lizzie will come back when they're ready," Farley said with certainty. "And you can stay here with me."

"Oh, right," Rue snapped, irritated not with Farley for making the suggestion, but with herself for wanting to go on sharing his life and his bed for as long as possible. "The good women of Pine River will love that."

Farley grinned. "No, they won't."

"You're being pretty cocky right now," Rue pointed out, annoyed, "but the truth is, you're afraid of those women, Farley Haynes. They have the power to make both our lives miserable, and you know it."

Farley's smile tightened to a look of grim obstinance, and Rue wondered hopefully if the night before had worked some ancient, fundamental magic in the deepest parts of his being, the way it had in hers.

"Those old hens will just have to do their scratching and pecking in somebody else's dooryard," he said.

"What the devil is that supposed to mean?" Rue countered, reaching for another slice of crispy bacon. The man made love with the expertise of a bard taking up the pen, and he had some pretty modern attitudes, but sometimes he talked in cowboy riddles.

Farley got up to refill his coffee mug and Rue's. "Hell," he grumbled, "even the prissy Eastern lieutenants and captains I knew in the army didn't boss a man around the way those old biddies do."

Rue stifled a giggle, but said nothing.

Farley came back to the table, set their mugs down and shook an index finger at her. "Mind you don't take to carrying on the way they do, because I won't put up with it."

Rue swallowed, unsure how to react. On the one hand, it was an affront, Farley's presuming to issue orders that way. On the other, though she would have chewed one of Aunt Verity's antique crystal doorknobs before admitting as much to him, she liked the gentle forcefulness of his manner. Here, at last, was a person as strong as she was.

"I don't see where my actions are any concern of yours," she finally managed to say.

He sighed and shook his head, as though marveling that someone so simpleminded could have reached adulthood without being seriously injured in the process. "After last night," Farley told her, making an insulting effort at clarity as he spoke, "there's nothing we can do but get married."

Rue wouldn't have been more stunned if he'd thrown his food all over her. *"Married?"* she squeaked. In that instant, she realized that it was the dearest, most secret wish of her heart to marry Farley Haynes. At the same time, she knew she'd have to be demented even to entertain the idea.

Okay, so she loved Farley, she thought. He didn't feel the same way toward her; in mentioning marriage, he was probably just following the code of the West, or something like that. And there was still the matter of their coming from two different centuries, two different *worlds*. To love Farley, to stay in this time with him, would be to give up everything she knew and much of what she was.

Rue was a strong woman, and that was both her blessing and her curse. Not even for Farley and a lifetime of the tempestuous dances he'd taught her in the night just past could she give up her own identity. She was of another time;

she was a journalist, a person with many more bridges to cross, both professionally and personally.

Of course, if she did marry the marshal, she would have a place to stay until she made contact with her cousin, found the necklace and returned to her own century. Farley would undoubtedly make thorough love to her practically every night, and the mere prospect of that brought all Rue's feminine forces to a state of hypersensitivity.

"I'll send somebody over to the next town for the justice of the peace," Farley said, as if the matter had been settled.

"Now just a minute," Rue protested, thumping the tabletop lightly with one fist. "I haven't said yes to your proposal, if you can call it that. It just so happens that I don't want to get married—I don't even plan to stay around here, once I've seen my cousin."

Farley looked untroubled by this announcement. "What if we made a baby last night?" he asked, figuratively pulling the rug out from under Rue's feet. "I don't think things are any different in Seattle or Boston or wherever it is you really come from. Life is damn near impossible for an unmarried woman with a child."

Rue laid both her hands to her stomach. Nature might very well be knitting a tiny being in the warm safety of her womb. She was filled with wanting and fear. "Oh, my God," she whispered.

Farley stood and carried his plate to the sink. Then he came back to the table, stood beside Rue's chair and bent to simultaneously taste her lips and rub her lower abdomen with one hand. "If there's no baby inside you now," he said huskily, "I'll put one there when I get back."

A hot shiver shook Rue; she was amazed anew at the depths of the passion this man could rouse in her with a few words and caresses. "When will that be?"

He nibbled at her lower lip before answering. "About noon, if nothing goes wrong," he said. Then he walked away to strap on his gun belt, reload his pistol and shrug into his duster. Farley put on his battered hat and reached for his rifle in a smooth, practiced motion. "Try to stay out of trouble until I can get you married," he urged, grinning slightly. Then he opened the door and left.

Rue was restless, and the choices confronting her seemed overwhelming. Go or stay. Love or pretend to be indifferent. Follow her heart or her head. Laugh or cry.

More to keep herself busy than because she was a devotee of neatness, Rue heated water on the cookstove, washed the dishes, wiped off the table and swept the floor. Following that, she made the bed. It was while she was doing that that she found the stash.

Her foot caught on a loose floorboard as she was plumping the pillows, and she crouched to press the plank back into place. The same curiosity that had made her such a good journalist made her a very bad houseguest; Rue couldn't resist peeking underneath.

A cigar box was tucked away in the small, dark place, and Rue lifted the lid to find a respectable collection of five-dollar gold pieces. This money, surely, was meant to be the down payment on Farley's ranch.

Kneeling now, Rue set the box on the side of the bed and studied one of the coins. Where she came from, the small, ornate bit of gold would be worth far more than five dollars, but here it was ordinary money.

Carefully, Rue closed the lid and set the box back in its place. If Farley had been anyone but who he was, she might have taken that money, used it to get to San Francisco, but she couldn't steal his dreams.

The best thing to do was look for the necklace.

The day was chilly, and Rue wished for a shawl as she walked along the sidewalks of Pine River, searching for the lost piece of jewelry that was her only link with the world she knew.

She searched all morning without any luck, and her shoulders were sagging with discouragement when she started toward Farley's office. Hopefully, since he was willing to give her a baby, he might also offer lunch.

As she was passing Ella Sinclair's boarding house, Rue realized there was one place she hadn't looked—the outhouse she'd materialized in. Her heart started to pound. She wasn't sure which one it was, but she knew it was in this neighborhood.

Lifting her skirts, Rue dashed around the house she'd been passing, avoiding manure and mud in the yard as best she could, and hurtled herself into the outhouse she found there, but to no avail—the necklace wasn't there. She began to run through backyards, entering and searching each outhouse she came to. So intent was she on finding the lost necklace that she was barely aware of the rumbles of consternation, shock and amusement around her.

When she spotted her pendant caught between two boards—thank the Lord—she let out a shriek of delighted triumph and snatched it up.

In practically the same instant, a strong arm curved around her from behind, and Rue was yanked backward against an impervious chest. She knew by the quivering in her spirit and the straightforward method of operation that she'd been apprehended by Farley Haynes. Again.

"I was only getting my necklace," she told him, wriggling to get free. "I lost it in the back of this wagon the other day, when I hitched a ride into town."

With his free arm, Farley swept off his hat and wiped his forehead with his sleeve. "That's just fine," he drawled, obviously furious. "Now I suggest you start apologizing to these people you've been disturbing."

Rue wanted to laugh and to cry, she was so relieved at finding the necklace. She dropped it into her skirt pocket. "Anything you say, Marshal," she responded sweetly. "Are we still getting married?"

The question stirred a buzz in the crowd that had gathered, and Rue was amused. Farley had just assumed she was up to no good, plundering the good citizens' outhouses for heaven only knew what scurrilous purpose, and she wouldn't have put it past him to arrest her. Therefore, in her opinion, a little embarrassment served him right, because after the previous night's activities, he should have trusted her more.

"Yes," he said as grimly as a judge pronouncing a death sentence.

Rue smiled all the while as she offered her apology to the crowd, every once in a while reaching into her pocket to make sure the necklace was there. She could not yet return to her own time because she hadn't found Elisabeth, but the door was no longer closed to her, and that was the important thing.

Chapter Eight

Some thoughtful citizen had brought fried chicken, biscuits and gravy for Farley's lunch, and he shared the feast with the solitary prisoner and Rue. The marshal's eyes were narrowed, however, as he regarded her across the surface of his messy desk.

"I thought I told you to stay out of trouble," he said.

Rue's cheeks pulsed a little as she thought of the episode. "I was only looking for my necklace, Farley," she answered reasonably. She took a bite from a crispy fried chicken leg and chewed thoroughly before going on. "If you had any idea how important that pendant really is, you wouldn't make such a big deal about a little disturbance."

Farley's frown deepened. He took another piece of chicken from the lunch basket, which was lined with a blue-and-white cotton napkin. "I know ladies like their trinkets," he allowed. "My mother had a brooch made of marcasite and jet that she wouldn't have parted with to save her own scalp. But I have a feeling this necklace of yours is important for some other reason.''

He was remarkably astute, Rue thought, but she wasn't about to explain the necklace's peculiar power—mainly because she didn't begin to understand it herself.

She reached into her pocket and touched the twisted chain, and that was when she felt the strange warning vibration. By instinct, she realized that the pendant was up to its old tricks again; she was about to be sent helter-skelter into some other part of history, and not necessarily the one she belonged in, either.

No, she thought desperately, *not now. Not without saying goodbye....*

The room seemed to waver and shift, like a reflection in old bottle glass. Glimpses of the orchard behind Aunt Verity's house were superimposed over the stove, the bars in the cell door, Farley himself. Rue wrenched her hand from her pocket and the visions faded instantly, along with the sense of an impending spiritual earthquake.

She gripped the edge of Farley's desk with both hands, swaying slightly with mingled sickness and relief.

Farley immediately jumped up to bring her a dipperful of cold well water from the bucket near the stove.

''Are you sick?'' he demanded. ''Do you want me to go and get the doc?''

Rue smiled thinly and squeezed her eyes shut for a moment, still trying to regain her equilibrium. ''Yes. Find Dr. Jonathan Fortner, please,'' she joked. ''And his wife Elisabeth, while you're at it.''

Farley crouched beside her chair, looking up into her face with troubled eyes, eyes of such a beautiful Arizona turquoise that it hurt Rue's heart to return their gaze. ''What just happened here?'' he demanded quietly.

I almost left you, Rue answered in stricken silence.

"Rue," Farley insisted, setting the empty dipper on the desk and holding both her hands in his. "Are you suffering from some sickness of the head? Is that your big secret? Did you run away from one of those mental hospitals?"

Rue laughed, a little hysterically, but with genuine amusement. She could answer only one of his questions with an unequivocal no. The other two he would have to take on trust. She shook her head. "I didn't escape from an asylum, Farley," she said softly.

She could see by his face that he believed her, maybe only because he wanted to, and that was the biggest relief she'd had since finding the necklace in the outhouse.

"I sent for the justice of the peace," he said. "He'll be here in a few hours."

Rue had never, in all her life, had to deal with such a degree of temptation. She wanted so much to marry Farley, to have the right to share his joys and sorrows, his table and his bed, but to vow eternal fidelity when she fully intended to return to her own time as soon as possible would be unthinkable. She would simply disappear, and Farley would be left to wonder, to the end of his days, what had become of her.

"We can't," she said.

"We will," he replied, rising and walking away to hang the dipper on its nail near the bucket.

Nothing was resolved when, fifteen minutes later, Rue left the jailhouse. Since she had nowhere in particular to go, she set out for the house in the country where all this had begun. She meant to find a tree in the orchard, climb up as high as she could and sit there and think, her back to the rough trunk, the way she'd done as a child, in a time far in the future.

She was surprised to find a fancy carriage in the yard next to the farmhouse. There was lots of bustle and activity; a little girl ran full tilt, first in one direction, then another, her small arms outspread in a child's joy at simply existing. A handsome, dark-haired man was taking bags and satchels from the vehicle's boot....

It was only then that the belated realization struck Rue. Elisabeth was back from San Francisco.

A tearful joy filled her. She struggled with the latch on the front gate, grew impatient and vaulted over the low fence, catching her skirts on the pickets. "Bethie!" she cried in breathless, exultant frustration; even though she had not yet caught sight of her cousin, she knew she was there somewhere.

Sure enough, Elisabeth came bursting through the doorway of one of the outbuildings at the sound of Rue's voice. She heedlessly dropped the crock she was carrying to the ground, and her blond hair tumbled around her shoulders as she ran.

"Rue!" she shrieked, laughing and sobbing the name. "Rue!"

Rue was dimly aware of the man and the little girl looking on in confusion, but she could only think of Elisabeth in those moments. Elisabeth, her best friend, her only real family.

"Bethie," Rue said, and then the two women were embracing and weeping, as women have always done, and probably will do, when meaningful separations end.

Finally, Bethie gripped Rue's upper arms in hands that had been strengthened by life in simpler but more physically demanding times, her blue-green eyes shimmering with tears, her face bright with joy.

"What are you doing here?" she wanted to know.

Rue laughed even as she wiped her cheek with one palm. "I sort of stumbled onto the place, the way I suspect you did," she confessed. "Once I got here, I was determined to find you, to make sure you were all right."

"I'm more than all right," Elisabeth answered, touching her stomach. "I never thought it was possible to be so happy, Rue. I'm going to have a baby."

The man and the child gravitated toward the two cousins while Rue was absorbing this news. She felt a pang of jealousy, which surprised her, and she even went so far as to hope she was pregnant herself—which was ridiculous, because that could only complicate matters.

"This is my husband Jonathan," Elisabeth said, and her skin took on the lustrous glow of a fine pearl as she introduced him. The child, who was as lovely as her father was handsome, huddled against Bethie's side and smiled shyly up at Rue. "And this is Miss Trista Fortner," Elisabeth added, as proudly as if she'd somehow produced the little girl herself, just that very moment. "Jonathan, Trista, I'd like you to meet my cousin Rue."

Elisabeth's husband was movie-star gorgeous, in a smooth, urbane way. Farley was just as good-looking, but he was the rugged type, exactly the kind of man Rue had always avoided.

"Hello," Jonathan said. He started to offer his right hand, which was scarred, then shrugged, grinned sheepishly and eased his arm back to his side. Rue recalled Farley saying the doctor had been injured.

Bethie smiled and linked elbows with Rue, marching her double-time toward the house. "I want to hear everything," she told her cousin. *"Everything."*

They sat at the kitchen table, and Rue, hardly knowing where to begin, told the story. She explained that the search had begun after she'd read Elisabeth's amazing letters about traveling through time, and admitted she'd first thought her cousin needed professional help. Then she'd found the necklace on the floor of the upstairs hallway, she went on, and made the trip herself.

For some reason she didn't fully understand—under normal circumstances Rue would have told Bethie *any-thing*—she didn't mention the passion she'd developed for Farley Haynes.

Elisabeth told Rue about her honeymoon, blushing intermittently and looking impossibly happy, and explained how Jonathan had hurt his hand. A fire had broken out and, while Farley had dragged Elisabeth out, Jon and Trista had been trapped upstairs. Jon had had the necklace in his possession and he'd escaped with the little girl over the threshold into 1992. The flow of time did not run parallel on both sides of the threshold, as Rue had already discovered, and when Dr. Fortner and his child finally managed to return, they'd found Elisabeth on trial for their murder.

Jon had made a dramatic entrance, Elisabeth said, eyes glowing with the memory, thus exonerating her of all charges, and they'd been married that day.

With help from Rue and Trista, Elisabeth began preparing dinner. She did it as naturally as if she'd been born in the nineteenth century instead of the twentieth. By then, the cousins had begun to speculate about the necklace. Although she couldn't explain why, Elisabeth believed the pendant's magic was different, depending on whose hands it fell into. She cautioned Rue to be careful about her choices.

Lanterns were lit as twilight tumbled silently down around the house and rose past the windows, and Jonathan moved, whistling, between the house and the barn.

"You truly do belong here," Rue marveled to her cousin later that night, when Jonathan had gone out to check on his regular patients and Trista was tucked away in one of the upstairs bedrooms.

Elisabeth nodded, lifting a kerosene lamp from the center of the table and leading the way into the parlor. A cozy fire crackled on the hearth and one other light burned on the mantelpiece. "I never knew it was possible for a woman to love a man the way I love Jonathan," she said softly, and there was a dreamy, faraway expression in her eyes as she gazed out the window toward the barn and the orchard and the covered bridge beyond. "It's like I was never whole before I came here. I felt like the odd woman out in some game of musical chairs—there was never a place for me to sit in that other world. The place is like a dream to me now, and I might even have convinced myself I'd imagined it all if it hadn't been for your appearance."

Rue thought of Farley and wondered if he was worried about her or if he'd even noticed she wasn't around. She sighed. "Don't you ever get scared? I mean, if a thing like this can happen, it changes everything. We're like players in some game, and none of us knows the rules."

Elisabeth turned to meet Rue's eyes. "They say that realizing how little we truly understand is the beginning of wisdom. But I've got a handle on this much—when you love with everything that's inside you, you take a terrible risk. I'm vulnerable in a way I never was before I knew Jonathan and Trista, and, yes, that scares me."

Reaching into her pocket, Rue found the necklace and brought it out, dangling it from her fingers. "Here's your ticket out," she said. "If you don't want to be vulnerable, all you have to do is go back home."

Elisabeth actually recoiled, her blue-green eyes round. "*This* is home," she said. "For heaven's sake, put that thing away before something awful happens."

Rue smiled and hurriedly dropped the pendant back into her pocket. After her experience in the jailhouse at lunchtime, when she'd seen one world taking shape on top of another, she was still a little shy about holding it for too long.

"Then I guess you've decided the risk is worth taking," she said, taking a place on a settee, resting one elbow on the arm and propping her chin in her hand. "Don't you miss it, Bethie? Don't you ever wish you could see a movie or eat frozen yogurt in a mall?"

Elisabeth moved to the fireplace and stood looking down at the fire on the hearth. "I miss hot baths," she said, "and supermarkets and books on tape. I *don't* miss traffic jams, jangling telephones and the probability of one marriage out of two biting the proverbial dust."

"Would you want to go back if it weren't for Jonathan and Trista?"

Bethie thought for a long time before answering, "I'm not sure. Things are difficult here—the old saying about a woman's work never being done certainly holds true—but there's an intensity to life, a *texture,* that I never found in the twentieth century. I feel as though I've come home from some long journey of the soul."

Rue sighed. "Well, I guess this completes my mission," she said. "I can go home now."

Elisabeth looked alarmed. "Oh, please say you'll stay for a few days, at least. After all, once you leave..." She paused, lowered her head for a moment, then finished bravely, "Once you leave, we may never see each other again."

"I can't stay," Rue said miserably. She reminded Elisabeth how the power of the necklace seemed to be changing, how she no longer needed to step over the threshold to return to her own century, how she'd seen images of the orchard in the middle of Farley's office that day.

In typical Victorian fashion, Elisabeth laid spread fingers to her bosom. "You're right," she said. "You mustn't take the risk. Do you suppose it's possible for a person to end up in another time period entirely, or another place? Say, medieval England, or Boston during Revolutionary days?"

"I'm the wrong person to ask, Bethie," Rue answered. Her heart was aching at the prospect of leaving her cousin and, she could almost admit it to herself, of leaving Farley. "I don't have any idea what laws govern this crazy situation, or even if there are any. Maybe it's covered by Einstein's Theory of Relativity or something."

Elisabeth's beautiful eyes were glazed with tears. "A day won't go by that I don't think of you," she said. "Oh, Rue, I want you to be as happy as I am. Will you try to go back tonight?"

Rue thought of Farley. "Yes, but there's something I have to do first," she said. She glanced at the clock on the mantel, then at the darkened windows. "Oh, my gosh! I forgot I was supposed to get married!"

"What?"

Rue was hurrying toward the front door. "I wasn't really going to marry Marshal Haynes," she babbled. "He just thought we should because we've slept together and everything." She pulled open the door and would have bolted out into the starry night if Elisabeth hadn't caught her firmly by the arm.

"Now just a minute!" Rue's cousin protested. "You can't just go traipsing off to town through the dark of night! And what's this about your sleeping with Farley?"

Rue sagged against the doorjamb, heedless of the biting chill of the November night, and she began to cry. "I'm in love with him," she whispered brokenly, then sniffled. Her eyes found Elisabeth's worried face in the dim light of the moon and the glow of lanterns from the parlor. "I'm not like you, Elisabeth. I can't stay here—I can't be happy in a place where there's no UPS, no PBS, no CNN!''

Elisabeth laughed and put an arm around Rue's shoulders. "Come in and sit by the fire. I'll brew us a pot of tea and we'll work out this whole problem."

When Jonathan returned an hour later, Elisabeth and Rue were no closer to a solution. However, the doctor had brought a surprise along with him, a coldly angry Farley Haynes.

"The justice of the peace came and went," Farley said when Jonathan had taken Elisabeth's hand and led her out of the room so that Rue and the marshal were alone. He rested his hands on the sides of her chair, effectively pinning her between his arms.

Rue studied Farley's craggy, handsome face fondly, trying to make a memory that would last for all time. "I'm sorry, Farley," she said, touching his beard-stubbled cheek with one hand. "But I'm not the girl for you, and you wouldn't be happy with me."

Farley set his hands on either side of her waist, stepped back and hauled Rue unceremoniously to her feet. The necklace slipped to the floor, with a *chink* that seemed to echo throughout eternity, and she bent to grab for it. The marshal's hand tightened around her upper arm, as though he thought she might try to escape his hold, and then it happened.

There was a wild spinning effect, as if the parlor were a merry-go-round gone berserk. Colors and shapes collided and meshed. Rue, hurled to the floor, wrapped both arms around Farley's right leg and held on with all her strength to keep from being flung into the void.

"Jumpin' Juniper," Farley said when the wild ride subsided.

Rue couldn't let go of his leg, but she did look around, seeing that while they were still in that same parlor, the furniture was different. There was a TV in the corner with a VCR on top.

"What the hell just happened here?" Farley whispered. Rue had to admire his cool. She was trembling as she shinnied up his thigh and finally stood on her own two feet.

She wanted to laugh, hysterically, joyously. She was home, and Farley was with her. On the other hand, she would probably never see Elisabeth again, and that made her want to weep.

"You've just aged almost a hundred years," Rue said, resting her forehead against Farley's shoulder and almost automatically slipping her hands around his waist. "I've got a lot to show you, Marshal Haynes, but first I'd better give you a little time to absorb the shock."

Farley went to the television set and touched one of the buttons. The head and shoulders of a late-night talk-show host appeared on the screen in an instantaneous flash of light and color.

The marshal recoiled, though only slightly, his wonderful, weathered face crumpled into a frown. "Where's the rest of that fellow?" he demanded. Before Rue could reply, he tapped the screen with his knuckles. "I'll be damned. It's a picture."

Rue set the necklace on the mantelpiece. Suddenly, she was filled with pizza lust and the yearning for a long, hot shower. She went to the telephone and punched out a number.

"One large pepperoni with extra cheese, sausage, green peppers and mushrooms," she said. Then she gave the address and hung up.

Farley had left the television to examine the phone. He picked up the receiver and put it to his ear, as Rue had done, then handed it back. "It's a telephone," she said. "A later version of those big wooden boxes with hand cranks and chrome bells." At his look of puzzlement, Rue added, "I'll explain later. Right now, I'm perishing for pizza." She looked down at her Victorian clothes. "I'd better change or the delivery person will spread a vicious rumor that we're having a costume party."

The marshal, who would certainly have carried off the prize for the most authentic getup at such a gathering, went over to one of the chairs and sank into it. He looked pale beneath his deep tan, and understandably bewildered.

"Where are Mrs. Fortner and the doctor?" he asked. "What happened here?"

"Listen, Farley," Rue said, sitting on the arm of his chair and slipping one arm reassuringly around his shoulders, "it's all pretty complicated, though if you'll remember, I tried to tell you about it before. Anyway, it's going to take a while for you to absorb the fact that this is really happening, let alone process a whole new universe. We just jumped a hundred years, you and I. Technically, Bethie and Jonathan are long dead. On the other hand, they're alive and well on the other side of some kind of cosmic chasm we don't understand."

"Thanks, Rue. That made everything clear as creek water," Farley said wryly. He was clearly still unnerved, as anyone would have been, but that lethal intelligence of his was stirring, too. Rue could see it in his eyes, hungry, wanting to comprehend everything. "Am I losing my mind?"

"No more so than I am, or Elisabeth. You just crossed from one dimension to another, somehow. All I know is that it has to do with my necklace."

"Good God," Farley sighed, rubbing his chin.

"Now you know how I felt," Rue said, polishing his badge with the sleeve of her dress. After that, she stood again. "Since you're company," she teased, "you can have the first shower."

"The first what?"

Rue laughed and took his hand. "Come on. I'll show you." She led the befuddled lawman up the stairs, along the hallway and into the main bathroom, reserving the one off the master bedroom for herself. There, she gave Farley soap and shampoo and showed him where to find the towels, then adjusted the shower spigots.

Farley's eyes went wide with puzzled amazement, but he was already starting to strip off his clothes when Rue slipped out of the room. She'd gotten only partway down the hall when a shout of stunned annoyance echoed from behind the door.

Thinking she should have explained that one spigot brought forth hot water and one cold, Rue smiled. She hoped it was ice Farley had just doused himself with, and not fire.

In the master bedroom, where all her things were still in the drawers and the closet, Rue had an urge to kneel and kiss the floor. She didn't, however. She just laid out jeans, underwear, socks and a bulky, white sweater, then took a shower.

The doorbell was ringing when she reached the upper hallway, and she heard voices roll up the front stairs.

"Here's the pizza, sir," said a voice, teenage and masculine. "That'll be fifteen dollars and seventy-five cents."

"For one flat box?" Farley boomed. "You'd better take your wares someplace else, boy."

Grinning, Rue hurried down the stairs. Farley was wrapped in a pink chenille bedspread taken from one of the guest bedrooms, and his freshly washed hair was standing up on top of his head.

"It's okay," Rue said quickly. She paid the young man, took the pizza and closed the door. Then looking up at Farley, she started to laugh. With the bedspread draped around him, toga-style, all he needed was a wreath of laurel leaves on his head to make him a very convincing Roman. "Don't tell me, I know. A funny thing happened to you on the way to the forum."

Farley was clearly not amused. "I'm in no mood for any of your fancy double-talk, woman," he said, glowering.

Rue opened the lid on the pizza box. "Mellow out, Marshal. This will fix you up—prepare to experience one of the best things about modern life." She pried a gooey slice loose and handed it to him. "Go ahead," she urged. "Eat it."

He took a cautious bite, tightened his bedspread toga with a nervous gesture of one hand and took another.

"Good, isn't it?" Rue said, talking with her mouth full.

Farley answered by taking another piece.

Rue had waited too long for this pizza to stand on ceremony. They went into the parlor and sat cross-legged on the floor in front of the empty hearth.

"Bet none of the Pine River ladies ever brought you anything like this for dinner," Rue said smugly.

He lifted a slice to look under it. "Damnedest pancake I've ever seen," he said in all seriousness.

Rue's attention had shifted to the bedspread. "We're going to have to get you some clothes, big fella. I think you're the button-fly-jeans type."

"I've got clothes," Farley protested. Rue hoped he wasn't going to pick now, of all times, to get stubborn.

"Chenille bedspreads have been out of style for a long time," she said. For Farley, the situation was gravely confusing, Rue knew that, but she couldn't help being happy that the two of them hadn't been separated. She would face the lingering pain of saying goodbye to Elisabeth later, and begin learning to live with it. She sighed. "Life is very complicated, Farley."

He glared at her, probably thinking she was a witch or a creature from another planet, that she'd deliberately uprooted him from the world he knew.

"Okay, so maybe that was kind of an obvious statement," Rue conceded. "I can't explain what happened to you, for the simple reason that I don't have the first idea myself. The fact is, you're in the 1990s instead of the 1890s, and you can probably go back if you want to just by holding the necklace in one hand." She started to rise to get the pendant from the mantel, but Farley stopped her by grasping her arm.

"Will you go with me?" he asked hoarsely.

Rue hesitated, then shook her head. "I belong here," she said. If she hadn't realized that before, she reflected, traveling back to 1892 had certainly cleared the matter up for her. She had a suspicion Farley belonged, too, because of his insatiable mind and progressive attitudes, but he would have to discover that for himself. It was not something she could decide for him.

Farley swallowed hard, the last slice of pizza forgotten in his hand, and Rue knew he was making a costly decision.

"I ought to go back where I came from," he finally said. "There are things I left undone and people I need to say goodbye to. But, damn it, scared as I am, I want to see this place." Farley gestured toward the TV set. "I want to see what other machines there are and how they work." He reached out from where he sat and touched the dangling cord of a lamp. "And these lanterns. Does the kerosene come in through this wire?"

Rue kissed his forehead. "You've got quite an adventure ahead of you, cowboy."

Farley finished the pizza, thoughtfully examining Rue's jeans and sweater. "I guess women must dress like that here, then?" he inquired, and it was obvious that he didn't wholly approve of the look.

She nodded. "Chinese women have worn pants for centuries," she said. "Here in the United States, the style didn't really catch on until the Second World War."

"There was a war involving the whole world?" Farley's eyes were wide and haunted with the horrible images of such an event.

"There were two," Rue said. "And all of us are praying like crazy that there'll never be a third."

Awkwardly, Farley got to his feet, still carefully clutching the bedspread that preserved his modesty, and started toward the back of the house. "The privy still in the same place?"

Again, Rue laughed. "The outhouse was filled in sometime in the thirties, Farley." She wriggled her fingers to summon him to the downstairs bathroom, showed him how to flush. "There's another one upstairs. I guess you missed it when you took your shower."

He whistled. "That's one fine invention."

"Wait until you see what we can do with computers," she countered, leaving the room and closing the door. She hung up Farley's sheepskin coat, his badge still gleaming on the lapel, and gingerly set his gun belt on top of the highboy in the smaller parlor. Then she dropped his socks, trousers and shirt into the washer. He'd need something to wear while they shopped for contemporary clothes the next day.

By this time, Farley was standing behind her, wearing just a bath towel around his middle now. Obviously, he was feeling a little more comfortable in the circumstances.

"What is that thing doing?" he asked, frowning at the washer.

Rue explained, and Farley grinned at the wonderment of such a thing, flashing his white teeth. He lifted the washer's lid to look inside. The agitator promptly stopped.

Rue closed the lid again and patted the top of the washer's companion appliance. "This is the drier. I'll put your shirt and pants in here after the washer stops, and they'll be ready to wear in less than half an hour."

Farley looked mesmerized. "Will you teach me how to work these things?" he asked.

"Count on it," Rue agreed. She was a firm believer in training a man right in the first place. That way, maybe he wouldn't be dropping socks and wet towels on the bathroom floor and leaving dirty dishes in the kitchen sink.

Upstairs, she gave him a new toothbrush from the supply in the linen closet, along with a tube of paste. He was standing at the sink in the main bathroom, happily foaming at the mouth when Rue retired to the master bath.

When she came out, Farley was sitting on the edge of the bed, still clad in the towel. Which was almost worse than nothing, because it sent Rue's fertile imagination spinning.

He discovered the switch on the bedside lamp and flipped it on and off three or four times before he was apparently satisfied that the same thing would happen ad infinitum, until either the mechanism wore out or he did.

When Farley turned his eyes to Rue and ran them over her short, cotton nightgown, she knew he'd gone a long way toward adjusting to his situation. He smiled broadly and said, "Hope you don't mind sharing your bed. I'm scared of the dark, and, besides, this was supposed to be our wedding night."

Chapter Nine

Rue hesitated in the doorway, fighting a disconcerting urge to fling herself at Farley in unqualified surrender. She'd always found other men highly resistible, no matter how famous or accomplished they might be, but this self-educated nineteenth-century marshal could send her pulse careening out of control with a look, a simple touch or a few audacious words.

"Are you sure it would be wise for us to sleep together?" she finally managed in a thin voice. "After all, we don't exactly know where our relationship is headed."

"Relationship," Farley repeated with a thoughtful frown, stretching out on the bed. At least *he* was comfortable. Rue was a mass of warm aches and quivering contradictions. "That's a peculiar-sounding word. If it means what I think it does, well, I don't believe all of that has to be worked out tonight. Do you?"

Rue ran the tip of her tongue nervously over dry lips. "No, but—"

Farley arched one eyebrow. "But…?" he prompted, not unkindly.

Rue hugged herself and unconsciously took a step closer. "I'm not sure you're going to understand this, being a man, but when we made love, I opened myself up to you in a way that I never had before. There was no place for me to hide, if you know what I mean, and intimacy of that kind—"

He rose, graceful in his bath towel, and came to stand directly in front of her. "Did I hurt you?" he asked.

Rue shook her head. "No," she croaked after a long moment of silence. "It's just that I felt so vulnerable."

Gently, Farley took Rue's hand, raised it to his mouth, brushed the knuckles with his lips. "I'll make you a bargain," he said. "If I'm loving you and you get scared, all you have to do is say stop, and I will. No questions, no arguments."

Gazing into Farley's eyes, Rue knew he was telling the truth. Color pooled in her cheeks. "You know as well as I do," she told him with a rickety smile, "that once you start kissing and touching me, stopping will be the last thing on my mind."

He eased her to the side of the bed, pulled the nightgown off over her head and tossed it aside. Then he feasted on her with his eyes, and that alone made Rue feel desirable and womanly.

Her breasts seemed to swell under Farley's admiring gaze, the nipples protruding, eager. Her thighs felt softer and warmer, as if preparing to cradle his hard weight, and the most secret reaches of her womanhood began a quiet, heated throbbing.

When Farley spread splayed fingers through her freshly combed hair and bent her head back for his kiss, Rue gave an involuntary whimper. She was terrified, and the sensation of his mouth against hers was something like hurtling down the face of Mount Rainier on a runaway toboggan.

Rue felt Farley's towel fall away as he gripped her bottom, raised her slightly and pressed her against him, never slackening the kiss. Most of her wits had already deserted her, but she knew somehow that Farley was afraid, too, as she had been when she'd suddenly found herself in an alien century. He needed her comfort as he might never need it again, and if Rue hadn't already been incredibly turned on, that knowledge alone would have done the trick.

Passion made her bold. Farley broke the kiss with a gasp of surprised pleasure when she closed her hand around his manhood and instinctively began a fiery massage. Finally, Rue knelt and took him into her mouth, and his fingers delved into her hair, frantic, worshiping. A low groan rolled beneath the washboard muscles of his stomach before escaping his throat.

Farley allowed Rue to attend him for a long time—it was amazing, but somehow he was still in charge of their love-making, even while she was subjecting him to exquisite rapture. Finally he stopped her, raised her to the bed and gently laid her there.

He said something to her in a low, rumbling voice, and then repaid her thoroughly for the sweet torment she'd given him. He did not bring her to the brink again and again, as Rue had done to him, however. Instead, Farley took her all the way, pursuing her relentlessly, until her heels dug deep into the mattress and her cries of satisfaction echoed off the ceiling.

When at last he took her, Rue didn't expect to have anything left to give. Her own instant, fevered response came as a shock to her, and so did the deep wells of sensation Farley plumbed with every thrust. He was exposing parts of her emotional life, places in her very soul, that had never seen the light.

Afterward, as before, he held Rue close, and her soaring heart returned from the heavens and settled itself inside her like a storm-ruffled bird that has finally found a roosting place. A tear brimmed the lower lashes of Rue's right eye and then zigzagged down her cheek, catching against the callused side of Farley's thumb.

Maybe he knew she didn't need consoling, that she was crying because life was life, because she was so grateful for the steady beat of her heart and the breath in her lungs. In any case, all Farley did was hold her a little tighter.

"It's strange," she said after a very long time, "to think that Elisabeth and Jonathan and Trista are in this house, too, even though we can't see or hear them."

Farley's hand moved idly against her hair, her temple, her cheek. "I'm still trying to figure out that thing you've got downstairs, the box with the pictures inside. There's no point in vexing my poor brain with how many people are traipsing around without us knowing about it."

Rue smiled, spreading her fingers over the coarse patch of hair on Farley's chest. "It's nice, though, to think Bethie and the others are so close by, that they're not actually dead but just in another dimension."

He reached over to cover her lips with an index finger. "I'm not even going to ask what you mean by 'another dimension,'" he said, "because I'm afraid you'll tell me."

She turned over, resting her leg on top of his and curling her foot partway around his ankle. Then she gave one of his nipples a mischievous lick before smiling into his eyes. "There is so much I want to show you, Farley. Like my ranch, for instance."

"Your what?"

"You remember. I told you I had a ranch in Montana."

He chuckled. "I thought you were just pulling my leg about that. How did you come to have your own land?"

"I inherited it from my grandfather. Let's go there, Farley—tomorrow. As soon as we've bought you some new clothes."

Farley stiffened, and his tone, though as quiet as before, had an edge to it. "The duds I've got will do just fine."

Rue sighed. "This is no time to have a fit of male pride, Marshal. Times have changed, and if you go around in those clothes, people will think you're a refugee from a Wild West show."

"I don't accept what I haven't earned," he replied. He'd clamped his jaw with the last word, and even in the thin moonlight Rue could see that his eyes had gone hard as marbles.

"Good," Rue said. "I need a foreman at Ribbon Creek anyway; my lawyers have been complaining about the one I've got ever since Gramps died."

In the next few seconds, it was as though Farley's masculine pride and desire for a ranch had taken on substance even though they remained invisible. Rue could feel them doing battle right there in the room.

"What are you going to do if you don't work for me, Farley?" she pressed quietly. "You're one of the most intelligent men I've ever known, but believe me, you don't have the kind of job skills you'd need to make a decent living in this day and age."

He was quiet for such a long time that Rue feared he'd drifted off to sleep. Finally, however, Farley replied, "Let's go and have a look at this ranch of yours, then."

Rue laid her cheek against his chest, smiled and closed her eyes.

When she awakened in the morning, Farley was sitting in a chair next to the bed, wearing his regular clothes. Although there were pulled threads shriveling the fabric in places, and the pants looked an inch or two shorter, he was still handsome enough to make Rue's heart do a happy little spin.

"I was beginning to think you meant to lay there till the Resurrection," Farley grumbled, and Rue ascertained in that moment that, despite the fact that he'd gotten up comparatively early, the marshal was not a morning person.

"Low blood sugar," Rue diagnosed, tossing back the covers and sitting up. She'd put her nightgown back on during the night, so she didn't feel as self-conscious as she might have otherwise. "Don't let it bother you. I have the exact same problem. If I don't eat regularly—and junk food is worse than nothing—I get crabby, too."

Farley was already at the door. "I don't know what the hell you're talking about, but if you're saying I'm hungry, you're right. I was planning to make breakfast, and I took some wood from the basket by the parlor fireplace, but I'll be damned if I could figure out where to kindle the fire in that kitchen stove of yours."

Rue grinned and preceded him out of the bedroom and down the stairs. "It's not the kind of stove you're used to, Marshal. Remember the cords on the lamp? Most everything in the kitchen works the same way, by electricity." She'd explained the mysteries of that science as best she could the night before, but in a way it was like trying to illustrate their trip through time. Rue couldn't very well clarify things she barely understood herself. "Never fear," she finished. "There's a set of books at the ranch that covers that type of thing—Gramps had a penchant for knowing how things worked."

She crossed the kitchen and opened the refrigerator, knowing ahead of time what she'd find. Nothing edible, except for three green olives floating in a jar. The other stuff had been there when she arrived at the house days—weeks?—before.

Rue opened the freezer and took out a box of toaster waffles. "I'm afraid this will have to hold us until we can get to Steak Heaven out on Highway 18."

Farley watched in consternation as Rue opened the carton, pulled apart the inner wrapper and popped two waffles into the toaster. While they were warming, she scouted out syrup and put two cups of water into the microwave for instant coffee.

"How does this contraption work?" Farley asked, turning to the stove that had so confounded him earlier.

Rue checked the oven on a hunch and found kindling sticks neatly stacked on the middle rack. She struggled not to laugh as she removed them, thanking heaven all the while that Farley had not gone so far as to light a blaze.

"These knobs on the top control everything," she said when she could trust herself to speak. With one arm, she held the applewood while pointing out the dials with her free hand.

Farley listened earnestly to her explanation, then nodded with a grin. It was plain that he was a quick study; no doubt he would take in information as fast as it could be presented.

They breakfasted on the waffles and coffee, and then Rue hurriedly showered and dressed. She wasn't afraid of her Aunt Verity's house, even after all that had happened to her and to Elisabeth here; she could never have feared that benevolent place. Still, Rue felt an urgency to be gone, a particular fear she didn't like facing.

Perhaps away from here, the necklace would have no power. If it did, however, Farley could disappear at any moment.

Getting the marshal to leave his gun belt behind required some of the fastest talking Rue had ever done, but in the end, she succeeded by promising him access to the big collection of firearms that had belonged to her grandfather.

It was almost noon when she and Farley locked the house and set out. Rue had brought her laptop computer, clothes and personal things, but she'd deliberately left the necklace behind; in its own way, the thing was as dangerous as the marshal's Colt .45.

Farley was fascinated by the Land Rover. He walked around it three or four times before getting in.

Thinking her guest might be interested in seeing how Pine River had developed over the decades since he'd been its marshal, Rue drove him down Main Street, showed him the movie house and the library and the local police station. She avoided the churchyard without looking too closely at her reasons.

Farley was, of course, amazed by the changes, and would have insisted on getting out and exploring, Rue was sure, if he hadn't been so fascinated by their mode of transportation.

He spent the entire ride to Steak Heaven opening and closing the glove compartment, turning the dials on the radio, switching on the heat, then the air-conditioning, then the heat again.

"Soon as we get to Ribbon Creek," Rue promised from her position behind the wheel, "I'll teach you to drive."

Farley beamed at the prospect.

When they reached the restaurant, Farley turned his attention from the dashboard and stared in amazement at the crowded parking lot. "Jumpin' Juniper," he said. "Does everybody in this place have one of these newfangled buggies?"

Rue smiled. "Almost," she answered, "but they come in all shapes, sizes and colors, as you can see."

Farley paused to inspect a pricey red sports car as they passed, giving a low whistle of appreciation. It only went to prove, Rue thought in amusement, that some things transcend time. Maybe men had always been fascinated by methods of transportation.

The noise and bustle of the inside of the restaurant made Farley visibly nervous. His face took on a grim expression, and Rue saw him touch his outer thigh once or twice while they waited to be seated. Probably he was unconsciously seeking reassurance that wasn't there—his gun.

"Smoking or nonsmoking?" a waitress asked pleasantly.

Farley's turquoise eyes widened as he took in the girl's short skirt, and Rue realized he'd never seen a female show so much leg in public.

"Non," Rue answered, linking her arm with Farley's and propelling him between the crowded tables as the girl led the way.

"Tarnation," Farley muttered, looking around and seeing that not only other waitresses but customers were dressed in the same way. "If the Presbyterians saw this, they'd be spitting railroad spikes."

Rue chuckled. "Some of these people probably *are* Presbyterians, Farley. This is an accepted way for women to dress."

They reached their booth, and Farley slid into the seat across from Rue, still looking overwhelmed. His eyes narrowed. "It's bad enough to see a woman in pants," he whispered pointedly. "I hope you don't plan on parading around in one of these getups you call a dress, with your knees sticking out. I'm the only one who should see you like that."

Rue rested her plastic-coated menu against her forehead for a moment, hiding her face while she battled amusement and her natural tendency to protest his arbitrary words. Finally, she met his gaze over the steaming cups of coffee between them, and said, "Even if we were married, which we're not, I wouldn't let you tell me what to wear, Farley. That would be like allowing you to tell me how to vote."

He stared at her. "You can vote?"

She sighed and rolled her eyes heavenward. "I can see this is going to be quite a project, acclimatizing you to the twentieth century."

The waitress returned, and Rue ordered a club sandwich and a diet cola, since it was lunchtime. Farley, having read his own menu, asked for sausage and eggs. Plainly, the toaster waffles hadn't seemed like breakfast to him.

When the food came, he loaded it down with pepper, except for the toast, and consumed every bite, leaving nothing on his plate but a few streaks of egg yoke.

Rue paid the check with a credit card, and when the cashier handed it back, Farley intercepted and studied the card intently.

"This is money?" he asked, handing the card to Rue as they crossed the parking lot a few minutes later.

"The plastic variety," Rue affirmed with a nod. She stopped and looked up into Farley's wonderful eyes, feeling so much love for him that it was painful. "I know everything seems pretty bewildering," she said gently, "but you're a very intelligent man and you'll figure things out."

He looked the Land Rover over speculatively as they approached. "I'd like to drive now," he announced.

"No way," Rue answered, pulling her keys from the pocket of her jeans. "Cars move a whole lot faster than horses, Farley, and when they collide, people get killed."

Although the marshal looked disappointed, he didn't argue.

Where before his attention had been taken up by the gizmos on the dashboard, now Farley was intent on the other cars, the buildings, the power lines alongside the highway. As they drove toward Seattle, he asked a million questions about the pavement, the road signs, the cars and trucks in the other lanes.

When Seattle itself came into view, with its busy harbor and the picturesque Space Needle, Farley was apparently struck dumb by the sight. He stared intently, as though his eyes couldn't take in enough to suit him, and he kept turning in different directions.

Rue drove through the city, knowing Farley couldn't have absorbed explanations just then, and kept going until they reached a large mall.

She parked and they entered the concourse. Rue still didn't speak because Farley was so busy absorbing the sights and sounds that he probably wouldn't have heard her anyway.

He studied a colorful display in front of a bookstore with an attitude that seemed like reverence to Rue. She was touched by the depth of his wonder, knowing it must be something like what she felt when he made love to her.

Suddenly she wanted to give him the world, show him everything there was to see.

"I remember that you like reading," she said, her voice a little shaky. She proceeded into the store, located the instructional section and found a comprehensive volume on how things work. Then from another shelf, she took a novel set in the twenty-fifth century. It was the only way she could think of to prepare Farley for the fact that human beings could fly now, that a few brave souls had even visited the moon.

Farley watched as she paid. "You can buy books with plastic money?" he asked as they left.

"You can buy almost anything with plastic money," Rue replied, handing him the bag.

They went on to the men's department of one of the big chain stores, and Farley was soon outfitted with jeans, shirts, underwear and socks. He refused to part with his boots, and Rue didn't press the issue.

Soon they were on the freeway again, headed east. Farley alternated between staring out the window and thumbing through the books Rue had bought for him. When he opened one and started to read, she protested.

"You shouldn't read in a moving car, Farley," she said, amazed at how silly she sounded even as she was saying the words. "It'll make you sick."

Farley wet the tip of an index finger, turned a page and read on. "If you can go around with your knees showing in one of those short skirts," he said without even glancing in her direction, "I can read whenever I want to. And I want to."

"Fine," Rue replied, because there was nothing else she could say. She was glad, in a way, that Farley hadn't given in, because his stubborn strength was one of the qualities she loved most. Without looking away from the road, she took a cassette tape from the box between the seats and shoved it into the slot below the radio.

Farley jumped and then lowered the book when Carly Simon's voice filled the Land Rover.

"I think the closest thing you had to this in 1892 was the music box," Rue said without smugness. She knew Farley's curiosity had to be almost overwhelming. "Or maybe a hand organ."

"I'm getting a powerful headache," Farley confessed, rubbing his eyes. "How could so much have happened in a hundred years?"

She didn't tell him about automatic-teller machines and laser surgery, out of simple courtesy. "There were many factors involved," she said gently. "A lot of historians think the nation turned a corner during the Civil War. There were other conflicts later. As wretched and horrible as war is, it forced science to advance, in both good ways and bad, because of the awesome needs it creates."

Farley sat up rigidly straight—clearly some dire thought had just occurred to him—and rasped, "The Union—it still stands, doesn't it?"

Rue nodded and reached out to pat his arm reassuringly. "Oh, yes," she said. "There are fifty states now, you know."

"Canada is a state?"

She laughed. "Hardly. Canada is still a great nation in her own right. I was talking about Arizona, Utah, New Mexico, Oklahoma, Alaska and Hawaii."

Farley was quiet.

That evening, they pulled in at a truck stop to buy gas and have supper. Rue showed Farley how to work the gas pump, and his pride in the simple task was touching.

In the bright, busy restaurant adjoining the filling station, Farley consumed a cheeseburger deluxe, fries and a chocolate milk shake. "Anything that good has got to be kissing cousin to original sin," he commented cheerfully, after making short work of the food.

Rue shrugged and smiled slightly. "Only too true," she agreed with regret, deciding to save the nutritional lectures for later.

Farley cleared his throat. "I suppose these folks have filled in their outhouse, too," he said seriously.

Rue laughed, pushed away the last of her own chef's salad, and slid out of the booth. "This way, cowboy," she said. She pointed out the men's room, which was at the end of a long hallway, and paid the bill for their supper.

Farley reappeared shortly, his thick hair damp and finger-combed.

They were cruising along the freeway toward Spokane, a star-dappled sky shining above, before he spoke again.

"I keep thinking I must have gotten hold of some loco-weed or something," he said in a low, hoarse voice. "How could this be happening to me?"

Rue understood his feelings well, having experienced the same time-travel process, and she was sympathetic. "You're not crazy, Farley," she said, reaching over to touch his arm briefly. "That much I can promise you. There's something really strange going on here, though, and I owe you an apology for dragging you into it the way I did. I'm sorry."

He turned to her in apparent surprise. "It wasn't your fault."

Rue sighed, keeping a close eye on the road. "If I hadn't attached myself to your leg the way I did when the necklace started acting up again and the room was spinning, you probably wouldn't be here now."

Farley chuckled and gave a rueful shake of his head. "I'd be back there wondering just how a lady could be standing in front of me one moment and gone without a trace the next."

"I think the thing that bothers me the most about this whole situation is not knowing, not being able to pick up a thread of reason and follow it back to its spool, so to speak. I don't like mysteries."

Farley was going through Rue's collection of cassettes. "Speaking of mysteries," he marveled, turning a tape over in his hand. "This is the damnedest thing, the way you people can put a voice and a whole bunch of piano players and fiddlers into a little box like this. Back there at that place where we ate, they were selling these things."

"Tapes are available almost everywhere. They don't just have music on them, either—you can listen to books and to all sorts of instructional stuff."

Farley grinned. "I saw one back at the truck stop that interested me," he said. "It was called, *Red-hot Mamas on Wheels.*"

Again, Rue laughed. "I didn't say it was all literature, Farley."

"What exactly is a red-hot mama?"

"I'll tell you when you're older."

"I'm thirty-six!"

"And then some," Rue agreed, and this time it was Farley who laughed.

Several hours later, they reached Spokane, and Rue stopped at a large motel, knowing Farley would be uncomfortable with the formality of a city hotel. As it happened, he was pretty Victorian when it came to the subject of sharing rooms.

"It didn't bother you last night!" Rue whispered impatiently. She'd asked for a double, and Farley had immediately objected, wanting two singles. The clerk waited in silence for a decision to be made, fingers poised over the keyboard of his computer, eyebrows raised.

Farley took Rue's hand and hauled her away from the desk. They were partially hidden behind a gigantic jade tree, which only made matters worse, as far as Rue was concerned.

"We're not married!" he ground out.

"Now there's a flash," Rue said, her hands on her hips. "We weren't married *last* night, either!"

"That was different. This is a public place."

Rue sighed. "Like the beds are in the lobby or something." But then she conceded, "Okay, you win. Explaining this is obviously going to be a monumental task, and I'm too tired to tackle the job. We'll compromise." She went back to the desk, credit card in hand, and asked for adjoining rooms.

Her quarters and Farley's were on the second floor, along an outside balcony.

"Good night," she said tightly, after showing Farley how to unlock his door with the plastic card that served as a key. There was an inner door connecting the two rooms, but Rue had promised herself she wouldn't use it. "Don't eat the peanuts or drink the whiskey in the little refrigerator," she warned. "Everything costs about four times what it would anywhere else."

Farley's tired blue eyes were twinkling with humor. "I'm only looking out for your reputation as a lady," he said, plainly referring to their earlier row over shared accommodation.

"I have a reputation as a reporter," Rue replied, folding her arms. "Nobody ever accused me of being a lady."

Farley put down her suitcase and curled his fingers under the waistband of her jeans, pulling her against him with an unceremonious jerk. "Somebody's accusing you of it right now," he argued throatily, and then he gave Rue a long, thorough, lingering kiss that left her trembling. "You're all woman, fiery as a red-hot branding iron, and the way you fuss when I have you, everybody in this place would know what was happening. I don't want that—those gasps and cries and whimpers you give belong to me and me alone."

Rue's face was crimson by that time. She'd heard much blunter statements—while traveling with other journalists and camera crews, for instance—but this was intimate; it was personal. "Good night," she said again, trying to wrench free of Farley's grasp.

He held on to her waistband, the backs of his fingers teasing the tender flesh of her abdomen, and he kissed her again. When he finally drew back, her knees were so weak, she feared she might have to *crawl* into her room.

"Good night," Farley said. Then he went into his room and closed the door.

Chapter Ten

That night, Farley experienced a kind of weariness he'd never had to endure before—not after forced marches in the army or herding cattle across three states or tracking outlaws through the worst kind of terrain. No, it wasn't his body that was worn out—he hadn't done a lick of honest work all day long—it was his mind. His spirit. There was so much to understand, to absorb, and he was bewildered by the onslaught of information that had been coming down on him in a continuous cascade ever since his abrupt arrival in the 1990s.

He moved to toss his hat onto the bed, with its brown striped spread, and stopped himself at the last second. Where he came from, to do that was to invite ill fortune. In this strange place where everything was bigger, brighter and more intense, he hated to think what plain, old, sorry luck might have developed into.

After a little thought, he went to the wardrobe, which was built into the wall, and put his hat on the shelf. The conveniences were right next to that, and he couldn't help marveling at the sleek and shiny bathtub, the sink and commode, the supply of thick, fluffy towels.

Except for Rue, who was just beyond a puny inside door, he was most attracted by the box on the bureau facing the bed. Rue had called the machine a TV, describing it as a shirttail relation to the camera, and Farley found the device wonderfully mystifying.

Facing it, he bent to squint at the buttons arrayed down one side, then touched the one that said Power.

Immediately, a black man with hair as flat as the top of a windswept mesa appeared, smiling in a mighty friendly way. He said something Farley didn't quite catch, and a lot of unseen people laughed.

Farley punched another button and found an imposing-looking fellow standing behind the biggest pulpit he'd ever seen in his life. Beginning to catch on to the system, the marshal pressed still another button.

A lady wearing one of those skimpy dresses appeared, pushing something that might have been a carpet sweeper. There was a block in one side of the window, listing several different figures.

Farley proceeded to the next button, and this time he got a faceful of a bad-natured galoot with a long, red mustache and six-guns as big as he was. He was moving and talking, this noisy little desperado, and yet he wasn't real, like the other TV people had been. He was a *drawing*.

Farley sat down on the end of the mattress, enthralled. Next came a rabbit who walked upright, jabbered like an eager spinster and would do damn near anything for a carrot.

Finally, Farley turned off the machine, removed his boots and stretched out on the bed with a sigh. This century was enough to terrify a body, though he couldn't rightly admit that out loud, being a United States marshal and all.

On the other side of the wall, he heard a deep voice say, "This is CNN," and smiled. A month ago, even a day ago, he'd have torn the place apart, hearing that. He'd have been convinced there was a man in Rue's room, bothering her. Now he knew she was only watching the TV machine.

He imagined her getting ready for bed, brushing her teeth, washing her face, maybe padding around in one of those thin excuses for a nightdress that made his whole body go hard all at once. He could have been in there with her—it was torture knowing that—but he didn't want anybody thinking less of her because she'd shared a room with a man who wasn't her husband. She was too fine for that, too special.

Farley got up after a time, stripped off his clothes and ran himself a bath in the fancy room with the tiles that not only covered the floor but climbed most of the way up the wall. When the tub was full, he tested the steaming water with a toe, yelped in pain, and studied the spigots, belatedly recalling that *H* meant hot and *C* meant cold.

He had scrubbed himself from head to foot and settled into bed with one of the books Rue had bought for him when the ugly contraption on the bedside stand started to make a jangling noise. Farley frowned, staring as though to intimidate it into silence. Then, remembering the brief lecture Rue had given him at her house, he recognized it as a telephone.

He picked up the removable part and heard Rue's voice, tinny and small, saying, "Farley? Farley, are you there?"

He put the device to his ear, decided the cord wasn't supposed to dangle over his eye and cheek, and turned it around. "Rue?"

"Who else would it be?" she teased. "Did I wake you?"

He glowered at the contrivance, part of which still sat on the bedside table. If the TV machine was family to the camera, this thing must be kin to the telegraph. Now that he thought about it, the conclusion seemed obvious. "No," he said. "I wasn't sleeping." Farley liked talking to Rue this way, there was a strange intimacy to it, but he surely would have preferred to have her there in the bed with him. "I was watching that TV box a little while ago."

There was a smile in her voice, though not the kind meant to make a man feel smaller than he should be. "What did you see?"

Farley shook his head, still marveling. "Pictures—drawings—that moved and talked. One was supposed to be a person, but it wasn't."

Rue was quiet for a moment, then she said, again without a trace of condescension in her voice, "That was a cartoon. Artists draw and paint figures, and then they're brought to life by a process called animation. I'll tell you more about it tomorrow."

Farley wasn't sure he was really that interested, not when there were so many other things to puzzle through, but he didn't want to hurt Rue's feelings, so he would listen when the time came. They talked for a few minutes more, then said good-night, and Farley put the talking part of the telephone back where he'd found it.

He'd mastered light switches—to his way of thinking it was diabolical how the damn things were in a different place on every lamp—so he twisted a bit of brass between his fingers and the room became comparatively dark.

He was as exhausted as before, maybe more so, and he yearned, body and soul, for the comfort Rue could give him. He closed his eyes, thinking he surely wouldn't be able to sleep, and he promptly lost consciousness.

He must have rested undisturbed for a few hours, but then the dream was upon him, and it was so real that he felt the texture of the sheets change beneath him, the firmness of the mattress. Indeed, Farley felt the air itself alter, become thinner, harder to breathe.

The traffic sounds from the nearby highway turned to the twangy notes of saloon pianos, the nickering of horses, the squeaks and moans of wagon wheels.

Farley was back in his own lifetime.

Without Rue.

He let out a bellow, a primitive mixture of shock and protest, and sat bolt upright in bed. His skin was drenched with sweat, and he was gasping for breath, as though he'd been under water the length of the dream.

The dream. Farley wanted to weep with relief, but that, too, was something unbefitting a United States marshal. There was an anxious knock at the door separating his room from Rue's, and then, just as Farley switched on the lamp, Rue burst in.

"Good grief, Farley, are you all right? It sounded like you were being scalped!"

He was embarrassed at being caught in the aftermath of a nightmare, and that made him a little angry. "Do you always barge in on people like that?"

Rue was wearing a white cotton nightdress that barely reached the top of her thighs. Her eyes were narrowed, and her hands were resting on her hips. "I seem to recall asking you a similar question," she said, "when I woke up in the master bedroom at Pine River a hundred years ago and found you standing there staring at me." She paused, drew a deep breath and went on, a fetching pink color rising in her cheeks. "Your virtue is in no danger, Farley. I just wanted to make sure you were okay. I mean, you could have slipped in the bathtub or something."

He arched one eyebrow after casting an eye over her nightclothes—there were little bloomers underneath the skimpy gown, with ruffles around the legs—and then her long, slender legs. Lordy, she looked as sweet as a sun-warmed peach.

"Suppose I *had* fallen in the bathtub," he responded huskily, leaning back against the padded headboard and pulling the sheets up to his armpits. One of them had to be modest, and it sure as hell wasn't going to be Rue, not in the getup she had on. "How would you have known?"

She ran impudent eyes over the length of his frame. "The walls are thin here, Marshal. And you would have made quite a crash." She folded her arms, thus raising the night-dress higher. "Stop trying to evade the subject and tell me what made you let out a yell like that."

Farley sighed. Now that he'd stalled long enough to re-gain most of his composure, he figured he could talk about what happened without breaking into a cold sweat. "I dreamed I was back in 1892, that's all," he said.

Rue came and sat on the foot of the bed, cross-legged like an Indian. "Was I there?"

Farley hoped the tremendous vulnerability he was feeling wasn't audible in his voice. "No," he said. "Don't you have a dressing gown you can put on? I can't concentrate with you wearing that skimpy little nightgown."

She gave him a teasing grin. "You'll just have to suffer."

He fussed with his covers for a few moments. He was suffering, all right; it felt like he had a chunk of firewood between his legs. He changed the subject.

"Can one or the other of us be sent back even if that damn necklace is nowhere around?"

Rue's smile faded. She bit her lower lip for a moment. "I don't know, Farley," she said quietly. "When I first found the necklace, I had to be wearing or holding it to travel through time, and I had to pass through a certain doorway in the upstairs hall of my aunt's house. It was the same for Elisabeth. Later, it was as though the two time periods were meshing somehow, and I no longer had to go over the threshold to reach 1892."

"But you always had the necklace?"

She nodded. "Things are obviously changing, though. It seems to me that if people can step backward or forward in time, anything can happen."

Farley had another chill, though this was only a shadow of the one that had gripped him during the nightmare. Maybe he wouldn't be allowed to stay in this crazy, mixed-up century, with this crazy, mixed-up woman. The idea was shattering.

Rue was as vital to him as the blood flowing through his veins, and there was so much he wanted to see, so much he wanted to know.

He moved over and tossed back the covers to make room for her. He hadn't changed his mind about the impropriety of sharing a bed in a public inn, but he needed to sleep with his arms around her.

She switched off the lamp and crawled in beside him, all warm and soft and fragrant. When she snuggled close, Farley let out an involuntary groan.

Rue smoothed the hair on his chest with a palm. "Let's hope we don't do any time traveling while we're making love," she teased. "We could make an embarrassing landing, like in the horse trough in front of the feed and grain, or on one of the pool tables at the Hang-Dog Saloon. I don't mind telling you, Marshal, the Society would be livid!''

Farley laughed, rolled onto his side and gathered her close with one arm. There was no use in trying to resist her; she was too delicious, too funny, too sweet.

"What am I going to do with you?" he asked in mock despair.

Rue started nibbling at his neck, and murmured, "I have a few suggestions."

When Rue awoke the next morning, Farley was already up. He'd showered and dressed in some of his starchy new clothes, and he was sitting at the requisite round table by the windows, reading *USA Today*. "It seems to me that politicians haven't changed much," he commented without lowering the newspaper.

Rue smiled. She was hypersensitive, but in a pleasant way; the feel of Farley's hands and mouth still lingered on her lips, her throat, her breasts and stomach. "Some things stay the same no matter how much time passes," she replied, sitting up and wrapping her arms around her knees.

He peered at her over the colorful masthead. "I agree," he said solemnly, folding the paper and setting it aside. Having done that, Farley shoved one hand through his gleaming brown hair. "It's wrong for us to—to do what we did last night, Rue. That's something that should be confined to marriage."

Rue would have rolled her eyes if she hadn't known Farley was dead serious. She reached for the telephone and punched the button for room service. "Are you trying to tell me that you were married to every woman you ever slept with?" she inquired reasonably.

"No, ma'am," replied the youthful masculine voice at the other end of the line.

Hot color surged into Rue's face, and she would have hung up in mortification if she hadn't wanted coffee so much. "I wasn't talking to you," she told the room-service clerk with as much dignity as she could manage. Farley had clearly figured out what had happened, and he was chuckling.

Rue glared at him, then spoke into the receiver again, giving the room number and asking for a pot of coffee, fresh fruit and toast.

The moment she hung up, Farley gave a chortle of amusement.

"Well?" Rue demanded, not to be deterred. "*Were* you married to everyone you've ever made love with?"

Farley cleared his throat and reddened slightly. "Of course not. But this is different. A nice woman doesn't—"

Rue interrupted with an imperious upward thrust of one finger and, "Don't you dare say it, Farley Haynes!" She stabbed her own chest with that same digit. "*I* slept with you, and I'm one of the 'nicest women' you'll ever hope to meet!"

"You only did it because I took advantage of you."

"What a crock," Rue muttered, flinging back the covers and standing. "Did I act like I was being taken advantage of?"

"You should have just stayed in your own room," Farley grumbled.

"So now it's my fault?"

The marshal sighed. "I think it would probably be easier to change General Custer's mind about strategy than win an argument with you. Damn it, Rue, what I'm trying to say is, I think we should be married."

Rue sat down on the edge of the bed again. She loved Farley, and she hadn't agreed to marry him in 1892 because she'd known she didn't want to stay in that dark and distant century. This proposal, however, was quite another matter.

"It might be difficult getting a marriage license," she said awkwardly after a long time. "Considering that you have no legal identity."

While Farley was still puzzling that one out, the food arrived. Rue wrapped herself in one of the big shirts they'd bought the day before to let the room-service waiter in and sign the check.

Once they were alone again, she sat at the round table, feet propped on the edge of the chair, and alternately sipped coffee and nibbled at a banana.

"What do you mean, I don't have a legal identity?" Farley wanted to know. He added two packets of sugar to his coffee and stirred it with a clatter of spoon and china. "Is there a gravestone with my name on it somewhere back there in the long ago?"

A chill made Rue shiver and reach to refill her coffee cup. "I can show you where Elisabeth and Jonathan are buried," she said, not looking at him. "But that's different, because they stayed in the past. You came here."

"So if we find my marker, say around Pine River someplace, that'll mean I'm going back. It would have to."

Rue's head was spinning, but she understood Farley's meaning only too well. Elisabeth had a grave in the present because she'd returned to the past and lived out her life. Coming across Farley's burial place would mean he wasn't going to stay with her, in the here and now, that he was destined to return.

"You're right," she blurted, "we should get married."

A slow smile spread across Farley's rugged face. "What are we going to do about my identity?"

Rue bit her lip, thinking. "We'll have to invent one for you. I know a guy who used to work with the Witness Protection Program—those people can come up with an entire history.''

After giving the inevitable explanations, Rue finished her breakfast and took a shower. Farley brought her things from the room next door, so she was able to dress and apply light makeup right away.

They were checked out of the motel and on the road to Montana while the morning was still new.

As they passed out of eastern Washington into Idaho and then Montana, the scenery became steadily more majestic. There were snow-capped mountains, their slopes thick with pine and fir trees, and the sheer expanse of the sky was awe inspiring.

''They call Montana the 'Big Sky Country,''' Rue said, touched by Farley's obvious relief to be back in the kind of unspoiled territory he knew and understood. She'd have to tell him about pollution and the greenhouse effect sooner or later, but this wasn't the time for it.

''Are we almost there? At your ranch, I mean?''

Rue shook her head. ''Ribbon Creek is still a few hours away.''

They stopped for an early lunch at one of those mom-and-pop hamburger places, and Farley said very little during the meal. He was clearly preoccupied.

''We should have stopped at the cemetery in Pine River'' was the first thing he said, much later, when they were rolling down the highway again.

Just thinking of standing in some graveyard reading Farley's name on a tombstone made Rue's eyes burn. ''I'll call the church office and ask if you're listed in the registry for the cemetery,'' she said. Even as Rue spoke the words, she knew—she who had never been a procrastinator—that this was a task she would put off as long as possible.

In the late afternoon, when the sun was about to plunge beneath the western horizon in a grand and glorious splash of crimson and gold, Rue's spirits began to lift.

Roughly forty-five minutes later, the Land Rover was speeding down the long, washboard driveway that led to the ranch house.

Farley had opened the door and gotten out almost before the vehicle came to a stop. Rue knew he was tired of being confined, and he was probably yearning for the sight of something familiar, too.

Soldier, a black-and-white sheepdog, met them in the dooryard, yipping delightedly at Rue's heels and giving Farley the occasional suspicious growl. There were lights gleaming in the kitchen of the big but unpretentious house, and Rue had a sweet, familiar sensation of being drawn into an embrace.

The screen door at the side of the house squeaked, and so did the old voice that called, "Who's that?"

"Wilbur, it's me," Rue answered happily, opening the gate and hurrying along the little flagstone walk that wound around to the big screen porch off the kitchen. "Rue."

Wilbur, who had worked for Rue's grandfather ever since both were young men, gave a cackle of delight. Now that he was elderly, he had the honorary title of caretaker, but he wasn't expected to do any real work. "I'll be ding danged," he said, limping Walter Brennan-style along the walk to stand facing Rue in the glow of the porch light. His rheumy blue eyes found Farley and climbed suspiciously to a face hidden by the shadow of the marshal's hat brim.

"Who might this be?" Wilbur wanted to know and, to his credit, he didn't sound in the least bit intimidated by Farley's size or the aura of strength that seemed to radiate from the core of his being.

"Farley Haynes," the marshal answered, taking off the hat respectfully and offering one hand.

Wilbur studied Farley's face for a long moment, then the still-extended hand. Finally, he put his own palm out for a shake. "Since it ain't none of my business," the old man said, "I won't ask who you are or what your errand is. If Miss Rue here says you're welcome at Ribbon Creek, then you are."

"Thank you," Farley said with that old-fashioned note of courtliness Rue found nearly irresistible. Then he turned and went back to the Land Rover for their things, having learned to open and close the tailgate when they left the motel that morning.

"He gonna be foreman now that Steenbock done quit?" Wilbur inquired in a confidential whisper that probably carried clear to the chicken coop.

Rue looked back at Farley, wishing they could have arrived before sunset. When he got a good look at the ranch, the marshal would think he'd been carried off by angels. "Mr. Haynes is going to be my husband," she said with quiet, incredulous joy. "That means he'll be part owner of the place."

The inside of the house smelled stale and musty, but it was still the same beautiful, homey place Rue remembered. On the ground floor were two parlors—they'd been her grandmother's pride—along with a study, a big, formal dining room, two bathrooms and an enormous kitchen boasting both a wood stove and the modern electric one. Upstairs, above the wide curving staircase, there were five bedrooms, one of which was huge, each with its own bath.

"This looks more like a palace than a ranch house," Farley said a little grimly when they'd made the tour and returned to the kitchen.

Rue took two steaks from the freezer in the big utility room and set them in the microwave to thaw. "This is a working ranch, complete with cattle and horses and the whole bit," she said. "Tomorrow, I'll show you what I mean."

Farley shoved a hand through already-rumpled hair. "What about you? What are you going to do way out here?"

"What I do best," Rue said, taking two big potatoes from a bin and carrying them to the sink. "Write for magazines and newspapers. Of course, I'll have to travel sometimes, but you'll be so busy straightening this place out that you won't even notice I'm gone."

When she looked back over one shoulder and saw Farley's face, Rue regretted speaking flippantly. It was plain that the idea of a traveling wife was not sitting well with the marshal.

She busied herself arranging the thick steaks under the broiler. After that, she stabbed the potatoes with a fork so they wouldn't explode and set them in the microwave.

"Farley, you must have already guessed that I have plenty of money," she said reasonably, bringing plates to the table. "I'm not going to be rushing out of here on assignment before the ink's dry on our marriage license. But I have a career, and eventually I'll want to return to it."

Farley pushed back his chair, found the silverware by a lucky guess and put a place setting by each of the plates. He was a Victorian male in the truest sense of the word, but he didn't seem to be above tasks usually regarded as women's work. Rue had high hopes for him.

"Farley?" She stood behind one of her grandmother's pressed-oak chairs, waiting for his response. Quietly demanding it.

His wonderful turquoise eyes linked with hers, looking weary and baffled. "What if we have a baby?" he asked hoarsely. "A little one needs a mother."

Rue smiled because he'd spoken gently and because the picture filled her with such joy. "I quite agree, Mr. Haynes," she said, yearning to throw her arms around Farley's neck and kiss him soundly. "When we have a child, we'll take care of him or her together," she assured him.

She turned the steaks and wrapped the microwaved potatoes in foil. Soon, Rue and Farley were sitting at the table, like any married couple at the end of a long day, sharing a late supper. Farley ate hungrily of the potatoes and steak, but he politely ignored the canned asparagus Rue had heated on the stove. To him, the vegetable probably looked as though it had been boiled to death.

When they'd finished, they cleaned up the kitchen together.

"Sleepy?" she asked.

Farley's wind-weathered cheeks blushed a dull red. He was going to get stubborn about the marriage thing again, she could tell.

"Look," Rue said with a sigh, "you can have your own room until after the wedding. After that, there will be no more of this Victorian-virgin stuff, understand?"

Farley stared at her for a moment, then smiled. "Absolutely," he agreed, his voice throaty and low.

Rue led the way upstairs. On the second floor, she paused in front of an electrical panel and switched off the downstairs lights. "This will be our room eventually," she said, opening the door to the large master suite with its fireplace and marble hot tub, "so you might as well get used to sleeping here. I'll be just down the hall."

Farley's throat worked visibly as he swallowed and nodded his agreement. Rue wanted him to sleep alone in the big bed, to imagine her sharing that wonderful room with him.

She stood on tiptoe to kiss the cleft in his stubbly chin. "Good night," she said.

"Good night," he replied. The words were rough, grating against each other like rusty hinges.

Rue went down the hall to her own room, whistling softly.

It was comforting to be back where she had sometimes slept as a child. When she was small, she'd spent a lot of time at the ranch, but later, her mother and grandfather had had some sort of falling out. That was why she'd ended up at Aunt Verity's when her parents had finally been divorced.

She unpacked, took a quick bath and climbed into bed. For a long time, Rue lay in the darkness, letting her eyes adjust, remembering. Once, a long time ago, she'd dreamed of living out her whole life on this ranch, marrying, raising her children here. Now it seemed that fantasy was about to come true.

Not that Farley wasn't going to have a hard time adjusting to the idea of having a working wife. He was fiercely proud, and he might never regard the ranch as a true home.

"Stop borrowing trouble," Rue scolded herself in a sleepy whisper. "Farley's always wanted a ranch. You know that."

She tossed restlessly from one side to the other. Then she lay flat on her back and spread her hands over her stomach. *Let there be a baby,* she thought. *Oh, please, let there be a baby.*

Imagining a child with turquoise eyes and unruly brown hair like Farley's made her smile, but her pleasure faded as she remembered his terrible dream the night before. He'd been flung back to his own time without her.

Rue squeezed her eyes closed, trying to shut out the frightening possibilities that had stalked her into this quiet place. It was hopeless; she knew Farley could disappear at any time, maybe without any help from the necklace. And if that was going to happen, there was a grave somewhere, maybe unmarked, maybe lost, and he would have to lie there eventually, like a vampire hiding from the light.

A tear trickled over Rue's cheekbone to wet the linen pillowcase. Okay, she reasoned, love was a risk. *Life* was a risk, not just for her and Farley, but for everyone. The only thing to do was ante up her heart and play the hand she'd been dealt with as much panache as possible.

Chapter Eleven

Rue was out of bed with the first crow of Wilbur's pet rooster, but when she reached the kitchen, wearing boots, jeans and a chambray work shirt left behind on her last visit, Farley was already there. He'd built a fire in the wood cookstove and had used Gramps's old enamel pot to brew coffee. He was reading intently from his how-things-work book.

She decided to demonstrate the automatic coffeemaker another time; Farley would have enough to think about, between grasping the ways ranching had changed since the 1890s and dealing with the cowboys. He would not be given their respect and allegiance simply because he was the foreman; he would have to earn them.

Rue kissed the marshal's cleanly shaved cheek and glanced again at the book he was devouring with such serious concentration. He was studying the inner workings of the combustion engine, and she could almost hear his brain cataloging and sorting the new information.

"'Morning,'" he said without looking up from the diagram that spanned two pages.

Rue got a cup and went to the stove for coffee. The warmth of the wood fire seemed cozier, somehow, than the kind that flowed through the heat vents from the oil furnace. "Good morning, Mr. Ford."

"Mmm-hmm," Farley said.

Rue was gazing out the window over the sink, watching as big, wispy flakes of November snow began to drift down past the yard light from a gray-shrouded sky. Silently, she marveled that she'd stayed away from the land so long, loving it the way she did. She'd let things go where the ranch was concerned, having her accountants go over the books, but never examining them herself, hiring one foreman after another by long-distance telephone without meeting them, sizing them up.

Sorry, Gramps, she said silently.

Wilbur had bacon and eggs in the refrigerator—he had spent the night in the bunkhouse with the other men now that Rue was back—so she made a high-fat, high-cholesterol and totally delicious breakfast. "We'll have to go into town and stock up on groceries," she said, serving the food. "Then I'll introduce you to the men, and you can choose a horse."

By that time, Farley had finished reading about car engine motors, but he looked sort of absentminded, as if he was still digesting facts and sorting ideas. A light went on in his eyes, though. "A horse?" he echoed.

Rue grinned, a slice of crisp bacon in one hand. "Horses are still fundamental to ranching," she said.

"Is this a big spread?"

She told him the acreage, and he whistled in exclamation.

"You raise mostly cattle?"

Rue nodded. "Some horses, too. I'd like to pursue that further, start breeding show stock." She got up and pulled a newspaper clipping she'd spotted earlier from the bulletin board. Wilbur had a habit of saving unusual accounts. "As you can see," she went on, placing the picture of a miniature pony and its trainer next to Farley's plate, "horses come in all shapes and sizes these days."

Farley frowned, studying the photograph. "Tarnation. That little cayoose doesn't even reach the man's belt buckle. Can't be more than two feet high at the withers."

"People breed miniature ponies to show and sell," Rue said, reaching for her coffee. She was prattling, but she didn't care. She enjoyed talking to Farley about anything. "Horses used to be about the size of house cats back in prehistoric times. Did you know that?"

"What good is a two foot horse?" Farley asked practically, letting the history lecture pass without comment. "I don't imagine you could housebreak them like an old lady's pet dog."

Rue laughed. "True enough. And just imagine what it would be like if they jumped up in your lap, the way a cat or a puppy might do." Seeing Farley's consternation, she spoke seriously. "I know in your time every animal had to have a distinct function. Nowadays, people raise all kinds of creatures just because they enjoy it. I know of a woman who raises llamas, for instance, and a man who keeps a little pig as a pet. It even rides in his car."

"You know some strange people," Farley said, and he clearly wasn't kidding.

Rue smiled. "Yes," she agreed. "And the strangest one of all is a United States marshal from 1892."

Farley smiled back, but he was obviously a little tense. He probably felt nervous about meeting the ranch hands; after all, up until then, Rue had been the only twentieth-century person he'd had any real dealings with. Now he would have to integrate himself into a world he'd only begun to understand.

Rue touched his hand. "Everything will be fine," she promised. "Hurry up and finish your breakfast, please. I'll show you the horse barn, and then I want to get the grocery shopping out of the way."

After giving her a humorously ironic look, Farley carried his plate to the sink. "Don't nag me, woman," he teased.

Widening her eyes in feigned innocence, Rue chirped, "Me? Nag? Never!"

With a lift of one eyebrow, Farley put on his hat and the canvas coat he'd been wearing when he and Rue were suddenly hurled into the latter part of the twentieth century. Rue put on a heavy jacket, gloves and a stocking cap, knowing the wind would be ferocious.

The sun had yet to rise, the snow was still coming down, and the cold was keen enough to bite, but Rue's heart brimmed with happiness all the same. Although she hadn't consciously realized the fact before, this ranch was home, and Farley was the man she wanted to share it with.

When they reached the horse barn, the lights were on and one of the hands was helping Wilbur feed and water the valuable geldings and mares. Soldier, the sheepdog, was overseeing the project, and he ran over to bark out a progress report when Rue and Farley appeared.

Farley grinned and affectionately ruffled the animal's ears, one of which was white, the other black. "Good boy," he said.

Rue proceeded along the center of the barn until she came to the stall that held her own mare, Buttermilk. It had been too long since she'd seen the small, yellow horse, and she longed to ride, but there were other things that had to be done first.

She went on to meet Wilbur, who was hobbling toward her.

"Where is that stallion you wrote me about? The one we bought six months ago?"

Wilbur ran his fingers through hair that existed only in his memory. "That would be Lobo. His stall is on the other side of the concrete wall. Had to keep him away from the mares, of course, or he'd tear the place apart."

"Lobo," Rue repeated, well aware of Farley towering behind her. "That's a silly name. You've been watching too many cowboy movies, Wilbur."

The old man winked, not at Rue, but past her right shoulder, at Farley. Obviously Wilbur had pegged the marshal as a kindred soul. "No such thing as too many cowboy movies," he decreed. "Ain't possible. Hell, when the Duke died, those Hollywood folks just stopped making good Westerns altogether."

Rue could feel Farley's questions and his effort to contain them until they were alone again.

"Movies," she said as they rounded the concrete wall Wilbur had mentioned, headed for Lobo's private suite, "are pictures, like on TV, put together to make a story."

"Who's this Duke Wilbur was talking about? I thought we didn't have royalty in America."

Rue grinned, working the heavy latch on the door to the inner stable. "There was a very popular actor called John Wayne. His nickname was the Duke."

Inside his fancy stall, the stallion kicked up a minor fuss. Rue supposed it was some kind of macho thing, a way of letting everybody know he was king of the stables.

"Easy, Lobo," she said automatically.

Farley let out a long, low whistle of admiration as he looked at the magnificent animal through the heavy metal slats of the stall door. "You broke to ride, fella?" he asked, stepping closer.

Rue had been around horses a lot, but she felt as nervous then as she would have if Farley had stood on the threshold of that mysterious doorway in Aunt Verity's house with the necklace in his hand. Either way, he'd have been tempting fate.

"Sure is," Wilbur replied from behind them, before Rue had a chance to answer.

She looked at the horse and then at Farley. "I don't think—"

"Where can I find a saddle?" Farley broke in. The line of his jaw and the expression in his eyes told Rue he would not be dissuaded from riding the stallion.

Wilbur produced the requested tack, along with a bridle and saddle blanket, and Farley opened the stall door and stepped inside, talking quietly to Lobo. Beyond the windows, the snow continued to tumble through the first gray light of morning.

Rue bit her lip and backed up, knowing Farley would never forgive her if she protested further. He was a grown man, he'd probably ridden horses most of his life, and he didn't need mothering.

Wilbur stood back, too, watching closely as Farley slipped the bridle over Lobo's gleaming, ebony head, then saddled the horse with an expertise that made a lump of pride gather in Rue's throat. Finally, he led the animal from the stall and through the outer doorway into the paddock.

Lobo was fitful, nickering and tossing his head and prancing to one side.

"You're sure that stallion is broken to ride?" Rue asked Wilbur, watching as Farley planted one booted foot in the stirrup and swung himself into the saddle.

"Pretty much," Wilbur answered laconically.

Lobo gave a shriek of outrage at the feel of a man's weight on his back. He set his hind legs, and his coal black flanks quivered as he prepared to rebel. Several of the ranch hands had gathered along the paddock fence to watch.

"Damn it," Rue ground out, "this isn't funny!" She was about to walk up to Lobo and grab hold of his bridle when Wilbur reached out and caught hold of her arm.

"Let the man show what he's made of," he said, and Rue could have sworn those words came not from the mischievous old man beside her, but from her grandfather.

"That's stupid," Rue protested in a furious whisper, even though she knew Wilbur was absolutely right.

Lobo had finished deliberating. He "came unwrapped," as Rue's grandfather used to say, bucking as if he had a twenty pound tomcat burying its claws in his hide.

Farley looked cool and calm. He even spurred the stallion once or twice, just to let Lobo know who was running the show.

Finally, with a disgruntled nicker, the stallion settled down, and permitted Farley to ride him around the paddock once at a trot. The watching ranch hands cheered and whistled, and Rue knew Farley had taken the first step toward making a place for himself at Ribbon Creek.

Farley rode over to the fence and spoke to the men who remained there, and soon he was bending from Lobo's back to shake hands.

Rue gave Wilbur a look fit to scorch steel, then crossed the paddock to speak to Farley. She smiled so that no one, least of all the marshal himself, would get the idea she was trying to boss him around.

"I guess we'd better be getting to town if we're going to get our business done," she said.

Farley nodded and rode toward the stables without protest, dismounting to lead Lobo through the doorway.

The cowboys at the fence greeted Rue pleasantly and then went on about their own tasks. When she stepped inside the stable, Farley had already unsaddled Lobo and was praising the horse in a low voice as he curried him.

"That was some fancy riding, Marshal," she said.

Farley didn't look away from the horse. "This is some pretty fancy stallion," he replied.

Rue nodded and wedged her hands into the pockets of her jacket. "The men seem to like you. I guess you know they'll play some pranks and bait you a little, to see if they can get a rise out of you."

"I know about ranch hands, Rue," he said with gentle amusement in his voice. "Don't worry yourself. The boys and I will get on just fine."

Rue sighed. "Maybe I'm like Wilbur," she said. "Maybe I've seen too many Westerns on TV."

He looked back at her over one shoulder, grinned and shook his head.

"In the movies, the new arrival on the ranch always has to prove himself by showing that he's got the hardest fists and the quickest draw," Rue said a little defensively.

Farley ran those saucy eyes of his over her in a searing sweep. "I haven't seen anybody around this place I couldn't handle," he said. He gave the horse a last wistful look before joining Rue to walk toward the house.

She put a hand on his arm. "Don't worry, Marshal. You'll be back here and in the saddle before you know it."

Since it was a two-mile stretch to the main highway, Rue let Farley drive on the first leg of the journey to town. He swerved right off the road once, and sent the Land Rover barrelling through the creek that had given the ranch its name, whooping like a Rebel soldier leading a raid.

Rue decided he was better at riding horses.

The drive into town took another half an hour. By the time they arrived, the community's one supermarket was open for business.

Even though he'd been to the mall outside Seattle and had driven across three states with Rue, Farley was still stricken mute with amazement when he walked into the market and saw the wide aisles and the colorful, complicated displays of boxes and cans and bottles. He jumped when the sprayers came on over the produce, and his eyes widened when he saw the pyramids of red apples and plump oranges. In the meat department, he stood watching a mechanized cardboard turkey until Rue finally grabbed his sleeve and pulled him away.

When they finally returned to the parking lot to load two bulging cartfuls of food into the back of the Land Rover, the marshal was looking a little dazed. All during the ride home, he kept turning around in the passenger seat and plundering products from the bags. He read the boxes and labels letter by letter, it seemed to Rue, frowning in consternation.

"No wonder you women are getting into so much trouble with your short dresses and all," he finally remarked when they were turning off the highway onto the ranch. "Everything can be cooked in five or ten minutes, and you've got all sorts of contraptions besides, like that washing machine. You've got too much free time."

Rue smiled. "I'm going to let you get by with that chauvinistic observation just this once, since for all practical intents and purposes, you're new in town."

"Chauvinistic?" Farley looked puzzled, but certainly not intimidated.

"It's another word for a hardheaded cowboy from 1892," Rue replied. Then she proceeded to explain the finer points of the definition.

Farley sighed when it was over. "I still think you've got too much free time," he said. He was gazing out at the snow-dusted plains of the ranch, and the longing to escape the confines of the Land Rover was clearly visible in his face.

"I guess you'll want to saddle one of the horses and look the place over on your own," Rue observed, pulling to a stop in front of the house.

He grinned with both relief and anticipation, and the moment they'd taken the grocery bags into the house, he headed for the barn.

Knowing Farley needed private time to acclimatize himself, Rue put away the food, then retired to the study to make some calls. Farley's old-fashioned insistence that they needed to be married had never been far from her mind and, due to her wide travels, she had contacts in virtually every walk of life.

It wasn't long before she'd arranged a legal identity for Farley, complete with a birth certificate, Social Security number, S.A.T. scores and even transcripts from a midwestern college. All the necessary paperwork was on its way by express courier.

Farley hadn't returned by noon, when a new snow began to powder the ground, so Rue made a single serving of vegetable-beef soup and sat by the big, stone fireplace in the parlor, her feet resting on a needlepoint hassock.

Once she was finished eating, Rue immediately became bored. She went to the woodshed and split a pile of pine and fir for the fireplace. She was carrying the first armload into the house when Farley appeared, striding toward her from the direction of the barn.

His smile was as dazzling as sunlight on ice-crusted snow as he wrested the wood from Rue's arms and carefully wiped his feet on the mat outside the back door. Obviously the ride had lifted his spirits and settled some things in his mind, and she found herself envying him the fresh air and freedom.

"At least you haven't come up with a machine to chop wood," he said good-naturedly, carrying his burden through the kitchen after seeing that the box by the cast-iron cookstove was full.

Rue followed, marveling at the intensity of her reactions to his impressive height, the broad strength of his shoulders, the muscular grace of his arms and legs. "We can get married in a few days," she said, feeling slightly foolish for her eagerness. "The system recognizes you as a real, flesh-and-blood person."

Farley laid the wood on the parlor hearth, pulled aside the screen and squatted to feed the fire. "That sounds like good news," he commented wryly, "though I've got to admit, I can't say I'm entirely sure."

Rue smiled. "Trust me," she said. "The news is good. Are you hungry?"

Farley closed the fireplace screen and stood. "Yes, but I can see to my own stomach, thank you." He went into the kitchen, with Rue right behind him, and took a frozen entrée from the fridge.

Rue watched with amusement as Farley read the instructions, then set the dish inside the microwave and stood staring at the buttons. She showed him how to set the timer and turn on the oven.

He took bread from the old-fashioned metal box on the counter, and his expression was plainly disapproving as he opened the bag and pulled out two slices. "If a man tried to butter *air,* it would hold up better than this stuff," he remarked scornfully, evidently wanting to let Rue know that not everything about the twentieth century was an improvement over the nineteenth. He held up a slice and peered at Rue through a hole next to the crust. "It's amazing you people aren't downright puny, the way you eat."

Rue laughed and startled Farley by jumping up and flinging her arms around his neck. "I never get tired of listening to you talk, lawman," she said, and her voice came out sounding husky. "Tell me you won't ever change, that you're always going to be Farley Haynes, U.S. Marshal."

He set the bread aside and cupped her chin in one hand. "Everybody changes, Rue," he said quietly, but there was a light in his eyes. She knew he was going to kiss her, and the anticipation was so intense that she felt unsteady and interlocked her fingers at his nape to anchor herself.

The bell on the microwave chimed, and hunger prevailed over passion. Farley stepped gracefully out of Rue's embrace and took his food from the oven.

It was a curious thing, being moved emotionally and spiritually by the plain sight of a man eating spaghetti and meatballs from a cardboard plate, but that was exactly what happened to Rue. Every time she thought she'd explored the depths of her love for this man, she tumbled into some deeper chasm not yet charted, and she was amazed to find that the inner universe was just as vast as the outer one.

Shaken, she tossed her hair back over one shoulder and stood with her hands resting on her hips. "I'm really in trouble here, Farley," she said, only half in jest. "It seems I want to cook for you and wash your clothes and have your babies. We're talking rapid retrograde, as far as women's rights are concerned.''

Farley smiled and stabbed a meatball with his fork. "I imagine you'll be able to hold your own just fine," he said, and Rue wondered if he knew how damnably appealing he was, if his charm was deliberate.

That afternoon, while Farley was out somewhere with Wilbur and the dog, Rue dusted off her grandmother's old cookbooks and hunted down a recipe for bread. When the marshal returned, the dough was rising in a big crockery bowl, and the air was still clouded with tiny, white particles.

Farley's turquoise eyes danced as he hung up his hat and gunslinger coat. "Somebody dynamite the flour bin?"

Rue was covered in white dust from head to foot, but, by heaven, those Presbyterians back in 1892 Pine River had nothing on her. As soon as the dough had puffed up for the second time, she would set it in the oven to bake, and Farley would have the kind of bread he was used to eating.

Sort of.

She thought of the vast differences between them, and the very real danger that they might be parted by forces they could neither understand nor control. All the rigors of past days caught up with her...all of a sudden, and Rue felt some barrier give way inside her.

She was stricken with what women of Farley's generation would have called "melancholia," she guessed, or maybe she was pregnant. The only thing she was certain of was that for the next little while, she wasn't going to be her usual, strong self.

Rue let out a wail of despair, covered her floury face with her floury hands and sobbed. Out on the utility porch, Soldier whined in unison.

Smelling of soap and clean, country snow, Farley came to her and gently pulled her hands down. His mouth quirked at one corner, and his eyes were still shining with humor.

"Stop that crying," he scolded huskily, wiping a tear from her cheekbone with the side of one thumb. "You're going to paste your eyelids together."

"I don't...even know...why I'm...acting like this!" Rue babbled.

Farley kissed her forehead, no doubt leaving lip prints. "You've been through a whole lot lately, and you're all tired out," he said. Then he led her into one of the downstairs bathrooms, ran warm water into the sink and tenderly, carefully washed her face.

The experience in no way resembled lovemaking, and yet the effect was just as profound.

After that, Farley carried her into the parlor, laid her on the big leather sofa and covered her with the lovely plaid throw she'd brought home from a trip to Scotland. She lay sniffling while Farley went to build up the fire.

"This is really unlike me," she whimpered.

"I know," he answered, his voice low and laced with humor. "Just close your eyes and rest awhile, Rue. I'll look after you."

Rue was used to taking care of herself, for the most part. Aunt Verity and Elisabeth had coddled her when she came down with a head cold or the flu, but having a man's sympathy was an entirely new experience. The sensation was decadently delicious, but it was frightening, too. She was afraid that if she laid down her sword even for a little while, it would prove too heavy to lift when the time came to fight new battles.

Chapter Twelve

Rue hadn't suffered through her bread-baking crisis for nothing. After she'd enjoyed the crackling parlor fire and Farley's pampering for half an hour, she returned to the kitchen and tackled the remainder of the job.

While the loaves were baking, filling the room with a very promising fragrance, Rue put game hens on the portable rotisserie, washed some russet potatoes for baking in the microwave and poured a can of cooked carrots into a saucepan to heat.

Farley had gone out to help with the evening chores, and when he returned, Rue had set the kitchen table with her grandmother's favorite china and silver. She'd exchanged her flour-covered clothes for a set of black lounging pajamas with metallic silver stripes, put on a little makeup and swept up her hair.

When the cold Montana wind blew Farley in, he stood staring at her, at the same time trying unsuccessfully to hang his hat on the peg next to the door. "How soon did you say we'd be getting married?" he asked.

Rue smiled, pleased, and lifted one shoulder. "Three or four days from now, if all goes well." She sighed. "Too bad you're such a prude. Montana nights can get very cold, and it would be nice to have somebody to snuggle with."

Farley was unbuttoning his coat. "Seems to me Montana nights can turn hot even in the middle of a snowstorm," he retorted hoarsely. He walked to the sink, rolling up the sleeves of his shirt as he went, and washed his hands as thoroughly as any surgeon would have done.

Proudly, Rue served the dinner she'd made, and Farley made it obvious that he enjoyed the fare, and even though the bread was a little on the heavy side, he didn't comment.

After eating, they washed and dried the dishes together—Rue never mentioned the shiny, perfectly efficient built-in dishwasher—and they went into the parlor. Rue had hoped for a romantic interlude in front of the fire, but Farley, having apparently absorbed everything in his how-things-work book, had gone to Gramps's bookshelf for another volume. This time, it seemed, he'd decided to investigate the secrets of indoor plumbing.

Resigned, Rue got out her laptop computer, and soon her fingers were flying over the keyboard. It seemed more important than ever to record what had happened to Elisabeth, and to her and Farley because of the strange antique necklace Aunt Verity had left as a legacy.

Rue had written several pages when she realized Farley was watching her. She glanced at him over her shoulder. He was next to her on the couch, holding his place in his book with a thumb. He'd already read nearly half the volume, which was incredible, given the technical nature of the material.

She smiled, reading the questions from his eyes and the furrows in his brow. "This is a computer, Farley. If I were you, I'd make that my next reading project. The modern world runs on these handy little gadgets."

Farley had seen the laptop before, of course, but never while it was running. "Light," he marveled. "You're writing words with *light* instead of ink."

As usual, his wonderment touched Rue deeply. He'd made such a profound difference in her life simply by being who he was, and even though she had been happy and fulfilled before she'd met him, Rue cherished the special texture and substance he gave to her world.

She showed him how to work the keyboard, and she watched with delight as he read from the screen.

All in all, it was a wonderful evening.

In the morning, Farley was up and gone before Rue even opened her eyes. She stumbled in and out of the shower, dressed warmly and went down to the kitchen for coffee. Since Soldier was whimpering on the back porch, she let him in to lie contentedly on the hooked rug in front of the old cookstove.

Farley had left a note on the table, and Rue read it while the water for her instant coffee was heating in the microwave.

Rue,
   It might be a long day. The snow is getting deeper, and Wilbur and the others think some of the cattle may be in trouble out on the range. Stay close to the house; folks have been lost in weather like this. Warm regards,

F.H.

"'Warm regards,'" Rue scoffed, turning to the dog, who lifted a single ear—the black one—in polite inquiry. "I give the man my body, and he signs notes 'warm regards.' And this command to stay in the house! What does he think I am? A child? A greenhorn? Next he'll be tying a rope between the back porch and the chicken coop so I don't get lost in the blizzard when I gather the eggs!''

Soldier whimpered and lowered his muzzle to his outstretched paws, eyeing Rue balefully.

"Oh, you're right," she conceded, though not in a generous way. "I'm being silly. Farley is a man of the 1890s, and it's perfectly natural that he sees things from a very different angle."

She went to the window and felt a vague sense of alarm at the depth of the snow. The drifts reached halfway up the fences and mounded on the sills, and shimmering, pristine flakes were still whirling down from a fitful sky.

Rue drank her coffee, poured herself a bowlful of cereal and began to pace. She was an active person, used to a hectic schedule, and the sense of being trapped in the house made her feel claustrophobic.

She went upstairs and made her bed, and even though she tried to resist, she couldn't. Rue opened the door to the master suite, intending to make Farley's bed, as well, and stopped cold on the threshold.

Farley had already taken care of the task, but that wasn't what troubled Rue so much. A golden chain lay on the bedside table, shimmering in the thin, winter light, and she knew without taking a single step closer it was *the* necklace, the magical, deadly, ticket-through-time necklace she'd purposely left on Aunt Verity's parlor mantel.

Rue sagged against the doorjamb for a moment, one hand cupped over her mouth. The discovery had been as startling as a sudden earthquake, and the implications crashed down on her head with all the weight of timbers shaken loose from their fittings.

Farley knew about the pendant, knew about its power. He could only have brought it along for one reason: he didn't intend to stay in the twentieth century with Rue, despite all his pretty talk about their getting married. This was only a cosmic field trip to him; he planned to return to 1892, to his jailhouse and his horse and women who never wore pants!

She started toward the necklace, possessed by a strange, tender spite, fully intending to carry the thing into the master bathroom and flush it. In the end, though, she retreated into the hallway, afraid to touch the pendant for fear that it might send her spiralling into some other period in time.

The distant toot of a horn distracted her, and she was grateful. She ran down the main staircase, one hand trailing along the banister, and bounded out onto the porch without bothering to put on her coat.

A white van had labored up the road from the highway. The logo of an express-courier company was painted brightly on its side, and the driver came cheerfully through the gate in the picket fence and up the unshoveled walk.

"Rue Claridge?" he inquired.

Rue nodded, hugging herself against the cold, her thoughts still on the necklace.

The courier handed her a package and pointed out a line for her signature. "Sure is a nasty day," he said.

Rue had long ago made a personal pledge to fight inanity wherever she encountered it, but she was too distracted to do battle that day. "Yes," she muttered, scrawling her name. "Thank you."

She fled into the house a moment later and tore open the packet. Inside were the papers her somewhat shady acquaintance had assembled for Farley.

Tears filled her eyes, and her throat thickened. Maybe he didn't intend to marry her at all. Or perhaps he'd planned to go through with the ceremony and then blithely return to 1892, leaving his bride behind to cope as best she could....

Soldier was in the kitchen, and he suddenly started to bark. Grateful for the distraction, Rue headed in that direction, the express packet still in her hand.

Through the window in the back door, she saw Wilbur standing on the porch, smiling at her from beneath the brim of his hat. She was surprised, having gotten the impression from Farley's note that the old man had gone out to help with the cattle.

Rue opened the door. "Hi, Wilbur. Got time for a cup of coffee?"

Her grandfather's old friend looked a little wan. "It isn't often that I turn down the opportunity for a chat with a pretty lady," he said, "but the truth is that I'm under the weather today. I wondered if you could pick up my prescription for me, if you were going to town or anything."

Rue took a closer look at the old man. "You come in here and sit down this instant," she ordered in a firm but friendly tone. "Of course, I'll get your medicine, but why didn't you have the store deliver it?"

"Costs extry," said Wilbur, hanging up his hat and slowly working the buttons on his ancient coat. He took a chair at the kitchen table and accepted the coffee Rue brought to him with a philosophical sigh.

"For heaven's sake," she scolded good-naturedly, sitting down with her coffee, "you're not poor, Wilbur." She knew that was true; Gramps had provided well for the faithful employee in his will. "Besides, you can't take it with you."

Wilbur smiled, but his hand trembled as he lifted his cup to his mouth. "You young people gotta spend a nickel or it burns a hole in your pocket."

Rue leaned forward, frowning. "What kind of medicine are you taking, anyway?"

"Just some stuff that jump starts the old ticker," he replied with a sort of blithe weariness.

In the next instant, as quickly and unexpectedly as Rue and Farley had been thrust from the nineteenth century into the twentieth, Wilbur's coffee clattered to the table. Brown liquid stained the cloth, and the old man clutched at his chest, a look of helpless bewilderment contorting his face.

"Oh, my God," Rue gasped, jumping up, rushing to him and grabbing his shoulders. "Wilbur, don't you do this to me! Don't you dare have a heart attack in my kitchen!" Even as she spoke the words, she knew how inane they were, but she couldn't help saying them.

He started to fall forward, making a choking sound in his throat. Soldier hovered nearby, whimpering in concern. Rue gently lowered her friend to the floor and loosened the collar of his shirt—a handmade one, Western cut with pearl snaps—that was probably older than she was.

"Hold on," she said urgently. "I'll have some help out here right away. Just hold on!"

She stumbled to the phone on the wall, punched out 911. Wilbur lay moaning on the floor, while Soldier helpfully licked his face.

"This is Rue Claridge out at Ribbon Creek," she told the young man who answered her call. "A man has collapsed, and I think he's having a heart attack."

"Is he conscious? Breathing?"

Rue glanced nervously toward her patient. "Yes. I think he's in extreme pain."

The operator was reassuringly calm. "We're on our way, Miss Claridge, but the roads are bad and the trip is bound to take some time. Are you trained to administer CPR?"

Rue nodded, then realized that was no help and blurted out, "Yes. Tell the paramedics to hurry, will you? We're in the kitchen of the main house."

"Would you like me to stay on the line with you?"

She looked at Wilbur, and her eyes filled with tears at his fragility. "I'd appreciate that—I think I'd better put some blankets over him, though."

"I'll be right here waiting," the dispatcher answered, and the unruffled normalcy of his tone gave Rue a badly needed dose of courage.

She quickly snatched thick woolen blankets from a chest in one of the downstairs bedrooms and rushed back to the kitchen to cover Wilbur, then rushed back to the phone.

"Should I give him water?"

"No" was the brisk and immediate response on the other end of the line. "Can the patient speak?"

Rue rushed back to the old man's side. He was looking up at her with glassy, frightened eyes, and she found herself smoothing his thin hair back from his forehead. "You'll be all right, Wilbur," she said. "Help is on the way. Can you talk?"

He grimaced with effort, but only an incoherent, helpless sound came from his lips. His hands were still pressed, fingers splayed and clutching, against his chest.

Rue spent the next half hour running back and forth between the telephone and the place where Wilbur lay, but it seemed like much longer to her. When she heard a siren in the distance, she felt like sobbing with relief.

"The cavalry's just about to come over the rise," she told Wilbur. "Hold on."

Farley and the others must have heard the siren, too, for the paramedics had just finished loading their charge into the ambulance when the whole yard seemed to be crowded with horses.

"What happened?" Farley asked, reaching Rue's side first. He was gazing speculatively at the vehicle with the spinning red light. "Is this what was making all that racket?"

Rue linked her arm through his and let her head rest against the outside of his shoulder. She hadn't forgotten that he'd brought the necklace to Ribbon Creek, knowing full well what could happen, but she was still in the throes of the current crisis and unable to pursue the point.

Yet.

"Wilbur came by to ask me to pick up his prescription if I went to town," she said. "After a few minutes, he grabbed his chest—" Emotion overcame her, and Farley held her close against his side.

Life was so uncertain, so damn dangerous, she thought. Here today, gone tomorrow. No guarantees. Catch as catch can.

One of the paramedics slammed the rear doors of the ambulance, then the vehicle was reeling away through the ever-worsening weather. The light flung splashes of crimson onto the snow, and the sound of the siren was like big needles being pushed through Rue's eardrums.

With Farley holding her close, Rue's heart was mended, if only briefly, and she could almost believe he hadn't planned to desert and betray her.

She forced herself to look up into his wonderful, rugged, unreadable face. "Are the cattle all right?"

He nodded, this man she loved, this man she'd hoped to spend her life with. "For the moment. Let's get you back in the house before you start sprouting icicles." With that, he ushered her away toward the warmth and light of the kitchen.

And the danger of the necklace.

Perhaps because she was used to crises, Rue quickly regained her composure. There was no point in worrying about Wilbur until she'd heard something from the hospital, and she wasn't sure how to broach the subject of the antique pendant.

"We can get married now," she said with only a slight tremor in her voice, after showing him the paperwork. They were in the parlor, by the fire, sitting on the raised hearth and drinking hot coffee laced with Irish cream. She watched him closely after making the announcement.

"Today? Tomorrow?"

Rue was heartened by his response, but only a little. "I think there's a three-day waiting period and, of course, it would be foolish to try to get into town today."

Farley grinned. "We could make it if we went on horseback."

Rue's heartbeat quickened, but she sternly reminded herself how sneaky men could be. Words were cheap; it was what a person *did* that counted. "Okay, cowboy," she said testily, thrusting out her chin. "You're on."

Farley looked at his feet and the gleaming hardwood floor immediately surrounding them. "On what?"

"I'm accepting your challenge. We're going to put the Land Rover into four-wheel drive and head for town. Just don't blame me if we get stuck and freeze to death!"

The marshal narrowed his eyes, not in hostility, but in confusion. "Wilbur was just saying the other day that women are odd creatures, and he was right. What the devil's gotten into you, Rue?"

"You kept the necklace!" she cried, surprising herself as much as Farley. "How could you do that? How could you pretend that I meant something to you, that you were planning to stay here with me, when all the time you intended to go back!"

Farley gripped her shoulders and lifted her onto her toes. While the gesture was in no way painful, it was certainly intimidating. "I thought you'd forgotten the damn thing," he said, his eyes darkening from turquoise to an intense blue. "I was trying to help."

Rue longed to believe him, and she felt herself wavering. "Sure," she threw out. "That's why you didn't mention it."

He closed his eyes for a moment, jawline clamped down tight, and if he wasn't feeling pure frustration, he was doing a good job of projecting that emotion. "It's not every day a man jumps a hundred years like a square on a checkerboard, Rue. I've been thinking about electricity and gasoline engines and computers and supermarkets and shopping malls—and how much I want to sleep with you again. There just wasn't room in my head for that blasted necklace!"

Rue felt herself sagging, on the inside at least. She wondered, not for the first time, whether this man sapped her strength or nurtured it. She let her forehead rest against his shoulder, and he slipped his arms lightly around her waist and kissed the top of her head.

"Let's hitch up your Land Rover," he said with a smile in his voice. "I think I'd better hurry up and marry you before you decide Wilbur's the man for you."

Rue laughed and cried and finally dried her eyes.

Then she grabbed the false papers proving Farley was a real person, smiling at the irony of that, and the two of them headed for town. The conditions were bad, but the snowplows and gravel trucks were out, and the Land Rover moved easily over the slippery highways.

At the courthouse in Pigeon Ridge, Farley and Rue applied for a marriage license, then went to the town's only restaurant to celebrate. The establishment was called the Roost, to Rue's amusement.

She called the hospital in the next town, while Farley's cheeseburger and her nachos were being made, and asked about Wilbur. He had arrived, the nurse told her, but was still in the emergency room.

Farley was poking the buttons on the fifties-style jukebox at their table, frowning the way he always did when something puzzled him.

Rue smiled, fished a couple of coins out of her wallet and dropped them into the slot. "Push a button," she said.

Farley complied, and a scratchy sound followed, then music. A country-western ballad filled the diner, an old song that would, of course, be totally new to the marshal. He grinned. "Cassette tapes," he said triumphantly.

"Close," Rue replied, fearing the strength of the love she felt for this man, the depth and height and breadth of it. She explained about 45-r.p.m. records and jukeboxes while they ate. After the meal, she called the hospital again.

Farley was having a second cup of coffee when she returned. "How is Wilbur?" he asked.

Rue sighed and slid back into the booth. "He's going to make it, thank God. He definitely had a heart attack, but he could live a long time yet, if he takes care of himself. I mean to see that he does."

"If Wilbur were a younger man, I'd be jealous."

Rue smiled at Farley's teasing, knowing he was trying to help her over a slick place, so to speak. "You should be. A guy like Wilbur can drive a woman mad with passion."

"Can we see him?"

She shook her head. "Not today. He needs to rest."

The trip back to the ranch was even more treacherous than the journey into town. Even with four-wheel drive, the Land Rover fishtailed on the icy highway, and finally Farley braced both hands against the dashboard and let out an involuntary yelp of alarm.

"For heaven's sake, Farley," Rue snapped, managing the steering wheel with a skill her grandfather had taught her, "get a grip!"

He thrust himself backward in the seat and pushed his hat down over his eyes, and Rue knew for certain that it wasn't because he wanted to sleep.

She spared one hand from the wheel just long enough to thump Farley hard in the shoulder. "I suppose you think you could do better!"

He pushed the hat back and glared at her. "Lady, I *know* I could do better."

"This superior, know-it-all attitude is one of the many things I don't like about men!" Rue yelled. She wasn't sure *why* she was yelling; maybe it was the stress inherent in the day's events, the tension of driving on such dangerous roads or frustration because it would be three days before she and Farley could be married and he had suddenly decided he had to be a virgin groom. Then again, it could have been because she'd thought she'd escaped the power of Aunt Verity's necklace, only to find that it had followed her.

Very carefully, she pulled to the side of the road.

"All right, wise guy," she challenged, "you can drive the rest of the way home. But when we're both in the emergency room, shot full of painkillers and wrapped in surgical tape and looking like a couple of fugitives from the King Tut exhibit, don't say I didn't warn you!"

Farley had already unfastened his seat belt, and he was opening the door before Rue even finished speaking. "I don't have the first idea what you're talking about," he said evenly, "but I know a dare when I hear one and, furthermore, I don't care for your tone of voice."

They traded places, Rue grimly certain they'd end up in the ditch before they'd traveled a mile, Farley quiet and determined. Much to Rue's relief and, though she would admit it, her disappointment, they reached the ranch without incident, and Soldier met them in the yard.

"There's a blizzard blowing in," Farley announced, looking up at the sky before he wrapped one arm around Rue and shuffled her toward the house. Even though the gesture was protective, there was something arrogant and proprietary about it, too.

Within an hour, the power had gone off. Farley built up the fire in the kitchen stove, and Rue lit a couple of kerosene lamps she'd found on the top shelf of the pantry. While she read the book she'd started earlier, Farley went over the account books for the ranch. He made notes, paused periodically to slip into deep thought, then went back to the study for more reports and files.

If Rue hadn't known better, she'd have sworn he was auditing her income tax return.

"I'm sorry," she said.

"About what?" Farley asked without looking up. He was making notes on a pad of paper, and every once in a while, he stopped to touch the tip of the pencil to his tongue.

"For yelling before. It's just that—well—it's the necklace. It's really bugging me."

That made him lay down the pencil and regard her somberly. " 'Bugging' you?"

"Troubling. Irritating. Farley, this is no time for a lesson in twentieth-century vocabulary. I love you, and I'm afraid. That necklace has the power to separate us."

Farley reached across the table and took her hand in his. For a moment, she really thought he was going to say he loved her, too, she believed she saw the words forming in the motion of his vocal cords. In the end, though, he simply replied, "We're going to be married. I don't know how to make my intentions any plainer, Rue."

She traced his large knuckles with the pad of her thumb. When Farley declared his love, it had to be by his own choice and not because she'd goaded him into it. She suspected, too, that men of his time had an even more difficult time talking about their feelings than the contemporary variety did.

"Okay," she finally responded, "but I'm still scared."

Farley gripped her hand and gently but firmly steered her out of her chair and around the table, then into his lap. "Don't be," he muttered, his lips almost touching hers. "Nothing and no one will hurt you as long as the blood in my veins is still warm."

Rue could certainly vouch for the warmth of the blood in *her* veins. She ached with the need to give pleasure to Farley, and to take it, and when he kissed her, tentatively at first and then with the audacity of a plundering pirate, her whole body caught fire.

"Just tell me," she pleaded breathlessly when Farley finally freed her mouth, "that you won't go back to 1892 without me."

The stillness descended on the room suddenly, with all the slicing, bitter impact of a mountain snowslide. Farley thrust Rue firmly off his lap and onto her feet. "I can't promise that," he said.

Chapter Thirteen

Rue clenched her hands into fists and stood beside the table, staring down into Farley's stubborn, guileless face. "What do you mean, you can't promise you won't go back without me?" The question was a whispery hiss, like the sound of water spilling onto a red-hot griddle.

Farley reached out and pulled her back onto his lap. He splayed his fingers between her shoulder blades, offering slight and awkward comfort. "Rue, I was the marshal of Pine River, and I had responsibilities. People trusted me. One day, I just vanished without a fare-thee-well to anybody. Sooner or later, I have to find a way to let those folks know I'm not lying in some gully with a bullet through my head, that I didn't just ride out one day and desert them. I can't make a new life with you until I've made things right back there."

Rue looked away, but she didn't have the strength to escape his embrace again. The day had been long and stressful, and she was drained. "So I was right in the first place," she said miserably. It wasn't often that Rue wanted to be wrong, but this time she would have given her overdraft privileges at the bank for it. "You brought the necklace to Ribbon Creek because you knew you were going back, just like I said. When you claimed you thought I'd forgotten it, well, that was just a smoke screen."

Farley paused, obviously stuck on the term "smoke screen," then he met Rue's gaze squarely. "I'm not the kind of man the Presbyterians entirely approve of," he confessed in a grave tone of voice, "but there's one thing I'm definitely not, and that's a liar. And if you'll search your memory, you'll find that I never promised to stay here."

Rue was aghast. "We took out a marriage license today," she whispered. "Didn't that mean anything to you? Was it just something to do?"

He laid his strong hands to either side of her face, forcing her to look at him, making her listen. "There's nothing I want more than to be your husband," he said evenly. "Unless you change your mind and call off the wedding, we *will* be married. We'll fill this big house with children, and I think I can even set aside my pride long enough to accept the fact that my place at Ribbon Creek came to me by marriage instead of honest effort. But the longer I talk, the more certain I get that I can't leave that other life unfinished."

Rue was exasperated, even though she could see the merit in his theory only too well. "What are you going to do, Farley?" she demanded, and something in her tone made Soldier whimper fretfully from his place on the hooked rug by the stove. "Grab the necklace, click your heels together, make a dramatic landing in 1892 and tell everybody you're a time traveler now?"

He shook his head. "I wouldn't talk about what really happened with anybody but Jon Fortner or your cousin

Elisabeth." He frowned, his brows knitting. "You don't suppose they're in any sort of trouble over our being gone all of a sudden like that, do you? After all, we were in their parlor when we disappeared."

Rue was ashamed to realize that the possibility had never crossed her mind. "I imagine the townspeople think I spirited you away to some den of never-ending iniquity. Besides, Jon and Bethie had no motive for foul play. Jon is—was—your friend, and everybody knew—knows."

Farley didn't look reassured, and Rue was almost sorry she'd ever confronted him about the necklace. It was plain that if he'd had any intention of using the pendant to escape her and an admittedly hectic modern world, he hadn't been consciously aware of the fact. No, the marshal had only begun to seriously consider returning to 1892 to tie up loose ends *after* Rue had reminded him that such a thing was possible.

She laid her head against his shoulder. "Don't try to send me off to bed alone tonight, Marshal, because I'm not stepping out of reaching distance. If I have to attach myself to you like one sticky spoon behind another, I'll do it. And I don't give a damn about your silly ideas about keeping up appearances, either. Everybody within a fifty-mile radius of this ranch thinks we're making mad, passionate love every chance we get."

Farley kissed her forehead. "We'll be married soon enough," he said.

The house was cooling off rapidly, since the furnace wasn't working, and the kitchen was the only logical place to sleep. Rue took one of the lamps and went in search of sleeping bags, making a point of going nowhere near the necklace. She returned sometime later to find Farley still absorbed in paperwork. He reminded her of Abraham Lincoln, sitting there in the light of a single lantern, reading with such solemn concentration.

She built up the fire in the wood stove and spread the sleeping bags within the warm aura surrounding it. "What are you doing?" she asked, sitting cross-legged on the floor to watch him.

He scribbled something onto a yellow legal pad and then glanced at her distractedly. "Doing? Oh, well, I'm just writing up some changes we could make—in the way the ranch is being run, I mean."

Rue was heartened that he was thinking of the ranch from a long-range perspective, but her fear of being abandoned hadn't abated. Afraid or not, though, she was tired, and after brushing her teeth and washing her face, she stripped to her T-shirt and stretched out on one of the sleeping bags.

The power outage wasn't bothering Farley a bit; lantern light and wood fires were normal to him. Rue wasn't above wishing he were a little spooked by the encroaching darkness and the incessant howl of the wind; she would have liked for him to join her in front of the stove. With his arms around her, she might have been able to pretend there was no danger, just for a little while.

She yawned and closed her eyes. Sleeping on the kitchen floor reminded her of other nights, long ago, when Aunt Verity had sometimes allowed Rue and Elisabeth to "camp out" on the rug in front of the parlor fire. They had turned out all the lights, munched popcorn and scared each other silly with made-up stories about ghosts and vampires and rampaging maniacs—never dreaming that something with equally mysterious powers, an old-fashioned pendant on a gold chain, lay hidden away among their aunt's belongings.

Waiting.

* * *

Farley continued to read and work on the rough outline of his plans for the ranch, but every once in a while, his gaze strayed to Rue, who lay sleeping in a bedroll in front of the cookstove. Looking at her tightened his loins and made barbs catch in the tenderest parts of his heart, but he wouldn't let himself approach her.

He sighed and took a cold, bitter sip from his mug, rather than pass Rue to get fresh coffee from the pot on the stove. If he got too close, he knew he'd end up pulling that peculiar-looking nightdress off over her head and making love to her until the sun came up.

The lights flared on just as dawn was about to break, and Farley switched them off so Rue wouldn't be disturbed, then he went upstairs to shower and change clothes. After last night's storm, there would be plenty to do.

As he entered the room he would soon be sharing with Rue, Farley looked at the big, welcoming bed and wondered if he was losing his mind. Rue was so beautiful, and he wanted her so much. Refusing to sleep with her now was like putting the lid back on the bin after the mice had gotten to the potatoes, and he knew she was right in believing that her reputation was long gone. Still, he wanted to offer her a tribute of some sort, and honor was all he had.

The necklace glittered on the nightstand, as if to attract his attention, and he reached for it, then drew back his hand. He'd be returning to 1892, all right, but only long enough to put his affairs in order. Then he would come straight back to Rue. He didn't intend to go before he'd married her, at any rate, nor would he leave without saying goodbye.

He made his way into the bathroom, kicked off his boots and peeled away his clothes. By then he'd figured out the plumbing system, thanks to one of the books he'd found in the study, and when there was no hot water, he knew it was going to take a while for the big heater downstairs to return to the proper temperature.

Resigned, Farley went back to the bed, crawled under the covers because he was naked and the room was still frigidly cold, and immediately felt the fool for being afraid of a little geegaw like that necklace. He reached out and closed his hand over it and, in the next instant, the room rocked from side to side. It was as though somebody had grabbed the earth and yanked it out from under the house like a rug.

Farley felt the firm mattress go feathery soft beneath him, and he bolted upright with a shout. "Rue!" He was sweating, and he could feel his heart thundering against his breastbone, as if seeking a way to escape.

He knew immediately that he was in a different room, in a different house. He could make out blue wallpaper, and the bed, an old four-poster with a tattered canopy, faced in another direction. And those things were the least of his problems.

Not only had Farley landed in a strange bed, there was someone sharing it. At his shout, a plump middle-aged woman in a nightcap let out a shriek loud enough to hasten the Resurrection, bounced off the mattress and snatched up a poker from the nearby hearth.

She continued to scream while Farley frantically clutched the necklace and willed himself back to the 1990s and Rue. The poker was coming toward his head when the mattress turned hard again and the wallpaper changed to paneling. He hadn't had more than two seconds to acclimatize himself when the bedroom door flew open and Rue burst in. She hurled herself over the foot of the bed and scrambled the rest of the way to Farley on her knees, throwing her arms around his neck when she reached him.

"I heard you yell. You saw something, didn't you? Something happened."

Farley tossed the necklace aside and embraced Rue. She was real and solid, thank God. "Yes," he finally rasped when his breathing had slowed to the point where speech was possible. "Yes."

"What?"

"I don't know. A woman with a poker in her hand—"

Rue drew back, her hands resting on the sides of his face, her eyes full of questions. "You're sure you weren't dreaming?"

Farley laughed, though amusement was about the last thing he felt. "I wasn't dreaming. That woman was as real as you are, and she wasn't pleased to find a naked cowboy in her bed, I can tell you that. Another second and she would have changed the shape of my skull."

Rue turned her head, looking at the necklace lying a few feet away on the carpet. "Farley, let's throw the pendant away before something terrible—and irrevocable—happens. Surely the good people of Pine River hired a new marshal, and Jonathan and Elisabeth *must* have found a way to explain your disappearance."

Farley gathered Rue close and held her, taking comfort from the soft, fragrant, womanly substance of her. "We can't do that, Rue," he reasoned after a long time. "There's no way of predicting what the consequences might be. Suppose somebody found it, a child maybe? No, we've got to hide that pendant and make damn sure it stays put."

She buried her face in his chest, that was all, but the surface of Farley's skin quivered in response, and he felt himself come to attention. "I'm scared," she said, her voice muffled by his flesh.

Farley wanted Rue more than ever, having been separated from her by a wall of time, but he was strong and stubborn, and so were his convictions. The next time he made love to Rue, she would bear his name as well as the weight of his body.

Her hand trailed slowly down over his chest and belly, leaving a sparkling trail of stardust in its wake. Then she captured him boldly.

He groaned in glorious despair. "Damn it, Rue, let go."

She did not obey. "You're bigger and stronger," she teased in a whimpery voice. "But I declare, Marshal, I don't see you trying to wrest yourself free of my sinful attentions."

Farley fully intended to pull her fingers away, but his hands went instead to the sides of her head. With a strangled cry, he kissed her, his tongue invading her mouth, plundering. And still she worked him mercilessly with her hand.

He broke away from the kiss, gasping. "Oh, God, *Rue—*"

She teased his navel with the tip of her tongue. "You promised not to make love to me again until we were married," she said, and he trembled in anticipation, knowing what was going to happen. "I, on the other hand, never said anything of the kind."

Farley felt her moving downward and groaned, but he could not make himself stop her. When Rue took him, he gave a raspy cry of relief and surrendered to her.

Later, Farley left the bed, showered and went about the business of running a ranch. Rue took a pair of tweezers from her makeup case, picked up the necklace, which was still lying on the floor where Farley had thrown it after his unscheduled flight into history, and dropped it gingerly into a big envelope.

She held the envelope by a corner, carrying it downstairs and laying it on the desk in the study. She opened the safe hidden behind her grandmother's bad painting of a bowl of grapes, expecting to find it empty since she had long since gone through all her grandfather's papers. To her surprise, however, there was a thin envelope of white vellum inside, and when she pulled it out, a chill went through her.

The handwriting on the front was old and faded and very familiar, and it read, "Miss Rue Claridge, Ribbon Creek, Montana." There was even a zip code, a fact that might have made Rue smile if she hadn't been so shaken. The date on the postmark was 1892.

She let the other envelope, containing the necklace, drop forgotten to the floor and sank into a chair, her heart stuffed into her throat.

Apparently the letter had been delivered to Gramps, and he'd saved it for her, probably never noticing the postmark or the antiquated ink.

Rue drew in a deep breath and sat up very straight. If the letter had been delivered to the ranch, why hadn't she found it before, when she'd settled Gramps's affairs? Come to that, why was any of this happening at all?

The only explanation Rue could think of was that Farley was going back to 1892 in the near future, if he hadn't done so already. And this was the only way he could contact her, by writing a letter that would be misplaced and passed from person to person for a hundred years.

Fingers trembling, Rue opened the envelope and pulled out a single, thin page. Stinging tears came instantly to her eyes. These words had been written a century before by a man she'd brazenly made love to only that morning.

My Dearest Rue,
I'm writing this to say goodbye, even though I know

my words will be confusing to you when and if you ever lay eyes on them. Maybe you'll not see this page at all, but I don't mind admitting I take some comfort from the writing of it.

I never meant to leave you forever, Rue, especially not on our wedding day; I want you to know that. My love for you is as constant as my breath and my heartbeat, and I will carry that adoration with me into the next world, where the angels will surely envy it.

I have every confidence that if a child is born of our union, you will raise our son or daughter to be strong and full of honor.

I'm staying here at the Pine River house, having been shot last week when there was a robbery at the bank. Oftentimes, I wonder if you're in another room somewhere, just beyond the reach of my eyes and ears.

When last I saw your cousin Lizzie, which was just a little while ago when she came to change my bandages, she was well. She saw that I was writing you and promised to help me think of a way to get the letter to you, and she asked me to give you her deepest regards.

I offer mine as well.

With love forever,
Farley.

Rue folded the letter carefully and tucked it back into the envelope, even though there was a wild fury of panic storming within her. She wanted to scream, to sob, to refuse to accept this fate, but she knew it would be useless.

Farley was going back; the letter was tangible proof of that. And he was dying from the wounds he'd received during the robbery. He hadn't come right out and said that, but she had read the truth between the lines.

She pushed the envelope under the blotter on the desk. She wanted to confront Farley with what she'd discovered, but she couldn't. For one thing, he hadn't done anything wrong; it was his life, and if he wanted to go back to 1892 and throw it away in a gunfight with a pack of outlaws, that was his prerogative. No, Farley wasn't the only one with integrity; Rue had it, too, and in those moments, the quality was her greatest curse.

Rue paced. She could warn him. Maybe if she did that, he would at least avoid stumbling into that bank at the wrong moment and getting himself killed.

Finally she remembered the registry at the graveyard in Pine River, got the number from information and put a call through. After half an hour and a string of hassles that heightened her frustration to new levels, a clerk in the church office finally unearthed an old record book and found Farley's name in it.

"Yes, he's listed here," the woman said pleasantly. "His grave would be out in the old section, under the oak tree. I hope that helps. It might be hard to find otherwise. Not everyone had a stone, you know, and a wooden marker would be long gone."

Rue squeezed her eyes shut, almost overwhelmed by the images that were filling her mind. "Does the record list a cause of death?" she asked, her voice thin.

"Gunshot wound to the chest," the clerk replied after a pause. "He was attended by Dr. Jonathan Fortner, a man who played quite an important part in the history of Pine River—"

"Thank you," Rue said, unable to bear another word, even though it meant cutting the woman off in the middle of a sentence. Her eyes were awash in tears when she hung up the receiver. Soldier came and leaned against her leg, whining in sympathy.

Rue knew it might be hours until Farley returned, and she couldn't stand to stay in the house, so she went out to the woodshed and split enough firewood to last through a second ice age. When that was done, she started up the Land Rover, Soldier happily occupying the passenger seat, and headed out over roads of glaring ice.

It took an hour to reach the hospital in the next town over from Pigeon Ridge. Leaving the dog in the Land Rover, Rue went inside and bought a card in the small gift shop, then asked to see Wilbur.

He'd spent the night and most of the day in intensive care, a nurse told her, but she supposed one visit would be all right if Rue kept her stay brief.

She found him in Room 447, and although there were three other beds, they were all empty. Wilbur looked small and forlorn, with tubes running into his nose and the veins of both his wrists.

"Hello, Wilbur." Rue set the card on his nightstand, then bent to kiss his forehead.

He looked surprised at his misfortune, and helpless.

Rue blinked back tears and patted his arm. "That's all right, I know you can't talk right now. I just wanted to stop by and to say hello and tell you not to worry about Soldier. I'm taking good care of him. In fact, he's out in the car right now—it was as close as the nurses would let him get."

Wilbur made a funny noise low in his throat that might have been a chuckle.

"I'd better go," Rue said. "I know you need to rest and, besides, you won't want me hanging around when all your girlfriends come in." She touched his shoulder, then left the room. In a glance backward, she saw him reach awkwardly up to catch hold of the get-well card she'd brought.

For all her activity, Rue had not forgotten Farley's letter for a moment. She circled the thought the way a she wolf might move around a campfire, fascinated but afraid to get too close.

The sun was out when Rue returned to the Land Rover, and the ice seemed to be thawing, but it still took forever to get home, because there were so many accidents along the way. When she and Soldier arrived, Farley and the other men were driving several hundred head of cattle into the big pasture west of the house, where a mountain of hay and troughs of fresh water awaited.

Rue started toward Farley, fully intending to tell him about the letter she'd found in the safe, but the closer she got, the more convinced she became that it would be impossible. She could barely think of being parted from him, let alone talk about it.

She stopped at the fence, listening to the bawling of the cattle, the yelling and swearing of the cowboys, the neighs and nickers of the horses. In those moments as she stood watching Farley work, she realized how simple the solution really was.

All she had to do was destroy the necklace. Once that was done, there would be no way for Farley to return to 1892 and get himself shot.

He rode over to look down at her, his face reddened by the cold and his mustache fringed with snow. His smile practically set her back on her heels.

"Where have you been?" he asked. He didn't sound annoyed, just curious.

"I went in to see Wilbur at the hospital. He's doing all right." The words brought an image of a wounded Farley to mind, a man dying in another time and place, close enough to touch and yet so far away that even science couldn't measure the distance.

Farley shook his head. "You've got no business driving on these roads."

Rue wanted to weep, but she smiled instead. "Are you jealous, Farley?" she teased, stepping close to Lobo and running a finger down the inside of the marshal's thigh. "Think I'm paying Wilbur too much attention?"

Farley shivered, but Rue knew it wasn't from the cold. He'd loved the game they'd played that morning, and her attempt to remind him of it had been successful. He bent down and exclaimed in a low voice, "You little wanton. I ought to haul you off to the woodshed and blister your bustle!"

"Very kinky," she said, her eyes twinkling even as tears burned at their edges. Then, before he could ask for the inevitable definition, she turned and walked toward the house.

That night, the power stayed on and the wind didn't blow. Rue and Farley curled up together on the couch in the big parlor and watched television. At least, Farley watched— Rue alternated between thinking about the necklace and about the letter hidden beneath the desk blotter.

Although they didn't make love, Farley seemed to know Rue would not be separated from him, and they shared the large bed in the master bedroom. He held her and for the time being that was enough.

Contrary to her expectations, she slept, and the next thing she knew, Farley was kissing her awake.

"Get up," he said, his breath scented with toothpaste. "Today is our wedding day."

Some words from the letter he didn't know he'd written echoed in Rue's heart. "I never meant to leave you forever, especially not on our wedding day." Unless she did something and soon, she would become Farley's wife and his widow without turning a single page of the calendar in between.

"I love you," she said, because those were the only safe words.

He kissed her lightly and quoted a mouthwash commercial they'd seen the night before. One thing about television, it had an immediate impact.

Rue got out of bed, passed into the bathroom and brushed her teeth. When she came back, Farley was gone.

Panic seized her. With another man, she would only have thought he'd left the room, or maybe the house. Farley might have left the century.

Dressed in jeans and a warm woolen shirt, she raced into the hallway and down the stairs. "Farley!"

He was in the kitchen, calmly sipping coffee, and he smiled at Rue with his eyes as he took in her furious expression. "A body would almost think you'd been left at the altar, the way you carry on when I get out of sight."

Looking up at him, Rue ached. Why did it all have to be so complicated? Other people had problems, sure, but not the kind that would have made an episode on *Tales from the Crypt.* "Farley, the necklace—"

"I know where it is," he said calmly. "The safe, behind that painting of the fruit."

Rue paled. "But you couldn't have known the combination."

He had noticed her terror by then, and he reached out with his free hand to caress her jaw. "I found it when I went through the ranch records, Rue," he said quietly. "I checked the safe to see if there were any more reports to go over."

Rue closed her eyes, swayed slightly and was steadied by Farley's firm grip. "But the necklace is still there?" she asked evenly, reasonably. "You didn't move it, did you?"

"No," he answered. "But I want your promise that you won't move it again, either. I need to know where it is, Rue. Now, for the moment, all I want you thinking about is becoming my wife." He bent his head, bewitched her with a soft kiss. "I hope you're planning to wear something pretty, though. I draw the line at a bride wearing trousers."

Chapter Fourteen

Rue struggled to maintain her composure; in all her travels as a reporter, she'd never faced a greater challenge than this one. "Farley," she began reasonably, "you've got to listen. If you go back to 1892, you'll die."

He touched her face. "Everybody dies, darlin'," he answered gently. "Considering that I was born in 1856, I've outlived a number of folks already."

She stepped back, raised her fingertips to her temples. It sounded as if Farley knew what was going to happen to him if he went back to 1892 and that he'd resigned himself to that fate. "You found the letter, too."

"By accident," he said. "I spilled a cup of coffee on the desk, and when I moved the blotter, I came across an envelope with my own handwriting on it. I would have put it aside if it hadn't been for that."

Rue sagged into one of the kitchen chairs. "You'd go back, knowing you were going to be shot by a bank robber and die of the wounds?"

"I have to settle my affairs, Rue. I told you that. And I'm still the marshal of Pine River, as far as I know. God knows, it wasn't a job the town council would be able to foist off on somebody else without a fight. If there's a holdup, I'll have to do whatever I can to intervene. Besides, I've been warned—I'll just be more careful than usual."

Rue felt sick. This was supposed to be one of the happiest days of her life. And she *was* happy, because she wanted the legal and spiritual bond with Farley no matter what lay ahead—or behind—but she was terrified, as well.

Apparently nothing would shake his determination to return to 1892. That left only one avenue open to his distraught bride-to-be.

"I'm going with you, then."

"Rue—"

"I mean, it, Farley," she interrupted, rising so fast that her chair toppled over backward behind her. She didn't pick it up. "I'm not marrying you so we can be apart. We belong together."

He looked at her for a long time, then sighed. "All right," he agreed reluctantly. He kissed her, then left the house without breakfast.

Rue was still inwardly frantic, but fortunately for her, she had things to do. She called the hospital for a progress report on Wilbur, who was doing well, then wired her mother, who had no doubt moved on from the spa to one of several favorite ski resorts.

Giving the credit-card number to pay for the wire took longer than dictating the telegram itself, a fact that seemed ironic to Rue.

"Mother," it read, "I'm marrying at last, so stop telling your friends I'm an old maid. His name is Farley Haynes, and I adore him. Love, Rue."

The message to Rue's father, who might have been anywhere in the world, but could be counted on to check with his answering service in New York on occasion, was even more succinct. "Dad. By the time you get this, I'll be married. Rue."

With those two tasks out of the way, Rue turned all her concentration to the upcoming wedding. She hadn't brought anything suitable for the ceremony—in fact, she didn't *own* anything suitable. But she remembered the line of trunks in the attic, filled with things from all phases of her grandmother's life. When she was younger, she'd worn those lovely, antique garments to play solitary games of dress-up during long visits.

Naturally, the room at the top of the house was dusty, and the thin winter sunlight barely found its way through the dirty panes of glass in the only window. Rue flipped the light switch and the single bulb dangling in the middle of the ceiling flared to life.

This was a friendly place, though cold and a little musty smelling, and Rue smiled as she entered. If there were ghosts here, they were merry ones come to wish the bride well on her wedding day.

After a few moments of standing still, feeling a reverence for the old times and wondering if her grandmother might not be here after all, young and pretty and just beyond the reach of Rue's senses, she approached the row of trunks.

The sturdy old chests had metal trim, tarnished to a dead-brass dullness by the passing of time, and the stickers plastered to their sides were peeling and colorless. Still, Rue could make out the names of a few places—Istanbul, Prague, Bora Bora.

She smiled. Grammie had been quite the traveler in her youth. What had it been like for such an adventurous woman to settle on a remote ranch in Montana?

Rue knelt in front of the first trunk and laid her palms on its dusty lid. She didn't remember her grandmother, though Gramps and Rue's own mother had spoken of her in only the most glowing terms.

She lifted the lid and right on top, wrapped tightly in yellowed tissue paper, was a beautiful pink satin dress. Rue took a few minutes to admire it, to hold the gown to her front and speculate as to whether or not it would fit, then carefully rewrapped it and returned it to the chest.

Time blew past like the wind flying low over the prairies, and Rue was barely aware of its passing. Going through the things her grandmother had so carefully packed away, she found a lovely calf-length dress of ecru lace, with a modest but enticing neckline, a pearl choker, pale satin slippers that were only slightly too small and a lovely, sweeping straw picture hat with a wide rose-colored ribbon for a band and a nosegay of pink and blue flowers for decoration.

Because the chests were lined with camphor, the fragile old clothes smelled only faintly musty. Totally charmed, the threat of Aunt Verity's necklace held at bay for just a little while, Rue carried the treasures down from the attic and hung the dress on the screen porch to air.

Upstairs again, she gave herself a facial, washed her hair and then took a long, hot bath. She was back in the kitchen sipping from a cup of noodle soup, a towel wrapped around her head turban-fashion, when Farley came in.

"Are you hungry?" Rue asked, lowering her eyes. She'd said and done outrageous things in this man's arms, and it wasn't as if he hadn't seen her in considerably less than a bathrobe, but suddenly she felt shy.

"Yes," he answered with a smile in his voice. "But I'm still planning to wait until after some preacher has said the words that make it all right."

Rue blushed. "I was talking about food."

"I wasn't," Farley replied. "Are we getting hitched here, or do we have to go into town?"

She felt another stream of color rush into her cheeks, but since the previous flood probably hadn't subsided yet, it wouldn't be so obvious. She hoped.

"I arranged for a justice of the peace to come out. It was the same day we got our license."

"Where was I?" Farley hung up his hat and coat, then crossed to the refrigerator and opened the door. It was an ordinary thing, and yet Rue pressed the image into her mind like a cherished photograph. Just in case.

She smiled. "You were playing with the drinking fountain," she said.

Farley took the milk carton out, opened it and started to raise it to his mouth. He went to the cupboard for a glass when he saw Rue's warning glare. "I don't have a ring," he said worriedly, "or a fancy suit."

"You're still going to be the best-looking groom who ever said 'I do,'" Rue retorted, taking the carton from his hand.

He squeezed her bottom through the thick terry cloth of her robe when she bent over to return the milk to the fridge. "And after I've said 'I do,'" he teased huskily, "you can bet that I will."

The justice of the peace, who ran a little bait shop at Ponderosa Lake in the summertime, arrived an hour later.

By then, Farley had showered and changed into clean clothes, and Rue had put on makeup, arranged her hair in a loose Gibson-girl style and donned the lovely, gauzy lace dress and the pearl choker.

A couple of the ranch hands came in to serve as witnesses, wearing shiny, ill-fitting suits that had probably been in and out of style several times. One of the old-timers, Charlie, brought along his relic of a camera, which had a flash attachment the size of a satellite dish, fully prepared to record the event.

Rue didn't allow herself to think beyond the now; she wanted to cherish every second for its own sake.

Being a civil ceremony, the wedding itself was short. Even though Rue was trying to measure out the moments and make them last, the whole thing didn't take more than five minutes. When Farley kissed her, the hat tumbled off her head and the flash of Charlie's camera glowed red through her closed eyelids.

Rue would have been content to go right on kissing her husband, but, of course, they weren't alone, so that was impossible. Hope overflowed her heart as she looked up into Farley's tender eyes, and in those golden moments, she found it impossible to believe that time or trouble or even death could ever separate them.

The justice of the peace left as soon as he'd been paid, but the ranch hands stayed for refreshments, since festive occasions were such a rare treat. Sara Lee provided the wedding cake, which had to be thawed out in the microwave, and coffee and soda completed the menu.

When Charlie wasn't eating, he was taking pictures.

Finally, however, one of the other hands elbowed him in the ribs, then cleared his throat pointedly and suggested that they get back to the bunkhouse and change into their working duds. Some of the cowboys started to protest, then caught on and pushed back their chairs, beaming.

Time was more precious now than ever, so Rue didn't urge the hands to stay. Despite her insistence that Farley take her with him when he went back to 1892, she hadn't forgotten that his letter said he'd gone alone—on their wedding day. She was glad when she and her new husband were finally by themselves.

She unbuttoned the top two buttons of Farley's shirt. "No more virginal protests, Farley," she said, sliding her hand under the soft chambray to find and caress a taut masculine nipple. "You're my husband now, and I demand my rights as a wife."

He chuckled, but the sound was raw with other emotions besides amusement. No doubt he, too, was wondering how much of their destiny could be changed, if any. He swept Rue up into his arms and mastered her with a thorough kiss, then carried her to the bedroom.

"You look so beautiful in that dress," he said after setting her on her feet at the foot of the massive bed. "I almost hate to take it off you."

For Rue time no longer stretched into the past and the future, forming a tapestry with no beginning and no end. Nothing and no one existed beyond the walls of that room, and their union would be eternal.

She didn't speak, but simply began unfastening the pearl buttons at the front of her gown, her chin at a high, proud angle, her eyes locked with Farley's, challenging him to resist her.

He couldn't; sweet defeat was plain in his face, and the knowledge made her jubilant.

The dress fell over her hips, and Rue hung it over the back of a chair, then kicked off the tight slippers. She kept stripping until all that was left was the wide, pearl choker at her throat.

Farley's throat worked visibly as he swallowed, looking at her as if he'd never seen a naked woman before. When Rue lifted her arms to unclasp the choker, Farley rasped, "No. Leave it," and she obeyed him.

He began taking off his own clothes, starting with his boots, setting them aside with a neatness that made Rue impatient. She watched with brazen desire as he removed his shirt, unfastened his belt, stepped out of his jeans.

Finally, Farley stood before her wearing only his skin, and he was as incorrigibly, magnificently male as a wild stallion.

He held out a hand to Rue. "Come here, Mrs. Haynes," he said.

It wasn't the time to say she meant to hyphenate both surnames into one; in that bedroom, alone with her mate, no title suited her better than Mrs. Haynes. Rue yearned to give herself to Farley totally.

She went to him and he drew her upward into his kiss, a tall shaman working his treacherous magic. Rue trembled as she felt his hand cup her breast, and she moaned into his mouth as his fingers lightly shaped the nipple.

As Rue's body was pleasured, so was her soul. There was a joy in the depths of her being that overruled all her fears and doubts and furies. She was, while Farley loved her, in step with a dancing universe.

He continued to worship her with words and kisses and caresses while she stood with her head back, lost in glorious surrender. When he knelt to pay the most intimate homage, she gave a soft, throaty sob and burrowed her fingers in his thick hair, holding him close, stroking the back of his head.

Their lovemaking was woven of silver linings plucked from dark clouds, golden ribbons of sunset and lengths of braided rainbow, formed at once of eternity itself and the most fleeting of moments. Farley's and Rue's souls became one spirit and did not exist apart from each other, and this joining sanctified their marriage in a way an official's words could never have done.

There was no room in Rue for any emotions other than soaring happiness and the most intense pleasure, not while she and Farley were still celebrating their wedding. Finally, however, she dropped off to sleep, exhausted, perspiration cooling on her warm flesh.

Farley held Rue for a long time. He'd heard other men talk about love, but he'd never imagined it could be the way it was for him with this woman.

He kissed the top of her head, even though he knew she wasn't awake to feel the touch of his lips, and his eyes stung. Returning to 1892 wasn't really his choice, as he'd implied to Rue earlier, but it was his fate—he knew that in his bones. The letter, penned in his own handwriting, was irrefutable proof of that.

Farley grew restless. If he managed to circumvent destiny, somehow, and stay in the twentieth century with Rue, would the letter stop existing? Would his fate, or anyone's, be altered?

The room was filling with gray twilight, and Farley felt a chill. He eased himself apart from Rue and went into the bathroom, where he took a shower. Then he put on the same clothes he'd worn earlier, because he'd been married in them and because they'd borne a vague hint of Rue's scent. He stood beside the bed for a long time, memorizing the shape of her face, the meter of her breathing, knowing his heart was beating in rhythm with hers, even though he could hear neither.

"I love you," he whispered raggedly. He knew he should wake her, since any parting could be a permanent one, but he turned away. If he looked into her eyes, he would see the reflection of his own despair, and the pain would be beyond bearing.

Downstairs, Farley put on his coat, took the necklace from the safe, left the house and strode toward the barn. Most of the men were in the bunkhouse, since the day's work was over, but he found Charlie puttering around in the barn.

Farley touched the brim of his hat as he passed the man, but he didn't trust himself to speak. He needed to ride, cold as it was, and let the fresh air clear his mind. Maybe then he could figure out some way to change things.

He entered the separate part of the barn where Lobo was stabled, led the big stallion out of his stall and saddled him. The animal nickered and tossed his head, as eager for the open spaces as Farley was, and it was then that a profound, almost mystical bond took shape between the man and the horse.

Farley led Lobo outside, under a full but icy moon, and swung up into the saddle.

"Everything all right, boss?" Charlie inquired. He was leaning against the paddock fence, Soldier at his side, both of them lonely for Wilbur.

Farley looked around him at the land, the kind of land that could soak up a man's blood and sweat and still make him happy. In his mind the ranch would always be Rue's, even if he managed to keep himself from getting shot back in 1892 and found his way home to her. One day, though, the land on either side of Ribbon Creek would belong to their child, if he'd been fortunate enough to sire one, and Farley wanted to guard the place and make it grow almost as much as he wanted to stay with Rue.

He looked toward the big house, adjusted his hat and finally answered the ranch hand's question. In a way. "You'll look out for her if something happens to me?"

"Exactly what is it you're expectin' to happen to you, Mr. Haynes?"

Farley lifted a shoulder. "Maybe nothing." He reined an impatient Lobo toward the south, where the moon spread silver over the snow.

He rode until neither he nor the horse could travel any farther, until he wasn't even sure he was still within the borders of the ranch. He pulled off his gloves and reached into his coat pocket for the thin cigars he loved, but instead of the package, he felt a cold, fragile chain between his fingers.

He'd tried to forget he was carrying the necklace.

"Go on," he muttered hoarsely, glad nobody was there to hear him talking to a trinket. "Do your worst and get it over with!"

Farley held the pendant up, watched the moonlight do a twinkling dance along the length of the chain. He considered flinging it aside into the snow, but he knew now that that would do no good. A force he did not begin to understand had brought the necklace into his life, for good or evil, and that force would not be denied. He had to tie up the loose ends of his old life so that he could live the new one to the fullest.

"Rue." Her name was a ragged, broken whisper on his lips. Once again, his vision blurred, and he wasn't sure whether the necklace was working its bitter magic or if he was finally giving way to the grief dammed up inside him.

Five minutes passed, then ten, while the stallion rested and Farley waited.

When the transition occurred just as the sun came up, it was a subtle one. There was a roaring in Farley's ears, and Lobo fretted and sidestepped beneath him. The power lines and the distant gray ribbon of the highway dissolved into nothingness.

Farley knew without consulting a calendar that he and the horse were back in his own century, and it was a long way back to Pine River from the Big Sky Country.

Still, he dropped the necklace into his pocket and rode back to the place where the house should have been, where Rue should have been drinking coffee in a warm kitchen and Soldier should have been barking. There was nothing except for an abandoned cabin and a single grave marked with a wooden cross.

Farley took off his hat for a moment, his throat thick with misery, his heart full of the kind of loneliness that can drive a person to do stupid, reckless things. He lowered his head for a few moments, struggling with his emotions, and then turned Lobo west, toward his destiny.

Rue stirred in her marriage bed, dreaming. She saw Farley riding alone through a winter dawn, his horse's gleaming onyx coat contrasting starkly with the pristine snow. Knowing she could never catch up with her husband, she struggled to awaken instead.

The instant Rue opened her eyes, however, she knew the nightmare was real and she hadn't escaped it. She and Farley had said their vows and consummated them, and now he was gone.

A frantic sob tore itself from her throat and she covered her face with both hands, trying hard to get a grip on her emotions. Farley was probably downstairs, reading one of his how-to books with one eye and watching his favorite TV program with the other.

She jumped out of bed, found her robe, pulled it on and dashed downstairs.

"Farley?"

The parlor fire was out, and the TV screen was blank.

Rue hurried into the study, but she knew before she reached it that Farley wouldn't be there. His presence had a substance, an impact all its own, and she felt nothing except a rising numbness.

"Oh, God," she prayed, unable to go farther, stumbling through the darkening house to the kitchen.

No fire in the cookstove, no coffee brewing, no Farley reading at the table.

Rue was still in shock, but she could feel her emotions moving underneath the hard layer of control. Soon they would break through and panic would reign.

She continued to entreat heaven as she ran back up the stairs to shower quickly and dress. Her hair was still damp when she followed Farley's boot prints along the path that led to the barn. She nearly collided with Charlie at the gate.

"He's gone," she choked out miserably when the aging man gripped her shoulders to steady her.

"He took Lobo out hours ago," Charlie said, his craggy, ancient face looking worried in the light of the moon. "I'm going to wake the other men so we can saddle up and start lookin' for him soon as the sun's up."

"I'm going with you," Rue insisted, as if anyone had given her cause to argue. "I think we should start right now."

"Mr. Haynes made me swear to look after you," Charlie said stubbornly. "And lettin' you ride out in the dark of night over dangerous ground ain't my idea of keepin' my promise."

Rue's heart stopped for a moment, and she felt her eyes widen. "Farley asked you to take care of me?" The certainty came to her then that they weren't going to find her husband, no matter how long or how thoroughly they searched, but since the realization wasn't one Rue was ready to accept, she pushed it to the back of her mind.

"That's right," Charlie responded with a nod. "Now, you just go back in that house and mind your p's and q's until we can head out. Remember this, too—you won't be a damn bit of good to the man if you've worked yourself up into a tizzy."

Doing fierce battle with a flock of instincts that bade her to do otherwise, Rue obeyed. She walked stiff legged into the house, brewed coffee, drank a cup and then ran to the bathroom to throw up.

That ruled out the idea of breakfast—she would only have been going through the motions anyway—and her knees were too shaky for effective pacing. She took a chair at the kitchen table and laid her head on her arms.

The shrill ringing of the wall phone made her jump a good six inches off her chair, and she snatched the receiver off the hook and yelled, "Hello! Farley?" before she realized he wasn't very likely to call.

Even in the face of logic, however, Rue's disappointment was keen when an operator announced that she had a telegram for Ms. Rue Claridge.

She closed her eyes. "Read it, please," she whispered.

"'A set of sterling is on its way. What do you know about this man? Is he a fortune hunter? Have they found poor Elisabeth yet? Do write. Love, Mummy.'"

"Thanks," Rue muttered when she was certain the operator had finished. Under other circumstances, the message would have embarrassed her, but she was too distraught over Farley to feel anything so mundane.

"Will there be an answer?"

"Not one you could send over a public-communications system," Rue answered with wooden sweetness. Then she hung up the receiver. At least the annoyance of her mother's passionate disinterest had put some starch in her knees and she was able to pace for a while.

Rue even drank another cup of coffee, but that proved to be a foolish choice. She was back in the bathroom, in the midst of violent illness, when she heard the back door open and close.

Quickly, Rue rinsed her mouth and washed her face, but when she hurtled into the kitchen, Farley wasn't there. Charlie was, and he stood, hat in hand, looking worried and authoritative, obviously trying to do and say the things Wilbur would have. The crisis had made him younger and stronger, if only for a little while.

Rue didn't speak. She just put on her winter gear and followed him outside. Her mare, Buttermilk, had been saddled, and all the hands were mounted and ready to ride out.

Lobo had left a trail of hoofprints in the hard snow, and they followed it for several miles, their breaths and those of the horses making white clouds in the bitterly cold air.

The tracks led to the middle of a vast clearing, and there they stopped. Rue, who had been riding in front, alongside Charlie and a younger man called Bill, closed her eyes, absorbing the shattering reality that Farley was gone.

Without her.

Recalling the words of Farley's letter, written from his deathbed, Rue reminded herself that he had left her reluctantly. It was that damn code-of-honor thing, the need to finish all his business before he took up something new.

He was gone, and he surely had the necklace, so there was no way to follow him.

The hands were circled around the pattern of tracks in the snow, exclaiming. Naturally, they'd never seen anything like that before. One even speculated that both Farley and his horse had been abducted by aliens, and Rue wondered disconsolately if that theory was really any stranger than the truth.

Reining Buttermilk toward the house, feeling too broken inside even to cry, Rue let the animal take her home. She was aware of the men riding with her, although she didn't look at them even once.

"I'll get the sheriff out here quick as I can, Mrs. Haynes," said one. "Don't you worry. We'll find your bridegroom."

Tears glittered in Rue's eyes, but she kept her chin high. "They won't find him," she managed to say. "Nobody could find him."

"You don't believe that crackpot idea of Buster's about the spaceship and the little green men, do you?" Bill asked.

Rue meant to laugh, but a sob came out inside. "Right now," she said when she could speak, "I don't know what I believe, but I'm sure of one thing—wherever Farley is, that's where I want to be."

The sheriff came, and he called in the state police. They summoned the FBI, and all the ruckus attracted reporters from the tabloids. A week passed, and no trace of Farley or the horse was found, and in every supermarket check-out line in the country, the front page of the *National Scoop* screamed, UFO SNATCHES MAN AND STALLION, STATE OF MONTANA ON RED ALERT.

If Rue hadn't been in mourning, she would have thought it was all a wonderful joke.

Chapter Fifteen

It took Farley a full week, riding hard, to reach Pine River. Having no money and no gun, he'd lived on what he could scavenge, which wasn't much, considering there was snow on the ground. Lobo, once fat from his winter confinement in the stables at Ribbon Creek, was now sleeker and leaner, the kind of horse a man could depend on.

Folks shouted from the sidewalks and waved from the windows as Farley rode through the center of town, but he not only didn't stop to talk, he didn't even acknowledge them. His whole being was focused on a single objective: getting back to Rue.

As he came abreast of Jon Fortner's office, Farley saw his friend waiting by the hitching rail out front, his arms folded, his gaze steady.

"That's a fine-looking horse, Farley," the doctor said.

The marshal drew back on the reins, dismounted and tethered the stallion to the rail. He needed to talk with Jon, but he feared to start because his emotions were so raw and sore and so close to the surface.

Jonathan came down the steps and laid a reassuring hand to Farley's shoulder. "I've been there, too, remember?" he said, keeping his voice low so the gawking townspeople wouldn't hear. "Come on inside, and I'll pour you a cup of my special medicinal coffee."

For the first time in more than a week, Farley smiled, though he knew the effort was probably somewhat on the puny side. "How about just giving me a cup of medicine with a little coffee in it?"

Rue was lying in bed one night, a month after Farley's dramatic disappearance, when the memory invaded her mind, three-dimensional and in full color.

She saw herself in Pine River, at the churchyard, talking with a dark-haired young man. Michael Blake, that was his name, and he'd said Elisabeth and Jonathan Fortner had been his great-great-grandparents.

Now her heart was pounding like some primitive engine, and the fog of pain and confusion was finally lifting. She heard the young man say cordially, *My grandmother would really like to meet you, since you're a shirttail relation and everything. She lives with my mom and dad in Seattle. Why don't you give her a call sometime?*

Rue threw back the covers and leapt out of bed. Michael had written a name and telephone number on a page from a pocket-size notebook. She squeezed her eyes shut. Where had she put that piece of paper?

At the same time she was pulling on clothes, Rue was ransacking her memory. Whenever someone handed her a business card or anything like that, she always slipped it into her pocket, and she'd been wearing a Windbreaker jacket that day....

Her stomach clenched into a painful knot as she strug
gled to pursue the recollection further. It was like trying t
chase a rabbit through a blackberry thicket, but Rue fol
lowed tenaciously, because finding Farley and saving hin
from the bank robber's bullet was so critically important t
her.

"My purse!" she yelled, flipping on the overhead lights
She snatched her bag from the bureau top and upended i
over the bed, sending pennies and gum wrappers, credit
card receipts and scruffy tissue all over. After a feveris
search, however, she unzipped the change pocket and foun
the paper folded inside.

On it, Michael had written a name, Mrs. Elisabeth R
Blake, and a telephone number.

Rue reached for the bedside telephone, then caught sigh
of the alarm clock and realized it was four o'clock in th
morning, and just three in Seattle.

"Hell," she muttered, wondering how she could contair
herself until a decent hour. Maybe Mrs. Blake was one o
those old ladies who have trouble sleeping, and she was sit
ting up, working a crossword puzzle or watching one of the
cable channels.

Rue's speculations changed nothing. Michael had said hi
grandmother lived with his parents, and *they* were proba
bly sleeping, with no clue of what a mystery their existence
really was.

She went downstairs and made herself a cup of tea, since
she could no longer tolerate coffee, a drink she'd once loved.
She felt dizzy sometimes, too, and she was cranky as a bea
recovering from a root canal, but she attributed these
symptoms to the stress she'd been under for nearly a month.
Pregnancy was both too wonderful and too terrible a pros
pect to consider.

Soldier, who had been sleeping on the hooked rug in front of the cookstove, as usual, traipsed over to give Rue a friendly lick on the forearm. Idly, she patted his head and went right on sipping her tea.

Perhaps this delay was a good thing. Rue didn't have any idea what to say to Mrs. Blake once she reached her, but she knew the woman was her only link with Elisabeth and Farley, now that the necklace was gone.

Slowly, the icy gray light grew brighter at the windows. Rue fed Soldier, let him out and wandered back to the study.

The photographs taken at the wedding were there, tucked into a place of honor in a drawer of her grandfather's cherrywood desk. Although it always did her injury to look at them, Rue could no more have ignored those pictures than she could have given up breathing or stilled the meter of her heartbeat.

She flipped through them, smiling even as tears pricked her eyes. Farley with coconut frosting all over his mouth. Herself wearing the gauzy dress from the attic. The bride and groom kissing right after the justice of the peace had pronounced them man and wife....

Rue carefully returned the photos to their envelope, then put on her coat and boots and made her way to the woodshed. She brought back an armload of pitchy pine logs, feeling better because of the effort of wielding the ax.

She made a fire and watched an early-morning news show in the study. When eight o'clock came around, Rue simply could not wait any longer. She sat down at the desk, pulled the telephone close and carefully punched out the number Michael had given her that day in the graveyard.

There were a few vague thumps on the line, then a long ring, then another.

"Blake residence," a pleasant male voice answered.

"My name is Rue Claridge-Haynes," Rue blurted. "I'd like to speak with Mrs. Blake—the senior Mrs. Blake—about some genealogy research I've been doing."

"That would be my mother," the man said. "If you'll wait just a moment. . . ." There was a thumping sound as he laid the receiver down, and Rue chewed a fingernail while she waited.

After what seemed like a long time, though it was probably not more than a minute or two, a woman's voice came on the line, almost drowned out by the racket of an extension being hung up.

"Rue Claridge?"

Rue shoved a hand through her hair. "Yes. Mrs. Blake, I'm calling about—"

"I know what you're calling about," the old lady interrupted, crisply but not unkindly. "I've been waiting all my life for this moment."

"I beg your pardon?"

"My grandmother, Elisabeth Fortner, left something for you under the flyleaf of her Bible."

Rue's heart was hammering. This, she realized, was what she had been subconsciously hoping for. Elisabeth had found a way to reach across a hundred years, to send word about herself or Farley.

"Miss Claridge? Are you there?"

"My name is Claridge-Haynes now," Rue said. It sounded totally inane, she knew, but she was in shock. "I'm married." She paused, cleared her throat. "Mrs. Blake, what did my cous—your grandmother leave for me?"

"It's an envelope," Bethie's descendant answered. "A letter, I suppose. I didn't look because Grandmother's instructions said I mustn't. No one but you is to open the packet, and I cannot send it through the mail or by messenger. The note on the front specifically says that you will contact me when the time is right and that I must insist on your coming for it in person.''

Rue was practically dizzy with excitement and suspense. "I'm in Montana, Mrs. Blake," Rue said. "But I'll be there as soon as I can."

Mrs. Blake gave Rue an address and told her to call the moment she arrived in Seattle, no matter what time it was. "I'll be waiting by the phone," she finished.

Rue immediately called the nearest airport, but there were no planes available, charter or otherwise, because of the weather. Rue accepted that disappointment. She told Wilbur, who was recuperating at the ranch house under the care of a nurse, that she was leaving and he was boss until further notice, then threw her suitcases into the back of the Land Rover and left.

The storm started out as a light, picturesque skiff of snow, but by the time Rue reached Spokane, it had reached blizzard proportions. She stopped there and forced down a hearty dinner while a man at a service station across the street put chains on her rear tires.

"You shouldn't drive in this, ma'am," he said, when Rue returned from the restaurant and was settling up the bill. "It's a long way to Seattle, and you've gotta go over the mountains. Snoqualmie Pass is probably closed anyway...."

Rue smiled, nodded, got behind the wheel and went right on.

Hours later, she reached the high mountain pass that connected the eastern and western parts of Washington state. Sure enough, traffic was backed up for miles, but the road was closed only to people who didn't have chains on their tires.

On the other side of the mountain range, there was hardly any snow, and a warm, drizzling rain was washing that away.

Just over an hour after that, Rue pulled into the parking lot of a convenience store in the suburbs of Seattle. She called Mrs. Blake, who was awake and waiting, as promised.

After washing her face, combing her hair and brushing her teeth in the rest room, Rue bought a tall cup of hot chocolate and went on.

She found the Blake house with relative ease, but even though her exhausted state made her feel slightly bewitched, Rue wouldn't let herself attribute the fact to anything mystical. She had always had a good sense of direction.

A white-haired old woman with a sweet smile and soft blue eyes came to the door only an instant after Rue rang the bell.

"Rue," she said, and something in the very warp and woof of the woman reminded Rue of Elisabeth and filled her with an aching sense of nostalgia. Bethie's *granddaughter*—how impossible that seemed. "Come in."

"I hope I haven't awakened anyone...."

"Mercy, no," Mrs. Blake said, linking her thin, age-spotted arm with Rue's and ushering her into a large, tastefully decorated room to the left. "Phillip, my son, is a surgeon, and he's been up and gone for hours. Nadine, my daughter-in-law, is at the health club, swimming, and, of course, Michael lives in one of the dorms at the university now. I pretty much have the place to myself, except for the maid. Won't you sit down?"

Even though she felt sure she would faint any moment, Rue was so tired, she was almost painfully tense. She sat in a graceful Queen Anne chair, upholstered in a pretty blue-and-white floral pattern, and tried to keep calm.

"Would you care for some coffee?" Mrs. Blake inquired, taking a chair facing Rue's and gesturing gracefully toward the silver service on the cocktail table.

Rue shook her head. "No, thank you," she said, and then bit down hard on her lower lip to keep from demanding the envelope Elisabeth had left for her.

"Well, then, there's no sense in dragging this out, even if it is the biggest thing to happen around here since Nadine's friend Phyllis crawled out on the roof during last year's Christmas party and made a world-class fool of herself. She sang twenty-two different show tunes before the fire department got her down, you know, and every note was off key."

Rue smiled and nodded and tapped the arm of the chair with her fingertips.

Mrs. Blake flushed slightly. "I'm sorry, I do get to running on." She pulled a battered blue vellum envelope from her bag, which was resting on the marble-topped table beside her chair, and held it out to Rue.

Rue forced herself not to snatch it out of Mrs. Blake's fingers. She must have looked calm on the outside, but inside, Rue was suffering an agony of hope. If this was nothing more than a cosmic postcard—"How are you? I am fine. Wish you were here"—the disappointment would be beyond tolerance.

Rue made herself read the faded but familiar lettering on the front of the envelope, and tears filled her eyes. Elisabeth's cryptic instructions were all there, just as Mrs. Blake had relayed them.

Finally, like a child opening a fascinating, fragile present found under the Christmas tree, Rue broke the old wax seal and pulled a single page from inside the envelope.

The necklace did not tumble to her lap, as Rue had hoped it would, but she'd mourn that oversight later. Now, she would read words that had waited a hundred years for her attention.

My Dearest Rue,

I know you probably expected to find the necklace folded inside this letter, so that you could return here to find Mr. Haynes, but, of course, once you think about it, you'll realize that I couldn't take a chance like that. You and I know only too well what magic Aunt Verity's pendant is capable of.

If you *must* find it, I can only tell you to remember that rainy afternoon when we were thirteen and we decided to make a time capsule.

I hate writing this part, knowing what an awful impact it's going to have, but you married Farley, and I think you have a right to the truth, so you can get on with your life. Rue, Farley was shot ten days ago while stopping a robbery, and last night he died of his wounds.

Rue stopped there, fighting to hold on to consciousness while the gracious room swayed around her, then forced herself to go on reading.

"There are no words I can say to console you, except that I know Farley loved you desperately, and that his greatest wish was to return to you.

Rue, I told you where to find the necklace because I know I don't have the right to withhold a choice that rightfully belongs to you, but I beg you not to try to return. The power of that pendant is unpredictable, we know that if hardly anything else, and it's dangerous. Anything could happen.

I love you, Cousin, with my whole heart, and I'm depending on you to do your grieving, then pull yourself together and go on.

Forever, and with a new understanding of the word,

Beth

When Rue let the letter crumple to her lap, Mrs. Blake was ready with a glass of cool water.

"Here, dear, drink this. You look as waxen as a ghost."

Rue might have smiled under other circumstances. As it was, she only reached out a trembling hand for the glass and drank with desperate thirst. Once she felt a little steadier, she thanked Mrs. Blake, carefully folded Bethie's letter and tucked it into her purse.

"I can't share it," she confessed softly. "I hope you understand."

Mrs. Blake's smile was reminiscent of Elisabeth's. "I won't say I'm not curious, dear," she replied, "but I understand. There are mysteries aplenty in this life, and I've learned to accept the fact."

Rue kissed the old lady's cheek lightly. "Thank you again, Mrs. Blake. And goodbye."

Barely an hour later, Rue was back in Pine River, her eyes puffy and sore. Alone in the Land Rover, insulated from a world that couldn't have comprehended her pain, Rue had screamed in rage and grief over her husband's unfair death. Tears had left acid trails on her cheeks, and her throat was so constricted, she could barely breathe.

Instead of heading for Aunt Verity's house, Rue stopped at the churchyard. She found Farley's grave, under the old oak tree as the clerk in the church office had told her. If there had ever been a stone or a wooden marker, no trace remained.

Rue was mourning a man who'd been dead a century, and there wasn't even a monument to honor his memory.

The cemetery was cold on that grim winter day, and Rue's strength was almost gone. She turned—she would visit Elisabeth's and Aunt Verity's graves some other day—and made her way back to the muddy Land Rover.

Moving like a person in a voodoo documentary, Rue bought soup and soap and tea and other supplies at Pine River's state-of-the-art supermarket, then drove to the house where all her adventures had begun.

The mail was knee-deep in front of the slot in the door, and there were so many messages on the answering machine that the tape had run out. Rue didn't play them back. She just put away her groceries, made a bowl of tomato soup and ate without actually tasting a single spoonful.

After rinsing the bowl, she went upstairs, put fresh sheets on one of the beds, took a shower and collapsed. She slept for fourteen hours straight, got up and made herself another bowl of soup, then went back to sleep for another seven.

When she awakened, rested at last, but still numb with sorrow, Rue took Elisabeth's earlier letters from their hiding place in the rolltop desk in the parlor and read them again.

Her heart began to thump. Time did not necessarily run parallel between then and now, she remembered, with growing excitement. If she found a way back—and the whereabouts of the necklace was teasing the edges of her consciousness even then—she would probably arrive after Farley's shooting. But she could also get there before it happened.

Maybe she could intercede.

She ran to find her purse—she'd discarded it on the floor of the downstairs hallway when she first returned—pulled out the letter Mrs. Blake had kept for her and scanned it.

Her gaze snagged on one particular sentence. " . . . I can only tell you to remember that rainy afternoon when we were thirteen and we decided to make a time capsule."

Rue yelped in frustration and began to pace. Her memory wasn't good when it came to things like that, though she could reel off statistics and stock prices and phone numbers until her voice gave out.

"Time capsule, time capsule, time capsule." She repeated the words like a litany, hoping they would trigger some rusty catch deep down in her mind.

Suddenly, gloriously, the memory was there.

Rain on a leaky roof. The smell of dam dust and moldy hay. Two adolescent girls, herself and Elisabeth, in the barn loft, talking about the distant future. They'd wanted posterity to know about their lives, so they'd swiped a lidded plastic bowl from Aunt Verity's kitchen and put in things they considered representative of Planet Earth in the 1970s. Lip gloss. Pictures of their favorite rock group, carefully snipped from fan magazines. A candy bar with peanuts and caramel. . . .

Rue hurried through the house and outside, crossing the dead winter grass in long strides. The barn was old and flimsy and should have been torn down years before, but safety was the last thing on Rue's mind as she went inside.

She did test the ladder leading up to the loft, but only in a quick and cursory way. The boards under her feet swayed a little when she reached the top, but that didn't stop her, either. She and Elisabeth had put their time capsule into the creaky framework where the floor and wall met with great ceremony.

"X marks the spot," she said breathlessly when she found the hiding place and knelt to wrench back a board. The whole loft seemed to shimmy at the intrusion, but again Rue was undaunted.

Behind the filthy, weathered board was a dirty plastic container riddled with the tooth marks of some creature that could probably qualify for top billing in a horror movie. Rue tossed the bowl aside without lifting the lid to look inside and peered into the crevice behind it.

At first, she could see nothing but darkness, dirt and spider webs, but after a few moments her vision seemed to sharpen. Well behind the place where her and Elisabeth's treasures had been hidden, a solid-looking shadow lurked in the gloom.

Rue grimaced, reached deep into the unknown and closed her hand around the object. Having found what she sought, she drew back so fast that a splinter or the tip of a nail made a long, shallow gash in her arm.

She paid no attention to the wound; all she could see was the round, rusted tin she held. Once it had held salve, and the distinct possibility that it was nothing more than a stray piece of trash raised panic into Rue's throat like bile.

"Please," she whispered, and it was at once the most sincere and the most succinct prayer she had ever said.

It was hard, and she broke a couple of fingernails, but Rue finally managed to pry off the lid of the tin. Inside, dusty and tarnished and as full of mystery as ever, lay the necklace.

Rue's eyes filled with tears of relief, and she clutched the pendant to her chest. Now, if only the magic would work again.

Nothing happened, so Rue carefully tucked the necklace into the pocket of her jacket. Only then did she notice that the bit of paper lining the salve tin had writing on it.

Carefully, Rue lifted it to the thin light coming in through one of the wide cracks in the barn wall. "I knew you wouldn't listen!" Elisabeth had scrawled.

Rue smiled, dried her eyes with the back of one hand and climbed cautiously down the ladder again.

Inside the house, she laid the necklace on the drainboard beside the kitchen sink and washed it with cotton balls, mild soap and water. When the pendant was clean, she patted it dry with a soft paper towel, draped the chain around her neck and carefully closed the clasp.

She shut her eyes, gripped the edge of the counter and waited. Hoped.

At first, nothing happened, but then a humming sound filled Rue's ears, rising steadily in pitch. The floor buckled and rolled under her feet, and it seemed that she could feel the spin of the earth itself.

Someone screamed and something crashed to the floor.

Rue opened her eyes to see Bethie's housekeeper standing there, aghast and staring, a shattered crockery bowl at her feet. Its contents covered the length of the woman's calico skirts.

"Ellen, for heaven's sake..." a familiar voice complained, and then Elisabeth appeared in the doorway leading to the main parlor. When she saw her cousin, her blue-green eyes widened and her face lit up with a dazzling smile. "Rue!"

"She just came out of nowhere, missus," Ellen blathered. "I'm telling you, I don't know about the goings-on in this house. I just don't know. And now I've got myself a sick headache."

"You'd better go and lie down," Elisabeth told her gently, but she didn't look at the housekeeper again. She gave Rue a gentle hug.

"Is he dead?" Rue whispered, unable to bear the agony of wondering for another moment.

"Who?" Bethie asked, and her look of puzzlement raised Rue's spirits considerably.

"Farley. Farley Haynes, the marshal." For the first time, the thought occurred to Rue that she might have come back not only before her husband's death, but before he knew her.

"Well, he hasn't been very happy about being separated from you," Elisabeth said with a fond smile, "but people don't usually die of a broken heart. They just *wish* they could."

Farley was alive, and he would know her. Rue's knees literally went slack with relief, and she might have collapsed if Elisabeth hadn't steadied her.

"I've got to go to him right now," she said after a few deep breaths.

"But you're shaken—you need to sit down and have a cup of tea—"

"I need to find my husband!" Rue said. "Is there a horse I can borrow?"

Elisabeth offered no further argument; she knew her cousin too well. "There's a chestnut mare in the barn. Her name is Maisie, and she prefers to be ridden bareback."

Rue hugged her cousin, bade her a good life with Jonathan and raced out the back door, nearly tripping because the steps were different from the ones she was used to. The barn that had been a teetering disaster the last time she entered it was sturdy now, and well maintained.

Quickly, Rue bridled the small mare and swung up onto its back. A woman in pants, riding astride no less, was going to come as yet another shock to the fine people of Pine River, but that could not be helped. The necklace had slipped beneath her shirt; it felt warm against her collarbone, and she was filled with a new and terrifying sense of urgency.

She'd gotten back in time, but just barely. There wasn't a second to lose.

Sure enough, Rue heard the shots just as she and Maisie hit the foot of the town's main street. Rue spurred the animal through the uproar and confusion—everybody was trying to take cover—weaving her way around wagons and buggies and other horses.

Undaunted, Rue rode hell-bent for the bank. If she had to, she would catch that outlaw's bullet herself before she let it strike Farley.

Two men ran out of the bank, their faces, except for their eyes and foreheads, covered by dirty bandannas. It was just like a scene in a John Wayne movie, except that here the bullets were real.

Rue looked frantically for Farley, which was why she was caught completely unprepared when an arm as hard as iron wrenched her off the mare's back and onto another horse. After that, everything was a dizzying blur.

Either she was dreaming, or she was sitting sidesaddle behind Farley, clutching his canvas duster with both hands. The magnificent animal carrying them both was Lobo. She felt the swift, skilled movement of the marshal's arm as he drew his .45. Then she heard two shots in rapid succession and felt the recoil in the muscles between Farley's shoulder blades, where her cheek rested. The air seemed thick with the smells of horse manure and burned powder, and Rue figured if she survived this, the first thing she was going to do was vomit.

In that moment, of all moments, she realized she was definitely pregnant.

A brief silence followed. Rue clung to Farley, soaking in the hard strength of his body in front of her. He was alive, and so was she.

He turned his head to look back at her, and although a muscle in his jaw jumped in irritation, Rue could see joy in his eyes. "That was a damn fool thing to do," he bit out. "You could have been killed."

The necklace was searing Rue's skin. She locked her hands together in front of his stomach, determined that even a brand new Big Bang wouldn't blast her loose. "I love you, too, Farley Haynes," she said.

The magic was beginning again; the air was filled with a vibrant silence so noisy that Rue could hear nothing besides her own voice and Farley's heartbeat. She threw back her head and shouted for joy, at the same time tearing the necklace from her throat and flinging it away.

They might land in heaven or in hell. Either way, the die was cast.

"Tarnation," Farley marveled when the spiritual storm subsided. The marshal, Rue and Lobo were square in the middle of the deserted parking lot at Pine River High School. It was twilight, and the wind was chilly, but to Rue, the sky had never looked brighter nor had the air felt warmer.

Farley turned, his beautiful teeth showing in a broad grin. "Well, Mrs. Haynes," he asked, just before he kissed her, "what do we do now?"

It was a long moment before Rue caught her breath. "That's easy, Mr. Haynes," she replied. "We ride off into the sunset."

* * * * *

Silhouette Special Edition®

Linda Lael Miller

Beyond the Threshold

Two stories linked
by centuries, and by love....

There and Now

The story of Elisabeth McCartney, a woman looking for a love she can't find in the 1990s. Only with the mystery of her Aunt Verity's necklace can she discover her true love—Dr. Jonathan Fortner, a country doctor in Washington—in 1892....

There and Now, #754, available in July 1992.

Here and Then

Desperate to find her cousin, Elisabeth, Rue Claridge searched for her in this century . . . and the last. She found Elisabeth, all right. And also found U.S. Marshal Farley Haynes—a nineteenth-century man with a vision for the future....

Here and Then, #762, available in August 1992.

Take 4 bestselling love stories FREE

Plus get a FREE surprise gift!